A PIZZA TO DIE FOR

I was making pizzas as fast as I could, with the conveyor belt full, and several more pies waiting to go through. I didn't even have time to look up when someone came through the kitchen door from the dining room.

"We're nearly out of dough," I said, "so I'm going to switch to what we've got in the freezer."

"And that's my problem how, exactly?" Kevin Hurley asked as he came into the kitchen.

"Chief, I'd love to chat, but I've got more orders than I know what to do with. I've never made so many pizzas so quickly in my life."

"Funny how that worked out, isn't it?"

I stopped and stared at him. "Hang on a second. Are you implying that I had something to do with Italia's postponing their grand opening? What happened, did Judson lose his pizza man? Or did his wood supply fail to show up?"

"It's a little more serious than that."

"What are you trying to tell me, Kevin?"

"The reason Italia's didn't open is because someone killed Judson Sizemore inside his pizzeria last night . . ."

Books by Chris Cavender

A SLICE OF MURDER

PEPPERONI PIZZA CAN BE MURDER

A PIZZA TO DIE FOR

REST IN PIZZA

Published by Kensington Publishing Corporation

A PIZZA TO DIE FOR

CHRIS CAVENDER

KENSINGTON BOOKS
www.kensingtonbooks.com

KENSINGTON BOOKS are published by

Kensington Publishing Corp.
119 West 40th Street
New York, NY 10018

All Kensington titles, imprints, and distributed lines are available at special quantity discounts for bulk purchases for sales promotion, premiums, fund-raising, educational, or institutional use.

Special book excerpts or customized printings can also be created to fit specific needs. For details, write or phone the office of the Kensington Special Sales Manager: Attn. Special Sales Department. Kensington Publishing Corp., 119 West 40th Street, New York, NY 10018. Phone: 1-800-221-2647.

Kensington and the K logo Reg. U.S. Pat. & TM Off.

ISBN-13: 978-0-7582-2953-3
ISBN-10: 0-7582-2953-4

First hardcover printing: May 2011
First mass market printing: April 2012

10 9 8 7 6 5 4 3 2 1

Printed in the United States of America

*To TM, EB, CM, MG, and CC, the sum of the parts
sometimes indeed exceeds the whole!*

You better cut the pizza in four pieces because I'm not hungry enough to eat six.
Yogi Berra

Chapter 1

The pizzeria was dark, and nothing moved among the scattered tables and chairs in the dining room or the counters and work areas in the kitchen. There was just a whisper of light filtering in through the windows in front, but back near the oven, most of the light had already dissipated into darkness.

At first, it was hard to make out the identity of the body lying on the floor, but after a closer look, it was clear to see the one thing that would shake the very core of the citizenry of Timber Ridge, North Carolina.

There on the floor was the pizzeria owner, and a status of dead or alive was too difficult to determine at that moment.

I knew it was bad news the second I heard there was going to be another pizzeria opening in direct competition with mine in our sleepy little town of Timber Ridge, North Carolina, but I never thought it would lead to murder. It was alarming enough that someone was going to try to steal my customers, but opening another pizzeria on the promenade a thousand feet from A Slice of Delight was just too much.

There was going to be trouble; I was certain of it.

I just didn't realize how much when I first heard the news.

"It's freezing out there," my sister, Maddy, said as she walked into A Slice of Delight before we opened one morning toward the end of October. "What happened to the concept that we're living in the South where it's supposed to be warm?" Maddy was tall, thin, and lovely, and whenever we stood side by side, I felt every extra pound I carried on my shorter frame. "I didn't think it was supposed to get this cold until January."

"You know our weather," I said as I continued kneading the dough I'd been working on. "It can change in an instant this time of year. It could just as easily be in the seventies and sunny tomorrow."

"Then again, it could be snowing," she said as she rubbed her hands together.

"Aren't you going to take your coat off and stay awhile? It's going to be tough to prep the veggies if you're bundled up like that."

"You turn up the thermostat and I'll take off my jacket."

I walked over and raised it one degree, but I really couldn't afford to heat the entire place when it was just the two of us, and Maddy knew it. Our operation was marginal, and we both realized it. We could stand one bad month, but two in a row could shut us down for good, and I wasn't about to give up my pizzeria without a fight. My late husband, Joe, and I had worked too hard establishing the place for me to give up on it.

My sister acknowledged my gesture by finally slipping off her coat. As she did, Maddy said, "Eleanor, I still wish that you and Joe had bought one of those wood-fired ovens instead of the conveyor system we've got. It would be nice to be able to warm ourselves up by the fire."

I laughed. "If you're that cold, go ahead and turn on that space heater in the corner. Sorry, but it's just going to have to do. Joe and I looked at wood-fired ovens when we first opened this place, but we couldn't afford the initial investment, let alone the hassle of collecting wood, keeping the fire going, and hauling off the ashes. Besides, you have to admit that it's a lot easier to make a pizza, put it on the conveyor, and then just wait for it to come out the other side. With a wood-fired oven, we'd have to be checking every pizza and sandwich constantly, and I know for a fact that you don't have the attention span that would require."

She smiled. "That may be true, but you've got to admit that I have other attributes."

"Too many to name," I agreed. "I hate to burst your bubble, but I heard on the radio that we might get a hint of snow flurries this weekend."

"Whatever happened to this global warming that everyone was making such a fuss about?" she said as she washed her hands and started prepping the vegetables and meats for our pizzas and subs.

I loved the morning hours before we opened. It was the only time of day that Maddy and I had a chance to work together and chat, and as much as

I objected sometimes to her subject matter, it was great having her close. My sister had been a real sport, moving back to town when my husband died to help me out in my darkest hour. It just so happened she'd been between husbands at the time, but I had a feeling that she would have found a way to come back anyway. Having her at the pizzeria made all the difference to me.

"Come on, you remember how much we both loved snow when we were kids," I said, trying to lighten the mood as I formed the dough into balls and stored them in the refrigerator until they were needed later in the day.

"I was quite a bit younger then," she said.

"Hey, so was I," I protested with a grin. "If you get to be younger, Sis, then I do, too."

Maddy studied me for a few moments, and then she said, "What's gotten into you today, Eleanor? You're awfully chipper for it being first thing in the morning."

"Halloween is next week," I said. "How can I not be excited about that? You know it's my favorite time of year."

She laughed. "You used to come up with some unique costumes, I'll give you that. Remember the ghoul-friend outfit you wore in high school?"

At the time, I'd been dating the guy who would become our current sheriff, and I wasn't certain I liked any reminders of the time we'd been a couple. Kevin Hurley had been handsome, a smooth talker, and younger than me. Against my better judgment, I'd gone out with him for quite a while until I'd caught him cheating on me with the girl who was now his wife. The Halloween we'd been together, he'd refused to dress up, so I'd donned zombie makeup and then created a sign with an arrow pointing to the left. Instead of it saying, I'M WITH STUPID, it proudly stated, HIS GHOUL-FRIEND. Kevin hadn't been all that amused, but I'd refused to take the sign off until Halloween was over.

"Those days are long gone," I said.

"Thank goodness for that." Maddy paused, and then asked me, "Did you hear that?"

"Hear what?"

"Someone's pounding on the front door."

"They can just wait until we open," I said. We'd been working hard prepping the place, and we were close to our opening time. I didn't realize how close until I glanced at the clock and added, "They just have to wait ten minutes. It won't kill them to stand out in the cold that long."

"It's your place," Maddy said. "I know how you hate not answering a door or a ringing telephone."

At that moment, my cell phone rang.

"How did you do that?" I asked my sister as I reached for my telephone.

"I'm just that good," she said with a sly smile.

"Hello?" I asked, after I'd quickly washed my hands and then dried them on one of our towels.

"Eleanor, have you both gone deaf? Would one of you mind coming up here and opening the front door and let me inside? It's freezing out here."

"Greg? What are you doing here? You're early." Greg Hatcher was our delivery guy and inside waiter, a student at the nearby college, and one of the best employees I'd ever had. Though he'd recently come into a substantial amount of money, I'd been relieved to learn that he had no intention of quitting his job at the pizzeria. It appeared that he enjoyed being with us as much as we loved having him around.

"Let me in where it's warm, and then I'll explain."

I was about to ask him more when he hung up on me.

"Wow, Greg's less of a fan of the cold weather than you are," I told Maddy.

"At least some of us around here have some common sense," she answered.

I shook my head. "It's October. I'm not sure what you both expect, but I for one like changing leaves, brisk weather, and snuggling up by a fire."

As I walked out front, Maddy asked, "I thought he wasn't supposed to be due for another half-hour?"

"He's not, but evidently he's got something to tell us."

Greg came in stamping his feet and rubbing a hand through his always-short haircut as though he was trying to warm up his scalp. He was built like a linebacker, solid and strong, but underneath that exterior was a young man who had a good heart, a deep soul, and a real desire to make the world a better place. I would never have admitted it out loud, but of all the high school and college employees I'd had over the years, Greg was my favorite. Josh Hurley, the police chief's son and the remainder of my current staff, was a close second, and I dreaded the thought of my favorite team breaking up someday, as they always did, sooner or later.

"What's so urgent?" I asked him out front as he took off his jacket.

"I found out what's going in The Shady Lady's place," he said as he rubbed his hands together. I didn't like it, but I had to admit that it was a fact of life that businesses on the promenade had a way of coming and going. I loved where A Slice of Delight was located, nestled in a blue building among a series of shops that were lined up in a nearly continuous block of storefronts, with a large brick promenade out front that made it easy to stroll around from place to place. I'd seen pictures of the location from the turn of the century, and it was decidedly strange to see a dirt street out front instead of those weathered bricks.

The Shady Lady's demise didn't surprise me. How on earth Myra Clark had stayed afloat selling just lamps, shades, and accessories had been a constant source of amazement to me. Since she'd closed her doors a month ago, the windows had been soaped over, and despite the buzz of activity around the place and the proclivity of townsfolk to dig out the most carefully guarded secrets, no one had an inkling about what was going in.

Apparently until now, at any rate.

"What's it going to be, another clothing store?" Maddy asked.

He shook his head. "Trust me, you could both take a thousand guesses, and you'd never get it."

"It's not going to be another restaurant, is it?" I asked.

"How could you possibly guess that?" Greg wanted to know. "I thought I was the only one who knew."

"I don't know anything," I said. "I was just guessing. Then it's true?"

"I'm afraid so," he said.

I shrugged. "I've got to admit that I'm not happy about having competition so close to the Slice, but we'll be okay. We've got a loyal fan base who love our pizza. They won't desert us." I wasn't sure I meant it, though. There were months where we barely squeaked by as it was. With another restaurant so close, it would make my life harder than I liked.

"I'm not so sure," Greg said as he handed me a flyer. "That's not the worst part of it."

What I saw printed there was enough to make my stomach drop.

Announcing Our Grand Opening This Saturday at Noon! ITALIA'S offers a wood-fired oven and a professional pizza maker who will spin your crust into the air as you watch, amazed! Come by for the show, and for a sample of what real pizza should taste like! We'll have free food, drinks, and prizes, so don't miss it!

"We're dead," Maddy said as she read over my shoulder.

"Not yet," I said. "Grab your coat."

My instruction surprised her. "Where are we going? We're supposed to open in ten minutes, Eleanor."

"Sorry to disappoint anyone who's in the mood for a slice, but this can't wait. We need to see just what we're going to be up against."

* * *

No one answered the door when I knocked at Italia's, which shouldn't have come as a great surprise to me, since the sign still wasn't up and the windows were soaped over, not letting even a speck of light through.

As he jammed his hands into his pockets, Greg said, "We're wasting our time, Eleanor. It's pretty clear that no one's here."

"Come on, we can't give up that easily," I said. "They have to be taking deliveries in back if they're going to open so soon. Let's go check it out."

Though her legs were longer than mine, Maddy had trouble keeping up with me as I raced around the promenade. "Sis, I don't think I've ever seen you this fired up," she said.

"No one's threatened my way of life before," I said. "You know what they say. This isn't personal. It's business."

The three of us went around back, passing the pharmacy and the bank along the way, and I was surprised to find the back door of the new pizzeria standing wide open. I knocked on the steel frame, but again, no one answered.

I started to go in when Maddy grabbed my arm "Hang on a second, Eleanor."

"Why should I? It's not like I'm going to tear the place up or threaten anyone. I'm just going to offer a friendly welcome to our new neighbors."

"Is that all?"

"Of course not," Greg said as he brushed past us both. "She's going to mop up in there. Let's go. I'll lead the way."

Greg was being entirely too enthusiastic, so I

put a hand on his shoulder. "I appreciate the gesture, but this is my battle, remember? I'm going in first, and I'll do the talking."

"Do you honestly see that happening in your wildest dreams, Eleanor?" Maddy asked.

"If you don't, then you both need to stay out here while I deal with it myself," I answered. From the tone of my voice and the expression on my face, they both knew I wasn't kidding.

"Fine," Maddy said, "but don't think for a moment that you're going to keep us standing out here while you go in and have all the fun by yourself."

"Do you agree to those terms, too, Greg?" I asked.

"You bet," he said with a grin. "It's going to be fun sitting back and watching you work. Let's go."

We walked inside the back room, and I had to admit that though I'd meant every word I'd said, I still felt better having Maddy and Greg with me.

At first I thought no one was there, but then a man wearing blue jeans and a flannel shirt came out of the front with a small bucket in one hand.

He looked startled to see us there. "Can I help you?"

"Do you own this place?" I asked, trying to keep my voice calm, though I wasn't nearly so tranquil on the inside.

He grinned at me. "No, ma'am. I'm the mason. I had to come by and put a few finishing touches on the pizza oven's façade before the grand opening. If you haven't seen it yet, you should sneak a peek. It's a work of art, if I say so myself."

"Is the owner around?" I asked.

"He just stepped out," the mason said. "Excuse

me, but I've got a window of opportunity here before the grout hardens, and it's closing fast. If I don't get to it, I'm going to have some nasty chisel work ahead of me."

After he was gone, Maddy asked, "Now what do we do? We're not going to just leave, are we?"

I looked at my watch, and saw that time was running out. I wasn't exactly sure how long the owner of Italia's would be before he showed up, and I couldn't wait around all day. We might just have to come back on our lunch break, but I wasn't all that pleased about doing it that way. I was ready and primed, spoiling for a fight, and I was afraid if I waited, I'd lose some of my fire. On the other hand, I couldn't afford to alienate any of my customers by opening the Slice late, especially with this place opening up so soon.

I was about to tell my sister that we were going to have to go back to the Slice when a tall, elegantly dressed man came in.

He took one look at us and sneered as he asked, "Are you the wait staff? I told the agency that you need to dress up for the interviews." He took in our apparel once more, and before I could say anything, he added, "It doesn't really matter. I'm not sure you're what we're looking for, but thank you for stopping by."

"I'm not here for a job interview," I said, the blood beginning to roar in my ears. "I own A Slice of Delight."

The man frowned as he shook his head. "Then you shouldn't be back here in my kitchen. So sorry, but you'll have to wait for our grand opening celebration before you can come spying on me."

"We weren't spying," Maddy said, despite my warning. Oh, well. It wasn't as though I actually expected her to abide by her agreement to remain silent. I knew in my heart that it was just too much to ask of her.

"Funny, that's what it looked like to me." The pizzeria owner walked us toward the back door, and Greg looked at me questioningly before he allowed himself to be moved. With Greg's size and strength, I would have loved to see the man try to physically remove him, but that wasn't the way I wanted to fight this battle.

I wanted to make one try at being nice, even though I felt little good will toward the man. I put out a hand and tried to give my best smile. "It appears that we got off on the wrong foot. I'm Eleanor Swift."

He looked distastefully at my extended hand, then he refused to take it. "I'm Judson Sizemore," he said. "Pleased, I'm sure."

"Not as much as you might think," Greg said, nearly growling out his words.

I had to handle this fast, before things got ugly. "What made you decide to open a restaurant in Timber Ridge?" I asked.

"Do you even have to ask? It was clear that this town was in desperate need of some authentic cuisine," he said.

"What we serve is good enough for the people around here," Maddy said with a frown.

"Perhaps they believe that now, but I daresay their tastes will change when they sample what we offer." He offered me a slight smile with a hint of condescension in it. "Perhaps you'll find another niche in the marketplace."

"Okay, I tried being nice," I said. "Clearly that didn't work. It looks like it's time to go to Plan B."

"And what might that be?"

"Don't worry. You'll find out soon enough," I said, since I had no idea what I'd meant myself. I turned to Maddy and Greg, and then said, "Come on, we're leaving."

"Fine by us," Maddy said.

As we walked out the door, I saw that Judson Sizemore had followed us.

Once we were outside in the alley, a delivery truck was just starting to unload when Judson called out a question to me. "Was that a threat you just made, Ms. Swift?"

"No, I wouldn't look at it that way. Think of it more as a promise," I said.

As we walked back to the Slice, I stared at the blue brick exterior. I'd been saving enough money to get it repainted to a more appetizing color, but that money was spoken for now. It was going to have to go into a war chest in a life and death struggle for my restaurant.

I was about to enter a battlefield, and I couldn't afford to be cash-strapped when I went to war.

"I can't wait to hear what you have in mind. What's Plan B?" Maddy asked me as I unlocked the front door of the Slice and we walked inside.

"I have no idea," I admitted as we moved back into the kitchen. It was officially one minute past opening, but no one had been waiting to get in, and we had things to talk about. Flipping our CLOSED sign to OPEN could wait a few more minutes.

"Not even a clue?" Greg asked. "Come on, I know you better than that. I can think of a thousand things we can do about this, if you need any suggestions."

"It can't be illegal," I said.

Greg nodded. "Got it. Then that narrows it down to a hundred, but that should still be enough to run him out of town."

"I won't stand for anything unethical, either," I added.

Greg frowned at me as he asked, "Then what am I supposed to do if you keep taking away all of my options?"

Maddy looked at me as she said, "Eleanor, this is no time to be squeamish. We can't let Mr. High-and-Mighty back there get away with it."

"I agree," I said. "But if I drag myself down to his level, I don't deserve to have a business. There has to be a way we can beat him fair and square. Don't we have loyal customers?"

"I would certainly like to believe that," Maddy said with a shrug. "But do you really want to bank on that?"

Her answer surprised me. "What do you mean?"

"Come on, Sis, I love the Slice almost as much as you do, but Judson's offering a wood-fired oven and a guy who tosses the crust in the air like it's some kind of show on the *Food Network*. Our sad little conveyor stashed away in back can't compete with that, and you know it. We need to upgrade to the big guns."

"We can't," I said, some of the fight going out of me. "If we have to do that, we've already lost. I just don't have that kind of money."

She frowned. "Then we're out of luck."

Greg said softly, "I can finance it, and we all know it. If money is all that it's going to take, trust me, it's not a problem."

I'd actually forgotten how much money he had; Greg had been living hand to mouth for so long that it was hard not to still think of him as a struggling college student. "Thanks, but I can't let you do that." It was time to open the restaurant. I couldn't delay it any longer, and besides, I needed to defuse the bomb Greg had just hurled.

He clearly wasn't all that pleased with my reaction to his generous offer. "Why not? I've got more money than I'll ever need, and if you can use some of it, I can't think of a better way to spend it."

I stopped in my tracks, twenty feet from the Slice's front door. "Greg, I cannot express how much I appreciate your generous offer, but I can't accept it, and we both know it."

"If she won't take it, I will," Maddy said.

"What do you need money for?" Greg asked, clearly concerned about my sister's well-being.

"*Need* might be a little strong, but I saw a new sports car on television the other day that I'd look just darling in."

I knew that Maddy was trying to ease the tension in the air, but it wasn't going to work by joking about money.

"I'm sorry, Greg. Win or lose, I have to do this within the limits of my own financial resources. Joe and I never believed in mortgages. That's one of the main reasons we bought a house that was such a wreck and fixed it up ourselves. In a world full of credit, we've always believed in paying as we go, and I can't change the way I do business now just because things are getting scary."

He shrugged. "I'm sorry, Eleanor. I didn't mean to offend you. I just thought it might help."

I gave him a big hug, and was quickly joined by Maddy. I wasn't sure what it would do to his reputation around town to have two women in their thirties embracing him so publicly near the Slice's front window, but if he minded, he didn't show it.

Maddy ran a hand over his buzz cut as she said, "You're not half bad; you know that, don't you?"

"Can you get her to accept the offer?"

My sister laughed. "I wouldn't even try. She's absolutely right. It's her place, good or bad, sink or swim."

"Then if we go down, we go down together," Greg said.

"But we still have some fight left in us," I said, suddenly buoyed by the show of support. "Let's figure out a way to beat him fair and square."

"I guess we could always try," Maddy said, and then added with a grin, "even if you are taking all the fun out of it by not letting us fight dirty."

I answered with a grin. "How about if we keep those ideas on the back burner in case things get really desperate."

"Really?" Maddy asked.

"Of course not," I replied. "But that doesn't mean they aren't fun to think about."

Chapter 2

"Eleanor, do you have a moment?"

I had been in the back making pizzas for the last hour, happy that at least for the moment, we still had customers who loved what we did. I looked up to see Bob Lemon, local attorney and Maddy's steady boyfriend, standing at the door between the kitchen and the dining room as if it were no-man's land. Bob was a distinguished man, older than my sister's usual love interests; I couldn't have chosen someone better for her if she'd given me the chance, which we both knew she never would have dreamed of doing.

"You can have all the time you want, as long as you don't mind if I keep working. You don't even have to ask."

"Maybe you should wait until you've heard what I've got to say to decide that," he replied sheepishly.

"What did she do, pull you into this?" I asked. I had a sudden suspicion that Maddy had enlisted

Bob in our fight against Italia's, and I wasn't going to allow it.

"What do you mean?"

"Don't play dumb with me, counselor, I know how smart you are. My sister has dragged you into our battle with the new pizzeria, hasn't she?"

Bob struggled to look offended by my accusation, but he couldn't bring himself to sell it even halfheartedly. "What can I say? You know me. I'm a weak, weak man," he answered with a smile.

I had to laugh at the expression of contrition on his face. "Go on and have your say. I know it's not entirely your fault. My sister can be very persuasive. No one in the world knows that more than I do. What did she ask you to do, try to shut them down with some kind of injunction?"

"No, nothing as dramatic as that," he said. "But she did ask me to do a little research about the property. I was already at the courthouse, so it was no problem to see who holds the lease on the building where Italia's is going."

"I'm sure it's no big secret. His name is Judson Sizemore, and he introduced himself to me."

Bob shook his head. "From the way the lease was set up, I'm not entirely certain that he's in charge."

"Why do you say that?" I had to give Bob a great deal of credit. He had a way of commanding attention wherever he was, which must have come in extremely handy in the courtroom, and he surely had mine at the moment.

Bob frowned as he answered, "It appears that a corporation called Mountain Properties and Trust holds the lease."

"So, who owns them?"

"That's what I'm having trouble tracking down. Ownership in these groups is usually fairly easy to establish, but the owners of MPT seem to have made a real effort to hide their true identities. In a town the size of Timber Ridge, that's no small feat."

"I'll agree with you that it sounds odd," I said, "but I'm not exactly sure how the information is going to help me, even if you're able to get it."

Bob raised a finger in the air. "Don't kid yourself. Knowing your opponent is half the battle in these situations."

"Well, thanks for trying," I said. "How would you like a specialty pizza on the house for your efforts?"

"Believe me, I'm not finished yet," Bob said. "I just wanted to let you know where things stand as of right now. I was doing this as a favor to you and your sister, but now I'm personally intrigued. Trust me, I'll sort out the paper trail and know who the real leaseholder is soon enough."

"What are you holding out for, two pizzas?"

He smiled at me. "As good as that sounds, I'll have to take a raincheck for both of them. I'm due in court in ten minutes, and I can't be late."

"What's so urgent?" It must be an exciting life, but it wasn't one for me. I had enough on my hands making pizza *and* keeping my employees out of trouble. Either option would have been a full-time job on their own.

"I really can't say what it's regarding," he said. "I'll keep you posted."

"Thanks, Bob. I appreciate it."

"I know you do, but we both know that's not the real reason I'm doing it. When it all comes down to it, I just seem to have lost the ability to tell your sister no. See you later, Eleanor."

"Good luck, Bob."

Soon after he left, I finished an order and walked into the dining room with it myself. I handed it to Maddy so she could deliver it to the proper table, and as I did, I asked her, "You just had to drag him into this, didn't you?"

"Are you crazy? I'd never do anything against your direct and express wishes. He volunteered."

As she delivered the pizza, I chuckled. "Do you honestly expect me to believe that?"

When Maddy came back, she said, "You'd better. When push comes to shove, he's got his own self-interest at heart."

"Do you mean he's willing to do all this work just to keep you happy?"

"Think about it, Eleanor. There's more reason than that," she said as she walked back into the kitchen with me. "What happens if you have to shut down?"

I'd never really given it much thought. "I'm not quite sure," I admitted.

"As much as I love you, Eleanor, you can be a little thick at times. If there's no pizzeria for me to work in, there's less reason for me to stay in Timber Ridge. Trust me, Bob's not doing this for you. At least that's not the only reason."

"Would you leave town again, Maddy, if I had to shut the restaurant down?" I'd grown so accustomed to having her there with me that I couldn't imagine my life without her again. I'd leaned heavily on Maddy when Joe had died, and I was just beginning to realize that I needed her more than I'd ever imagined.

"Let's not worry about that right now, okay?" she asked. "We'll burn that bridge when we come to it."

I wasn't all that pleased with her reply, but there was nothing I could really do about it. "That's fine with me. But Maddy, you should know one thing."

"What's that?"

"All things being equal, no matter what happens with the pizzeria, I want you to stay."

She gave me a quick hug, and smiled at me. "I know you feel that way, but it's nice to hear it every now and then."

Greg came into the kitchen, and when he saw we were hugging, he started to back out.

"Come on in," I said as I broke free from my sister.

"I don't want to interrupt," Greg said.

"You're not," I said. "What can I do for you?"

He looked at my sister and said, "Maddy, if you're finished wrapping things up in here, I could use a hand out front."

"Why, have we suddenly gotten crowded?" she asked.

"You tell me," he said as he held the door open. Coming into the restaurant was a long stream of people, each one sporting a green baseball cap with blue and cinnamon stripes prominently featured.

"Who are they?" I asked.

Maddy laughed. "Can't you tell by their caps? They're fans of the Sparrows. Did you know they were coming, Eleanor?"

"I don't even know who they are," I said. "How could I know they were on their way here? I assume by *Sparrows* you don't mean actual birds."

Greg shook his head. "How long have you lived in Timber Ridge, Eleanor? They're the middle school soccer team."

"I can't keep track of every sports team and group in town," I said in my defense. "But at least they look hungry."

"Then we'd better get busy," Maddy said as she and Greg went out to face the crowd. I wondered how long I could count on getting so much patronage from the townsfolk with a competing pizzeria just down the promenade, but I was determined that no matter what, I was going to enjoy it while I could.

A dozen pizzas later, all of us were worn out from the intensity of the Sparrows fan-club visit. I glanced at the clock and saw that it was nearly two, the start of our own lunch break, before we had to get ready for our dinner crowd.

"Why don't you go ahead and lock the door," I told Greg as our last customer paid his bill. "We could use an extra few minutes to get a jump on things."

I didn't have to tell him twice. He flipped the sign over, engaged the lock, and stood by the door until our last customer left. Greg never said anything, but it could be a little unnerving for him on sentinel duty there. Even so, it was better than the way Josh reacted when I'd ask him to close a little early. He'd been known to make up stories just to run off any diners he felt were moving a little too slowly for his taste. At least I would be saved from having to deal with his teenage temper reacting to the new pizzeria for the moment. Josh wouldn't be in until later, since he was scheduled to work the evening shift, and I wondered how he'd react to the news. At least I had a break before he'd arrive and I'd have to deal with his outrage at the news.

Once the last customer left, Maddy looked around the dining room and said, "I can't believe how much of a mess they made."

"Don't think of it that way," I said as we all started getting the place back in order. Greg was on table duty, Maddy helped him bus, and I retrieved food and napkins from the floor so I could clear enough of a path to get the vacuum.

"How should I think of it?"

"As dollars in our register," Greg said before I could reply. He looked sheepishly at me and said, "Sorry, I didn't mean to speak out of turn."

"It's not a problem. You said exactly what I was thinking myself," I answered as I picked up an errant soiled paper napkin from the floor. Sometimes I wished I wore gloves, but my hands would be in scalding water soon enough as I washed dishes, and I wouldn't touch anything else until they were clean again. I liked to keep my restaurant clean, and I'd do whatever it took to make it happen.

Like most messes, it wasn't as bad as it had originally looked. We had the dining room in good shape in short order, and Greg took off, with my blessing.

As soon as he was gone, Maddy turned to me and asked, "What do you want to do now? Should we do all of the dishes, or should we forget about them for the moment and do a little more digging into Mr. Sizemore's life?"

I was tempted, but I wasn't all that certain that I could focus on anything else with a sink full of dirty dishes, and more waiting to be washed. "Let's go back and see just how bad it really is. With both of us working, we might be able to knock them out in no time."

Maddy shrugged. "Hey, it's your place. I'm just your number one employee." She looked at me and added, "I am number one, right?"

I laughed at that as I opened the door to the kitchen.

"What?" Maddy said. "Does that mean you aren't going to comment?"

"I thought my reply was on the nose," I said with a smile.

We walked back into the kitchen, and I looked at the mess. If anything, it was worse than I had expected.

I turned to Maddy and said, "I don't know about you, but I don't think I can face another dirty dish."

She grabbed my apron from me and threw it onto the counter. "Let's leave them for Josh, then."

I took my apron, sighed, and put it back on. "We both know that I can't do that, no matter how much I'd love to. I can delegate most things, but I can't make anyone else do something that I'm not willing to do myself."

She grinned. "I can always hope otherwise, but how can I say that I'm surprised by that reaction? Let's get to it, then. You wash, and I'll dry. We'll be out of here in no time."

"Why don't we make something to eat while we're working? That way we won't have to deal with it later."

"That sounds great to me. What did you have in mind?" she asked.

"Surprise me."

As I started on the dishes, I could see Maddy pulling pizza dough out of the refrigerator.

She was just starting to knuckle the dough into the pan when she caught me watching her. "Hey, no peeking."

I turned back to the dishes and, after a few minutes, she rejoined me and started drying the rinsed items from the rack.

I kept waiting for her to tell me about her latest concoction, but when she didn't say anything about it, I finally broke down and said, "I give up. You win. What kind of pizza are we having?"

"I honestly don't know what I would call it," she said, "because I'm not entirely sure anyone's ever made one quite like it before. But I'm hoping it's good."

"That makes two of us," I said.

Whatever it was, it smelled delicious. I found my gaze drifting back to the conveyor oven, wondering what she'd put together. I knew our operation wasn't fancy like having a wood-fired oven and pizza dough flying through the air would be, but our place was friendly and functional and, at least so far, it had allowed me to make a living doing something I'd grown to love. I couldn't imagine my life without A Slice of Delight, any more than I could envision living in Timber Ridge without Maddy.

I was going to have to do something to make sure that the pizzeria stayed open regardless of anything that happened outside its doors, and whatever I finally came up with was going to have to be good.

"So, are you going to try some, or just sit there staring at it all afternoon?" Maddy asked me as I plated a piece of her pizza concoction. We'd knocked the dishes out as the pizza had been cooking, and I had no problem with leaving the few dirty dishes we'd created for later. Now we were sitting in a booth out front looking outside. We'd decided to sit there as we ate and discussed possible plans to combat Italia's. It wasn't that I didn't love my kitchen, but I spent enough time back there working during the course of a day to want to get out of it now and then. We kept the lights off and the sign switched to CLOSED, and no one bothered us.

I got my nerve up and took the first bite.

"It's interesting," I said. "I've had pineapple and ham on a pizza before, but never combined with spicy sausage, mushrooms, jalapeno peppers, and Tabasco sauce. If you had to give it a name, what would you call it?"

She grinned at me as she said proudly, "I don't know about you, but I kind of like 'the Volcano.' Should we add it to the menu?"

I thought about it and realized that updating the menu, and what we offered to our customers, might not be such a bad idea. "Why not? We can create a whole new section on our menu and update our prices at the same time," I said.

Maddy stared at me for a few seconds, and then she finally burst out laughing. "It's really not that bad, is it? I made it as a joke to perk you up a little, but honestly, I kind of like it."

As I dropped the slice in my hand onto my plate, I said, "It's not something I'd ever order, but you never know. Some folks might like it."

"Wow, just think what else I might be able to create if I have the chance," Maddy said.

"Tell you what. Why don't we see how this does before we get too carried away?" I was still hungry, so I took another bite despite the heat in my mouth, and to my surprise, I found it starting to grow on me as well.

Maddy finished another bite, and then said, "It has a little sweetness, a little saltiness, and a little heat."

I must have bitten into a pepper, because my mouth started burning and tears were welling up in my eyes. "More like a lot of heat," I said as I grabbed my water glass and drained it.

"Maybe I'll back off on the peppers a little next time," Maddy said.

"I'd keep it exactly like it is. After all, a lot of folks love spicy food."

"All we can do is offer it and see if we get any takers." She pushed her plate away as she added, "A little of it goes a long way, doesn't it?"

"I'm through, too," I said.

After we pushed our plates away, I asked, "Should we clean this up and get started digging?"

"I don't think we should leave the pizzeria again," Maddy said.

"Come on, don't be such a baby. It's not that cold out. Maybe you just need a warmer coat."

"It's not because of the cold, Eleanor," Maddy answered. "I just think our time might be better spent if we came up with some kind of plan instead of just rushing into this headfirst."

I looked closely into my sister's eyes for a few seconds, and she asked me, "What are you doing?"

"I just can't believe those words came out of your mouth. You're usually the one who wants to stir up trouble and see what happens."

Maddy nodded. "Maybe this time I need to be the sister who offers a reasoned perspective."

I couldn't believe she could say that with a straight face. "I'd love to know how you plan to do that."

Maddy grinned at me and said, "It's easy. I'll just pretend that I'm you."

We sat there going over dozens of possibilities, but we weren't having much luck, and the time kept moving forward.

We were both lost in thought since we still hadn't come up with anything even approaching a game plan when Josh and Greg tapped on the glass door. I glanced at the clock on the wall and saw that we still had ten minutes before we were due to open for our evening shift. It was rare for one of them to come early, but the fact that they were together meant that something was up, and from the expressions on their faces, it wasn't good.

I let them in. "Josh knows what's going on," Greg said.

Wonderful. "I suppose you two are ready to go confront Judson Sizemore again," I said.

"That's one way to go," Josh said, and I marveled again about just how much he looked like his father had at that age. "Can we eat first, though?"

Both young men went straight to the new pizza before I could warn them about its combustible properties.

"What is it?" Josh asked as he took a piece and smelled it. I'd noticed that about him long ago, an odd habit indeed: Nothing went into that boy's mouth until he smelled it first, and if it didn't pass his sniff test, he refused to eat it.

"It's Maddy's new experiment," I said. "You aren't under any obligation to try it."

Josh shrugged, and then took a bite. He chewed it slowly, and then, after careful consideration, said, "I like it."

"You're kidding," Maddy said.

"No, really, it's good."

Greg leaned over and took a piece for himself. He had a bite, chewed it, and then dropped his slice onto my plate. "Man, that's awful. It's way too hot and spicy."

"If you don't want it, I'll take your share," Josh said.

I pushed the platter toward him. "You're welcome to the rest of it."

"Sweet," he said as he took the remaining slices to another table.

"I'm still hungry," Maddy said. "Shall I make us something else?"

"Why don't I take care of this one?" I asked as I stood. I'd had enough of my sister's creative approach to pizza-making to last me a while. "Greg, would you like me to make you something, too?"

"No thanks. I had a burger at Brian's Grill. You all go ahead, though. I'll keep you company."

I went back into the kitchen, and to my surprise, the three of them followed me, including Josh holding the remnants of that abomination of a pizza in one hand as he ate the final slice. I wasn't sure I'd ever be able to get that taste out of my mouth. Something simple was needed to cleanse my palette, the way a sorbet does, so I decided to make a plain cheese pizza for Maddy and me.

As I slid it onto the conveyor, she said, "You're not putting any toppings on it at all? Really?"

"I think I've had my fill of extras at the moment. Something simple might be good, but I can make you something else, if you'd like. What do you think?"

"Maybe you're right," she said after a moment's pause.

"Why are you two so early?" I asked, now that the pizza was on its journey through the oven. It might not be as fancy as the wood-fired one they had at Italia's, but it made good, consistent pizza time after time, and that was all I could ask of it.

"We came to help," Greg said.

I looked around the clean kitchen. "Thanks, but

you're a little late. Maddy and I took care of the dishes as soon as you left."

"Not with that," Josh said. "We're talking about the new pizza place."

"I can't believe you bothered him with this before he even came to work, Greg."

"He didn't have to," Josh said between bites. "I heard about it on the radio."

"He's advertising?" I asked, unable to believe he could afford to, in such a small market.

"Oh, yes. It's a regular media blitz. You've got to do something about it, Eleanor. This guy is not fooling around."

"That's what we told her," Greg chimed in.

"Go ahead. One of you come up with a plan. I'm listening," I said.

"We're one step ahead of you," Greg said. "Josh and I are going to stand in front of his restaurant when he opens and block people from going in."

I looked at Josh for a second before I trusted myself to speak. "And you don't think your father will have a problem with you doing that, what with him being the chief of police and all?"

"What's he going to do, lock me up?" he asked with a grin. "Mom would never forgive him."

"I can't say anything about that, but we all know that your father will find a way to blame me for it." I had to get their attention. As I looked at each of them in turn, I said, "Let me be perfectly clear. There will be no human barricades or demonstrations of any kind anywhere near Italia's. We need to attack this problem with a positive response, not a negative one. Do we understand each other?"

They both said that they did, and I only hoped it was true. At the very least, if they disobeyed me now, they couldn't claim ignorance.

"Good," I said. "I'm glad we got that settled. Now, does anyone have any ideas about what we can do to make sure our customers keep coming here instead of going there?"

"We could always cut prices," Josh said.

"Only if we're all willing to work for free," I said. "Our margins here are pretty slim as it is. It wouldn't take much for us to win the battle by selling more pizzas and end up losing the war by being forced to shut down."

"Forget about price cuts," Maddy said. "How about doing some kind of giveaway? We can put a ticket on the bottom of every large pizza pan and takeout box, and at the end of the week, we have a big drawing to see who wins."

"What's the prize going to be?" I asked, intrigued by the concept, but not sure how much foot traffic it would generate.

She smiled at me. "We could always give away a date with the owner."

"I don't think so," I said. Since David Quinton had left town to live in Raleigh, potential beaus weren't exactly lining up to take his place. I couldn't really blame them. There were folks in town whispering behind my back that I'd driven him off by refusing to date him, and I wasn't so sure they were wrong. I'd tried my best, but the memory of my late husband, Joe, was still so strong in my heart that I doubted I'd ever be able to let anyone else in.

I decided to turn the tables on my sister. "We could give a date away with you, instead."

"I'm not sure how Bob Lemon would feel about that," Greg said.

Maddy smiled at him. "Are you kidding? He'd be good for ten pizzas every night. That alone might be enough to get us solidly in the black."

I'd had enough of that particular topic. "Nobody's going out with anyone as a prize in a drawing. There's got to be something else we could give away. How about a free pizza to the winner?"

Maddy arched an eyebrow. "That's not exactly a big incentive, is it?"

"You come up with something, then."

"I have an idea," Josh said.

"Does it require any of us to go out on a forced date?" I asked.

"No."

"Then at least you've got my attention."

"We could name a pizza after the winner for a week, like Bob's Specialty Pizza. Then, the next week, we'll have a new drawing and do it again."

"Do you think that would be a draw?" I asked.

Josh shrugged, but Maddy answered, instead. "If we play it right, it could. We can put the winner's name in the window, and make a big deal out of it. Kids from the high school would love it, and even some of your older customers might get a kick out of having their names up on the wall. We can even keep track of the winners by keeping a master list posted all the time. I like it, Josh."

I nodded and looked at Greg. "What do you think?"

He looked reluctant to respond, so I said, "Now's the time to voice any concerns, before we do something that turns out to be a mistake."

Greg nodded, and then said, "It's a great idea, but I'm not sure it will make enough of a difference to keep us afloat."

"It's a start, though," I said. "Good job, Josh."

I saw our pizza coming out of the oven, so I said, "Let's take this back out front. Maddy, if you'll grab some drinks, I'll bring this. Are you sure you don't want to join us, Greg?"

He looked at the bubbling cheese and the golden brown crust and said, "Maybe I'll have one slice."

"I'll have one, too," Josh said.

I looked at the platter and saw that Maddy's abomination was gone. "I think you've had enough for one meal," I said with a laugh.

"Hey, I'm a growing boy."

"Let's just make sure the direction you're growing isn't out."

He nodded. "Yeah, you're probably right."

The mood was lighter, which was what I'd been trying for, and I was beginning to feel that things weren't quite as hopeless as I'd felt earlier.

We opened for dinner as soon as we'd finished cleaning up our own mess, and I was making the fourth order when I heard a commotion out front. What on earth was going on now? I slid the latest pizza onto the conveyor and walked out.

Judson Sizemore was in the middle of my pizzeria, handing out what had to be notices of his grand opening.

It appeared that he wasn't going to wait for me to attack first.

He was coming straight for me before I had a chance to do a thing.

"You need to leave," I said as I approached him.

"I already told him that," Maddy said, her face flushed with anger. "He says it's a free country, and he can do whatever he wants."

Greg started toward him as he said, "If you won't leave on your own, I'll give you a hand."

I looked around the restaurant to see who was witnessing this confrontation. Among the regulars were several townsfolk, and in particular, Karen Green, a woman who ate with us every day we were open. She, along with just about everyone else, looked dismayed by the scene, and I couldn't blame any of them.

"Nobody's going to do anything," I said firmly, stepping between Greg and Judson. "Josh, call your father. Tell him that we have a trespasser on our premises who refuses to leave."

"With pleasure," Josh said as he pulled out his cell phone.

"This is a public restaurant," Judson said loudly. "I have as much right to be here as anyone else."

I pointed to a sign near the register that we'd had posted since we'd opened. "Think again. We have the right to refuse service to anyone we choose for whatever reason, and we're invoking it right now. You're not welcome here, and that's the last time I'm going to ask you nicely."

"What are you going to do, turn your goon on me?" Judson didn't look the least bit afraid. All it would take would be a nod from me, and the stranger would find himself suddenly sitting on the sidewalk out front wondering how it had happened so quickly.

"We don't need Greg," Maddy said with grim determination. "I'll kick his scrawny little carcass out of here myself. What do you say, Judson? Care to get your tail whipped by a woman?"

I was trying to head her off when I saw Kevin Hurley walk in. I was rarely happy to see our police chief in my pizzeria, but this time I was tempted to give him a giant hug and an extra large pizza with whatever he wanted on it.

"What seems to be the problem here?" he asked me.

"This woman just threatened me with physical violence," Judson said as he pointed a bony finger at Maddy.

"Is that true?" he asked Maddy.

"Hang on a second," I interrupted. "This is getting out of hand."

"I'm not talking to you, Eleanor," he said without looking away from Maddy. "Did you threaten him?"

"We asked him politely to leave, and he refused," she said a little petulantly. "It looked like he needed a little extra incentive, so I offered to give him a hand if he wasn't sure he could make it on his own."

Chief Hurley shook his head. "Maddy, what have I told you about that temper of yours? It's going to get you into some serious trouble some day."

"She didn't do anything wrong, Dad. He was passing out flyers for his new pizzeria in here," Josh said. "It's not right you're chewing Maddy out."

Kevin Hurley looked as though he was regretting coming into the Slice at his son's insistence. I pointed to the sign again and said, "We have the right to refuse service to anyone who walks through that door, and that's what I'm doing. Would you please escort this gentleman out of the restaurant?"

"That I can do," the chief said.

He turned to Judson. "It's time to leave, sir."

Judson gave Maddy one last icy glare, and then said, "It would be my pleasure. This place has an unpleasant odor anyway, and I'm certain the pizza is inedible."

Once he was gone, I turned to Maddy and said, "You didn't help. You know that, don't you?"

"Eleanor, I'm not about to just stand here while he destroys our business," she said sharply.

I looked around and noticed that our customers were sitting in silence, watching us as though we were some kind of dinner theater. I could swear I saw tears on Karen's face. This had to end right here.

I turned to my customers and said, "Folks, we're sorry about the disturbance. Your meals are on the house, as our way of apologizing for the scene you just had to witness. We hope you enjoy them."

I went back into the kitchen, with Maddy close on my heels.

It was clear from the storm clouds on her face that she was not at all happy with me at the moment. "Why did you do that?" she asked.

"It's better than the alternative. I can't afford to lose any customers, especially not right now. If it means giving away a little food, so be it."

"They weren't that upset," Maddy said.

"Did you see Karen Green? She was in tears."

"Oh, please, the woman cries at television commercials." Maddy was not about to let this go, but I was finished talking about it, and the sooner she realized that, the better off we'd both be.

I waved a hand in the air. "I don't want to talk about it anymore."

Greg came back with a sour look on his face. Before he could say anything, I cut him off. "Don't you start in on me, too. I did what I had to do."

"That part is fine with me," Greg said. "That's not what I'm upset about. I just can't believe that Bobby Bannister and Jim Vance upped their orders to extra large specials to go once they heard your offer."

I shook my head and had to laugh. "Tell them they're both crazy, they'll get what they first ordered. I'd be happy to make them anything else, but tell them that they're paying for it."

"Two small pizzas it is," he said with a grin.

"Why are you smiling?" I asked Greg before he went back out front.

"I told them both that was exactly what you'd say, but they were pretty insistent that I try anyway."

"Would you like me to tell them myself?" I asked.

Greg thought about it a second, and then shook

his head. "No, but you might want to talk to Karen Green. She's still pretty upset about what just happened."

I nodded. "Maddy, handle the kitchen for me for the next few minutes. I'll be right back."

"Eleanor, are you punishing me for standing up for you?" she asked.

"Believe it or not, it's not a bad thing working back here. I just need you to cover for me while I talk to Karen," I said.

"Okay, but don't be long." I knew my sister wasn't all that excited about running the kitchen by herself. That was only fair. When I had to wait tables and run the cash register instead of running the kitchen, I always felt out of my element, too.

She'd have to deal with it, though.

I had a customer to keep.

Karen was waiting by the kitchen door as I walked out. Before I could say a word, she said in a distressed voice, "Eleanor, is it true? I don't know what I'll do. Are you really going out of business?"

The woman's voice carried all through the dining room, and the last thing I needed was for her sense of panic to spread to my other regulars.

"Of course not," I said, matching her decibel level. "We're here to stay, and you can count on it."

She shook her head. "He's trying to run you out of business though, isn't he? He can't, Eleanor, he just can't."

"Don't worry," I said. "We'll be all right."

"Why don't I believe you?" she asked.

"Have some faith in me, Karen. Can I get you anything while you wait for your pizza?"

"I'm too upset to eat," she said. That really was

serious. The woman never went a day without pizza from us. I was about to say something when she added, "I'll eat it later. Could you make my order to go?"

"You've got it. I'll be right back."

I ducked back into the kitchen just as her pizza came out of the oven. Maddy looked gratefully at me and started to take off her cooking apron, but I had to dash her hopes of escape. "You might as well leave it on. I'm just grabbing a pizza for take-out," I said as I grabbed a box.

She did so, albeit reluctantly, and then leafed through the orders. "We didn't have anything to go," Maddy said.

"We do now. Karen's decided to take hers home with her."

I boxed the pizza, cut it, and shut the top. "I'll be right back," I said.

"You'd better."

I handed Karen the pizza. She had the money out in her hand to pay, and tried to shove it to me.

I refused it, though. "Remember? It's on the house," I said.

"How are you going to survive if you start giving your food away?" she asked. "I insist that you take my money."

Taking it would be a sign of weakness, one I couldn't afford to show. "Thanks, but we're fine."

She put her money away, and then walked out of the pizzeria muttering softly to herself. At least I could count on her staying a customer.

I walked over to Jim and Bobby's table. "Do you two need to talk to me?"

"No, ma'am," they said in perfect unison. "We're good."

"All right then."

I went back into the kitchen, and said, "Okay, you can work the front again."

"Thanks," Maddy replied, the relief thick in her voice. As she headed for the door, Maddy added, "Sis, I'm sorry I lost my cool in there."

"Don't worry about it. Thanks for sticking up for me."

"I have to. We're family," she said with a grin.

The rest of the evening was pretty uneventful, and we were ten minutes from closing for the night when Maddy came into the kitchen.

"Do you have another order?" I asked. "It's late, but I can probably squeeze one more in."

"This isn't about food. There's someone here to see you."

"Show them back, then," I said. "I can talk while I start cleaning up."

"Okay. Whatever you say."

I wasn't sure who was about to walk into my kitchen—but it certainly wasn't anyone I would have guessed in a thousand tries—when the door opened and my visitor walked in.

Chapter 3

"Hey, Eleanor," David Quinton said as he walked in.

"David, what are you doing here?" I asked. He looked good, strong, and tan. There was something about the way he carried himself that told me he was not the same man who'd left town a few months before.

"Don't I get a hug?" he asked with a smile.

"You don't want any part of this," I said as I looked down at my dirty apron. "I'm a mess."

"I don't care," he answered with a laugh. "I'll take my chances."

I hugged him, and as I did, I was surprised to find that there was still a spark there, no matter how much I'd been trying to deny it. I thought David was out of my life for good, and here he was, showing up again unexpectedly and catching me with my guard down.

"It's good to see you," I said as we broke apart.

"You look beautiful," he said simply.

I put a hand to my hair. "Don't even try to lie to me. I know exactly what I look like right now."

He grinned. "I didn't say you were at your best, just that you look really good to me. How have you been?"

"Fine," I said.

"Despite the competition down the promenade?"

"How in the world did you find out about that?"

He laughed, and I realized how much I'd missed the sound of it. "Timber Ridge is a small town. I don't have to tell you that."

"Funny, I never heard a word that you were coming back. How long have you been in town, anyway?"

"Actually, I just got in. The home office asked me to come back and clear up a few things. I'll be in town for three or four days, and I was hoping we could get together for a meal while I'm here. I know how crazy your schedule is, so I'll make it breakfast, lunch, or dinner; your choice. Listen, don't worry about it if you can't make it. I understand completely, but it might do you some good to get out, and I know I'd love to spend some time with you."

It wasn't as though he was moving back. What could one lunch hurt? "Sure, why not? Are you free tomorrow?"

A frown crossed his lips. "I should have mentioned earlier that tomorrow will be tight. Are you still interested?"

"Of course I am," I said, surprising myself with my enthusiasm. What was that all about?

David looked around the kitchen and said, "I know you're busy, so I'll let you get back to work." He paused at the door and then he added, "It was good seeing you again, Eleanor. I'm looking forward to getting together soon."

"It was good seeing you, too, David." I was impressed. The old David I knew would have dropped everything at an invitation to see me. Had he grown stronger since he'd moved to Raleigh? That had been my main problem with him before, his lack of assertiveness when it came to our relationship. I had to admit that I liked the change I'd seen in him.

The second David was out of the kitchen, Maddy came bursting through the door. "Wow, was it just me, or did he look good?"

"It wasn't just you," I admitted.

"Eleanor, life doesn't give you many second chances. I hope you're not going to blow it this time."

"He's not moving back to Timber Ridge permanently," I said. "He's just here for a few days on business."

"The least you can do is ask him out to lunch," Maddy said.

"I can't," I said.

My sister was clearly unhappy with that response. "Would you mind telling me why not?"

I grinned at her as I explained, "Because he already asked me. We're going out tomorrow."

Maddy nodded her approval. "That's my girl." She looked around the kitchen, and then added, "This is going to take awhile. Why don't we jump on this mess early?"

"I'm game if you are. Tell Greg and Josh they're handling the front, and we'll get started on cleaning up."

Maddy nodded, and as she left the kitchen, I couldn't help remembering the changes I'd just seen in David. It was as though in the short amount of time he'd spent in Raleigh, he'd grown more confident in himself. I had to admit, I really liked this new and improved version of the man.

It was just too bad he wasn't back to stay.

As I ran hot water in the sink, I tried to clear my mind of daydreams about what might have been with David Quinton, though it was more difficult than I ever could have imagined. I had enough problems of my own to focus on without adding the complications of a love life into the mix. I couldn't afford any distractions at the moment, and that included tall, handsome men who suddenly reappeared in my life.

Saturday, the morning of the grand opening for Italia's, was incredibly beautiful, crisp and clear with just a hint of the cold to come. The sun shone through the dappled leaves, and if I was being honest with myself, I was disappointed we weren't having freezing rain with dark, overcast clouds low enough to reach down and grab whoever dared show their face outside.

So much for good luck being on my side.

I drove to the Slice, parked in my usual space in back, and walked through the passageway that led between the alley and the front of the businesses on the promenade. The city's crew always decorated this pleasant little brick path in an effort to get folks to use some of the parking in back. I wasn't sure how effective it was, but I always enjoyed the changing tableaus. In honor of autumn, there were stacked bales of hay sporting pumpkins and a scarecrow that didn't look out of place at all.

Two years before, they'd done it all up in Halloween style, with ghosts, goblins, and ghouls, but one complaint from a tourist from out of town, and the display had come down. I knew the decorated Christmas trees filled with offerings of seed and suet ornaments would likely be next to go, but I hoped not. I myself enjoyed seeing a lit menorah, even though I wasn't Jewish, and some of my friends who were eagerly admitted that the sparkling and brightly decorated trees were among the things they looked forward to seeing in December every year. It was one thing I didn't like about the modern age, despite advances in science, medicine, and just about every other thing that touched our daily lives: Some folks took themselves way too seriously and managed to wreck things for everyone who was just trying to spread a little beauty wherever they could manage it.

When I got to the Slice, I was surprised to find Bob Lemon standing at the front door, though we weren't due to open for hours.

"Were you supposed to meet Maddy for breakfast?" I asked as I reached for my keys. "She didn't say anything to me about it."

"Actually, I was hoping to speak with you before she arrived."

I unlocked the door and let him in, then locked

it behind us. "Bob, I'm flattered that you'd ask me, but I'm sorry, I already have a date for lunch today."

He looked startled. "Eleanor, I'm not here to ask you out."

"I know that," I said with a smile. "I was just trying to be funny."

He nodded. "That's good, then."

"You don't have to look so relieved," I said. "Believe it or not, some people find me quite pleasant to be around."

He was clearly not in any mood for my particular brand of humor. "Eleanor, this is serious. I found out who is backing your competition, and trust me, you're not going to be pleased when you hear who's behind this."

That wiped the smile off my face. "Who is it?"

"Nathan Sizemore," he said grimly.

"Are you sure?" Why was Bob acting so upset about the news?

"I'm positive," he said.

"Hang on a second. We're talking about that kook who lives on the edge of town, right? How can he afford to back a restaurant?" Nathan was famous in Timber Ridge, but not because of his wealth. If he were rich, he'd be labeled eccentric, but as far as I knew, he was just plain nuts. "The man goes around town claiming he invented dirt, Bob."

The attorney shook his head. "It's just a little joke of his. He didn't invent it, but he certainly owns enough of it around here. I kept coming across his name in my research for the owners of Mountain Properties and Trust, so I did some digging into his assets. Nathan Sizemore owns ten thousand acres full of timber in North Carolina, Virginia, and Tennessee, and he could buy everything in Timber Ridge with the interest he earns from just one of his accounts. This is not a man you want to go up against."

I slumped down into a booth before I could fall down. "So, it's over before it even begins. With pockets that deep, I don't stand a chance."

"It's grim," he agreed. "I thought you should know."

"Thanks. I'll tell Maddy you were by."

He looked up and said, "There's no need. She's already here. I'll go out and share the bad news with her myself, so you don't have to deal with it."

He unlocked the door and let himself out, while I just sat there, wondering what I could do now. Judson, I could have handled; at least the playing field would have been even. But with Nathan Sizemore backing him with more money than I had ever known he possessed, there was no doubt in my mind that I didn't stand a chance. I wasn't going to shut down A Slice of Delight yet, no matter how much fiscal sense that might make, but it was clear my days as a pizzeria owner were probably numbered. Not all of my customers would defect, I was sure of at least that, but enough would start buying their pizzas at Italia's to effectively put me out of business. There just weren't enough Karen Greens in the area to keep me going.

Maddy came in a few minutes later, and I was still sitting in the back booth feeling sorry for myself.

"Why aren't you making the dough?" she asked. "We're not going to just roll over, are we?"

"No, we'll keep fighting," I said as I stood and tried to shake the gloom off me, trying to put on a brave face for her benefit, if not my own.

"That's the spirit."

We walked into the back, and I started gathering the ingredients for my pizza dough. I'd done it a thousand times, and I could make it by heart, though I always glanced at the recipe every morning just for a little insurance.

As I worked on that, Maddy got out her cutting board and waved a knife in the air as she spoke. "Hey, you've got a big date today, don't you?"

I'd forgotten all about meeting David after hearing Bob Lemon's news. "I did, but I'm probably going to cancel it now. I doubt I'd be very good company, and David deserves better."

"That might be true, but then again, he might be just what you need," she said. "Staying here and stewing all day isn't going to make things any easier on you."

"I suppose you've got a point."

"Besides, you might never have this chance again. I'm sure Greg and I will be able to handle things while you're gone. He doesn't have any classes today since it's Saturday, so I asked him to come by and work. Is that okay?"

"It's fine," I said.

Too bad we didn't need him. Though it was two hours before Italia's grand opening, we had only one customer visit our restaurant, a young woman who wanted a Diet Coke to go, and nothing else.

By the time David arrived, I'd just about given up hope, at least for today.

"How about a picnic?" David asked as he met me outside the Slice holding two large plastic bags. "I got two hibachi steak orders from Nara's."

He held the bags up in the air, and his grin was infectious, as he added, "Why not? It's certainly pretty enough out."

I glanced over at Italia's, where a crowd was already starting to gather for their grand opening, though it was still ninety minutes away. "That sounds fine, but do you mind if we eat someplace besides the promenade?"

He looked over at the new pizzeria. "Sorry about that. I would never have done this if I'd remembered that place was opening today at noon." David frowned, and then suggested, "Why don't we eat on one of the benches on the shortcut? I saw the decorations yesterday, and they're really nice."

"That sounds perfect," I said as I followed him. I half hoped the two benches would be taken so we could get even farther away, but, again, I was out of luck.

We took the bench across from the mural and the stacks of hay, and David served us both.

"I must admit, this isn't what I'd pictured," I said as he handed me a paper plate and a set of plastic silverware.

"You still like Nara's, don't you?"

"I really do. I guess I was just expecting you to try to impress me a little more than this."

He laughed. "Trust me, I've been dreaming about this food since I left town. Besides," he added with a grin, "if anyone around here knows how hard you are to impress, it has to be me. Remember how much I used to try?"

"So what changed?" I asked, unable to hide my curiosity any longer.

He took a bite of steak, carrot, mushroom, and rice, and then asked, "What do you mean?"

"You've changed, David," I said.

"How so?"

"You're more confident, and not nearly so needy as you were before."

I wasn't sure if he'd be upset by my candor, but his smile surprised me. "Wow, don't hold back, Eleanor. Tell me what you really think."

I felt bad immediately. "I'm sorry. I didn't mean to be so blunt."

He laughed at that statement. "It's fine. I've known you a long time, you don't have to apologize to me for anything." He took another bite, and when he was finished with it, he added, "I'll be honest with you. Moving to Raleigh was the best thing that ever happened to me."

"It's only been a few months," I said after finishing a bite of my own. "How could that have happened so quickly?"

He waved his fork in the air as he explained. "Try moving to a place where you don't know a soul, and then get thrown into a job that's way over your head. It will make you change perspectives in a hurry. It didn't take me long to realize that I'd grown a little stale here, since we're both being so brutally honest. Going to a new city was exactly what I needed." He took another bite, and then added, "If I'm being honest about it, there was only one thing I missed in Timber Ridge."

I waved a piece of carrot at him. "Nara's cooking?"

He smiled. "Close, but no." David put his fork down, and then looked at me. "I'm not trying to scare you, and there's nothing I want from you, but the only thing I missed was you. I know I drove you away before, and there's no chance left for us now, but it's important to me for you to know that the only thing I regret in my life is the way I pursued you."

I shrugged. "You were earnest, I'll give you that."

"I was a golden retriever," he said with a laugh. "I'm sure it must have driven you crazy the way I followed you around hoping for a bit of your attention."

"Okay then, it's my turn to be candid. I was probably more than a little flattered by your interest," I admitted. It was true. I just wasn't sure what made me admit it to him. Maybe his rush of honesty was having more impact on me than I realized.

"But you were right to put me off. I can see that now. I fell for you, Eleanor, and when you didn't respond in kind, I started pushing you harder. I finally figured out that was exactly the wrong thing to do, and I hope you can forgive me."

"There's nothing to forgive," I said after I finished another bite. "It's like they say, another time, another place, who knows what might have happened."

"Well, it's another time right now, and I'm certainly in another place. I know you're not ready for anything more right now, and I respect that, but if you ever change your mind, I hope you'll call me.

"Don't tell me you'll be waiting for me," I said.

He grinned as he shook his head. "I won't lie to you. If I happen to meet someone else, it will be too bad. But if we're both free and interested, I'd be a fool not to pursue it. And that's the end of the sales pitch. I promise."

"Not so fast," I said, closing the white clamshell container. "I can't believe you'd be interested in a long-distance relationship with me, when we couldn't even manage to get together when we both lived in the same town."

"Try me. I don't mind driving, and my schedule's pretty flexible. It helps having a branch office here, so just give me an excuse, and I'll be here." He shook his head as he laughed. "I promised myself I wouldn't say anything today. I just wanted to enjoy your company, but what can I do? You seem to have that effect on me." He looked down at my lunch. "Are you finished?"

"I'm stuffed," I said as I pushed some of the remaining rice around in the box.

"Me, too." As he gathered up our trash, I couldn't help noticing again the air of confidence he had about him. This was indeed a changed man, and he was clearly still interested in me, which was a nice stroking for my ego. But Joe was still in my heart, and I wasn't sure there would ever be room for anyone else there.

If there was, though, I couldn't imagine anyone better than David to find his way into my heart.

"I'd walk you back," David said, "but I lost all track of time, and I'm going to be late for a meeting as it is. I'm working seven days a week right now. Thanks for seeing me, Eleanor. It was great fun."

He leaned in to kiss my cheek, and I caught the hint of aftershave on his neck as he did. I had to admit that I enjoyed his proximity, and wouldn't have minded one bit if it had gone on a little longer.

As he started for the alley, I said, "If you have a chance, stop in and say goodbye before you go."

"I will," David said, and I watched him walk away with a new spring in his gait.

My, my, my, how things could change.

I walked back to the Slice, and found Maddy, Greg, and Josh standing out in front of the pizzeria.

"Our lunch breaks are over," I said as I glanced at my watch. "What happened, did you forget your key, Maddy?"

"No, it's right here," my sister said. "The only thing we're missing is a single customer to serve." she gestured to the area of the promenade in front of Italia's. It was full of dozens and dozens of people, many of whom I recognized as our regular customers. "We can't really blame them. Everyone wants to see what Italia's has to offer."

I'd nearly forgotten about the opening, which was a true indicator of how much I'd been enjoying David Quinton's company.

"I've got an idea. Why don't we go, too," I suggested as I reached past Maddy and locked our door.

"Are you serious?" she asked.

"Why not? It couldn't hurt to scout out the competition, and it's not like anyone's going to come to us."

I started toward the new restaurant, and the other three followed close behind. Maddy caught up with me and asked, "How did it go? Did he take you somewhere elegant?"

"In Timber Ridge? You're joking, right?"

"Well, someplace nicer than the Slice, anyway."

"We had a picnic at the shortcut," I said. "He'd been craving hibachi steak from Nara's since he moved to Raleigh, so we dined alfresco."

Maddy frowned. "Eleanor, maybe I was wrong about David. I just don't understand it."

"What don't you get?" I asked.

She shrugged as she admitted, "I thought for sure he'd pull out all the stops on his chance to take you to lunch."

"The old David would have, but I've got to tell you, Maddy, the man's changed."

My sister touched my arm lightly, and as I turned to look at her, I found her staring into my eyes. "What are you looking for?"

"To see if you've changed, too," she said.

"No, I hate to disappoint you, but it's the same old me," I replied.

"Then why are you grinning like a teenager?"

"I hadn't realized that I was," I said, trying to wipe any expression from my face that might be misinterpreted.

"Too late," she said. "Are you going to see him again?"

"He's coming by to say goodbye before he leaves," I admitted.

Maddy deflated. "That's it? He didn't try any harder than that to get another date with you?"

I considered not telling her about our conversation, but I knew that she wouldn't be satisfied until she heard it all. "He told me that if I'm ever willing to date again, he wants to be first in line."

"That's the spirit." My sister frowned at me, and after a moment's pause, she said, "But I'm willing to bet that you brushed him off."

"Actually, I left the door wide open," I said.

"I'm so proud of you," Maddy said as she stopped us and hugged me.

"There's not exactly a reason to celebrate," I said. "There's a real possibility that day might never come."

She laughed as she said, "But there's a chance that it might. That's all that counts, just knowing that there's a possibility you might say yes."

"You are a hopeless romantic, aren't you?"

"I thought you already knew that," my sister said as we joined the crowd. "No woman gets married as many times as I have without being one."

"You've got a point." I looked at my watch. "What time is Italia's supposed to open?"

A man beside me must have overheard, because he said, "They should have been open thirty minutes ago. I understand wanting to build suspense, but this is ridiculous. I wonder if there's anyplace else to eat around here."

"A Slice of Delight is just over there," Maddy said as she pointed back to our pizzeria.

"Nope, they're closed. I checked them half an hour ago."

"Try again in ten minutes," I said, that being all the time I was going to give Judson Sizemore before I gave up on him.

He shrugged, and I decided to let it go at that. A stage had been set up in front of the new pizzeria, and I saw that I wasn't the only one growing impatient with the delay. The mayor was whispering with the head of the city council, and they both kept looking back over their shoulders toward the restaurant.

I was about to say something to Maddy when I noticed Kevin Hurley mount the steps to the stage. He went directly to the mayor, whispered something to him, and then left as fast as he'd come.

The mayor immediately took the stage, approached the microphone, and then said, "Ladies and gentlemen, I'm afraid that the grand opening of Italia's has been delayed indefinitely. I'm sure the owner appreciates your support, but there's nothing that can be done about it. Enjoy the rest of your day." With that, he practically sprinted from the stage before a reporter from *Timber Talk*, our local paper, could interview him. I noticed a TV truck from WHKY in Hickory standing by, and a reporter holding a microphone as he conveyed the news to his viewers.

There were some grumbles from the crowd, and as they started breaking up, Maddy shouted, "I've got great news, folks. A Slice of Delight is open right now, if anyone's hungry."

There were murmurs and nods from the crowd, and several folks started off in our direction.

"Why on earth did you do that?" I asked as I hustled back to unlock the front door and get ready to make pizza.

"Their loss is our gain," she said with a grin. "Why not take advantage of it?"

I couldn't argue with her logic. "It looks like we're going to be busy. Why do you suppose Judson called off the grand opening?"

"Does it matter? We're getting some free publicity from it, and enough customers to help add to our rainy-day fund—and we both know it's about to pour."

I decided to go along with Maddy's idea, not that I had any real choice. If these folks wanted pizza, it wasn't up to me to tell them no.

I was making pizzas as fast as I could, with the conveyor belt full, and several more pies waiting to go through. I didn't even have time to look up when someone came through the kitchen door from the dining room.

"We're nearly out of dough," I said, "so I'm going to have to switch to what we've got in the freezer."

"And that's my problem how, exactly?" Kevin Hurley asked as he came in to the kitchen.

I was in no mood to deal with him at the moment. I had my hands full. "Chief, I'd love to chat, but I've got more orders than I know what to do with."

"Sorry, Eleanor, but this can't wait."

I shoved a loose strand of hair out of my face. "Do you want to see me throw a fit, because I'm not far from that right now. I've never made so many pizzas so quickly in my life."

"Yeah, funny how that worked out, isn't it?"

I stopped and stared at him. "Hang on a second. Are you implying that I had something to do with Italia's postponing their grand opening? What happened, did Judson lose his pizza man? Or did his wood supply fail to show up?"

"It's a little more serious than that," Police Chief Hurley said.

"I can't imagine that I could find it in me to care," I said flippantly.

"You should care about this," he said solemnly.

There was something in his tone of voice that made me stop what I was doing instantly. "What are you trying to tell me, Kevin?"

"The reason Italia's didn't open is because someone killed Judson Sizemore inside his pizzeria last night."

Chapter 4

"What? How did it happen?" I asked as I nearly dropped the pizza I'd just made onto the floor. I hadn't been a big fan of Judson Sizemore or the arrogant way he'd treated me, but that didn't mean I wanted to see him dead.

"I'm the one asking the questions, if you don't mind," Kevin said.

"Not until you tell me how he died," I said. "Otherwise, you're just wasting your breath."

He seemed to chew that over, and then he admitted, "This isn't for public knowledge, but he was hit from behind with a piece of firewood he used in that pizza oven of his."

What a horrible way to go. No matter how I felt about him, I hoped it had at least been quick. "Thank you for trusting me with that. Now, what do you want to know?"

"Let's cut to the chase. I understand the two of you had some very public arguments over the past few days."

I couldn't believe he'd actually put any credence in them. "You don't believe for one second that I would do anything to him, do you?"

Chief Hurley shrugged. "I'm not in the believing business. I'm just gathering facts right now, Eleanor." He looked around, and then said calmly, "You've got plenty of motive, even you can't deny that."

"Just because I wasn't thrilled about him opening his pizzeria doesn't mean I'm the one who killed him."

"You didn't get along, either."

I paused long enough to stare at him a moment before I trusted myself to speak again. "If I murdered everyone I ever had an argument with, the body count would be too high to measure."

The police chief was clearly not buying my argument. "This is different. It could have easily buried this place forever, and we both know it. You had a great deal to lose if Italia's did well. In fact, some might say your entire life."

"I don't agree with that for one second."

It was his turn to look hard at me. "That's your right." Kevin took a deep breath, and then asked, "Eleanor, where were you between the hours of midnight and six A.M. this morning?"

I shook my head in disbelief. Was this really happening, or was I in some kind of nightmare and couldn't wake up? I took a deep breath to calm myself before I replied, but it didn't do any good. This wasn't the first time the chief of police had implied that I was involved in a murder, and I was getting tired of it. "I was home in bed, and before you even think about asking me if anyone can confirm it, we both know that I was there alone."

"I figured as much," he said as he jotted the information into his little notebook. "I wasn't even going to ask." There had been times that I would have loved to shred that notebook into confetti, but there was nothing I could do about it at the moment. "I'm surprised you and your sister didn't have one of your famous movie nights and sleepovers."

"Even that would have been too convenient for you," I said. "I doubt you would have believed either one of us if we'd been playing Monopoly with the mayor."

"There you go, talking about belief again. Eleanor, since you haven't denied your public disagreement with the deceased, would you care to help me out here and speculate on anyone else who might have wished him harm?"

I could think of three other people, all members of my waitstaff now serving customers in the other room, but I wasn't about to name any of them. "Sorry, I'm at a loss who might want him dead. I really didn't know the man at all."

"It doesn't matter," he said as he flipped his notebook shut. "We'll find them ourselves."

"Good. When you do, I'll be waiting right here for an apology."

With a grin that reminded me so much of the boy I'd dated in high school, Kevin Hurley said, "Then you might be in for a long wait. We'll talk again later, Eleanor."

"Believe me when I tell you that I'm not looking forward to it."

He turned and looked at me one last time and

then said, "Now that I believe completely, regardless of what I said before."

"Can you imagine the nerve of that man?" Maddy asked the second Kevin left the kitchen. "He was back here grilling you, wasn't he?"

"Of course he was, but we'll have to talk about it later," I said as I pulled another pizza off the line, cut it, and shoved it toward her. "We have too many customers in the Slice right now to drop everything and worry about what Kevin Hurley is doing."

"I know that," she said, "but there's no way that we can afford to let him accuse us all of murder."

"I'm guessing he said something to you, too," I said as I prepped another dough round. Knuckling the dough into place onto the pan wasn't as fancy as tossing it in the air, and I doubted anyone would ever classify it as a "show," but it had to be a faster and more efficient way to make pizzas in a hurry.

"Oh, yes," she said. As Maddy picked up the waiting pizza, along with its twin, she headed out the door. "This makes things worse than they were before, Eleanor. We're going to have to come up with a plan."

I knew what that meant. Maddy and I had meddled into murder investigations in the past, and while it was never my choice, trouble seemed to continue finding me. Still, I wasn't about to back down from a fight, and I wouldn't stop digging into Judson's murder.

Josh came in a minute later for the next load of pizzas.

As he grabbed two and headed back out, I asked, "Is it slowing down any out there?"

"Are you kidding? We're being overrun."

"Make an announcement," I said, making an executive decision. "Tell anyone coming in that we've run out of dough, but if they'd like sandwiches, we'd be more than happy to make them."

"They aren't going to like that," Josh said.

"The dough in the refrigerator is gone with this pizza," I said. "We really don't have much choice."

"Use the fresh you made this morning."

"That was gone quite awhile ago," I replied. "Tell Maddy to do it if you don't want to. She's never been afraid to speak in public."

"I've got it covered, Eleanor. I'll tell them," he said.

I slid the last pizza onto the conveyor and started to clean up my prep stations while I waited for sandwich orders. The sauce I made every week was getting low, and if we ran out of that, I wasn't sure what we'd be serving, since that went on just about everything we made.

Maddy came back to the kitchen for another pickup minutes later. "Smart move. That will clear some of them out."

"It wasn't a ploy," I said. "It happens to be true."

"Wow, we had a bigger run than I thought."

"Has the announcement had any effect on the folks waiting?" I hated the idea of losing customers, not that there was anything I could do about it.

"A few of them drifted out," she said, "but it's not exactly like we had any tables for them anyway. I think the worst of it is over."

"Thank goodness. We're closing in an hour, regardless of who's still waiting to eat," I said as I glanced at the clock and I knew some of our dinner patrons would be unhappy with it. I could always make more quick dough given enough time, but I was exhausted, and I was sure the other three were, too.

Maddy looked relieved by the news. "If you weren't going to pull the plug, Greg and Josh wanted me to come back here to urge you to close soon. We're beat."

"Trust me, I'm worn out, too," I said with a slight smile. "I think we deserve a little break this evening. Do you want to make a sign for the door, or should I?"

"I'll handle it," she said as she looked around the kitchen, which was messier than I ever liked to see it. "You've got your hands full back here."

"I was told you were back here," Bob Lemon said as he walked into the kitchen to join us.

"Sorry, Bob, I can't talk," I said.

He ignored me completely. "Madeline, you are not to investigate this man's murder, and that's final."

Maddy hated her given name, and I could see her bristling at its use, not to mention the direct order her boyfriend had just given her. I looked around for something I could use as a shield when she exploded, but my sister surprised me by smiling at him.

It was clear that Bob was puzzled by her reaction as well.

"Did you hear me?" he asked in a halting voice.

Her smile never wavered as she said, "I must not

have. It sounded as though you were telling me what to do, and I know you're more intelligent than that."

His voice had a deeper pleading quality to it as he said, "The police chief is going to make this case his number one priority. If he finds you interfering with his investigation, you might get into a mess that even I can't get you out of."

I was watching his face, and it was clear that he realized he'd made a mistake as the words left his mouth. "What I mean to say is . . ."

One look at my sister's stare was enough to silence him.

After a brief pause, Maddy said to him softly, "You may leave," her tone calm and even.

"Maddy, I . . ."

"Now," she said, with just the slightest hint of force behind it.

He started to say something else—I could almost see the words forming on his lips—when he decided he'd buried himself deep enough, turned, and left.

"Wow, you've got to teach me how to do that sometime," I said.

"What?"

"Intimidate someone like that," I replied. "I had chills and a fever from seeing it, and it wasn't even directed at me."

"Not now, Eleanor."

I could tell from her voice that she was in no mood to be jollied out of her anger.

"Got it," I said.

As Maddy left the kitchen, I started cleaning up between pulling pizzas out of the oven and preparing them for delivery. Bob should have known better, but I could relate to his sentiment. He cared for my sister, maybe he even loved her, but if he wanted to be with her, he was going to have to learn how to deal with her better than he'd been managing lately. It was his problem, though, not mine. I had enough of my own grief and concern without taking anyone else's on.

Greg came into the kitchen forty-five minutes later and announced, "The last customer just left and the front door's locked."

"I thought we were staying open for another fifteen minutes," I said as I glanced at the wall clock.

"We had a hunch that no one else would want to come in, given the fact that we had already locked the door and put up the CLOSED sign," he said with a smile. "Would you like some help with the dishes?"

I'd been steadily working on them as the orders had decreased, and I'd been through four sinks of suds so far. "Thanks, but I think I've got it under control. How's the front look?"

"Like a herd of angry llamas stormed through it," he said. "But we're getting it in good shape."

Maddy came back, followed by Josh. "We're here to help you tackle the back," she said. My sister looked around the kitchen and whistled. "Wow, I've got to hand it to you, Eleanor. You work fast."

"It pays to keep on it all the time," I said. "That way, it's usually not as bad at the end."

"I can see that. We've got the front in pretty good shape."

"What about the llamas?" I asked.

"What?"

Greg said, "Maybe I exaggerated a little."

"Maybe. Why don't you all go on home? Everyone deserves to have an early evening, and I can handle the rest of this myself."

Greg and Josh were headed for the front door when Maddy said, "I'll let them out, and then I'm coming back."

"It's okay. You can go, too," I said.

"Why?"

"Don't you have a date tonight?"

She frowned. "The key word is 'had,' not 'have,'" she said.

"Are you sure?"

Maddy bit her lip and then asked, "Eleanor, do I look like I'm kidding?"

I could see that she was in pain, but for the moment, there was nothing I could do about it. "Okay, I'll gladly take the help, if you're sure."

She came back a minute later, smiling. "Man, I didn't know how fast those two could move when they had incentive."

"Were they in that big a hurry to get out of here?"

She laughed, a sound I always liked hearing. There was something about a laugh that infected me with a touch of joy myself, and I just couldn't get enough of it. "They were both afraid you'd change your mind."

"I'm not that bad to work for, am I?"

"You have your moments," she said as she took up the drying towel, "but most of the time you're a wonderful boss."

As we worked our way through the rest of the dishes, I said, "I still can't believe Judson is dead."

"Are you kidding me? After the way he treated us? I can't believe he lasted as long as he did, if that was his standard of behavior toward people."

"Nonetheless, it looks bad for us, doesn't it?" I asked as I handed her another glass to dry.

She nodded. "That's exactly why we have to ignore what Bob said and dig into this ourselves."

I thought about that for a few seconds, and then said, "At the risk of having a pot thrown at me, can I say there's a chance that Bob might be right?"

Maddy looked at me with a serious expression, and then smiled broadly. "Of course he's right, but we can't let that stop us, can we? Since when have we been afraid of stepping on Kevin Hurley's toes? We both have a stake in this, and you know it."

"So we start digging into Judson Sizemore's life. What do we really know about him?" I asked.

"Other than the fact that he was a pretentious bore?"

"Maddy," I said.

"Okay, I'll get back on track. The only thing we really know is that he was being backed by one of the richest men in Timber Ridge, someone we thought was just about stone broke. That's as good a place to start as any, as far as I'm concerned."

"Then we need to talk to Nathan Sizemore."

As we drove to Nathan's house on the outskirts of town, I realized that I didn't really know much about the man other than the reputation he had around town. He was an odd bird, there was no denying that, and I was still trying to accept the fact that he was wealthy beyond my wildest dreams as we headed over to speak with him. I'd only seen his house a few times as a kid, and I hadn't really thought much about him since then, if I was being honest about it.

When we arrived, I stared at Nathan's home, trying to peer through the heavy vines that covered the front porch. It was difficult to see the bones of the basic house underneath it all. The place was in dire need of some serious landscaping, a good scrubbing, and a fresh coat of paint on the outside, and some of the columns on the front porch were showing signs of decay. But as I stared at it, erasing the clutter and disrepair in my mind, I began to see that it was an Arts and Crafts bungalow, much like my own.

"I never realized that it was just like my house," I said.

Maddy looked at the house, and then stared at me. "Eleanor, are you okay? Did you hit your head in the kitchen and not tell me?"

Her sarcasm was thick, but I wasn't about to be dissuaded from my point of view. "Maddy, look at the frame and forget everything else and you can see it. It's a bungalow, and I'm willing to bet the builder used the same crew that constructed mine."

She looked at the house again, this time longer and harder, and then finally said, "I don't see it."

"That's because you didn't spend a year of your life refurbishing one."

We were about to approach the porch when a wiry old man with a shotgun threw open the front door and pointed it in our direction.

"Get off my land, or I'll shoot you both where you stand."

It was time for some fast talking, and that shotgun gave me plenty of incentive. "Mr. Sizemore, I'm Eleanor Swift, and this is my sister, Maddy. We came to talk to you about..." I wanted to say Italia's, but instead, found myself finishing with "your house. I own an Arts and Crafts bungalow myself."

His shotgun started to lower as I said it. "You trying to tell me that you own the place on Farrar?"

"My late husband, Joe, and I rehabbed it from top to bottom," I admitted.

"I wouldn't mind seeing it," he said, the shotgun now pointed straight down at the porch floor. "I've always wondered what it looked like on the inside."

I had a sudden inspiration. "Why don't I show it to you right now? It's not clean, or ready for any company, but you can see the work we did."

He nodded. "I never worried about a mess I made myself in my life. Maid services are for sissies."

Nathan started to walk off the porch when I asked him carefully, "Did you forget something?"

"I surely did," he said as he walked back and locked his front door soundly.

That wasn't what I'd meant.

I pointed to his weapon and said, "There's no need to go there armed."

Nathan shrugged. "You never know," he said,

but he got the hint and unlocked the door again so that he could stow the shotgun inside. "You never can be too careful these days," he said. "Are you driving, or should I?"

I'd seen the rusty old pickup he drove through town, and I didn't want to chance getting lockjaw from sitting in it.

I decided to volunteer my services. "I'll be glad to drive," I said.

Maddy got in the back, and Nathan sat up front with me. As we drove, I wondered how I might bring up the pizzeria and what had happened to its owner. I was about to say something about it when Maddy tapped me on the shoulder. When I looked back at her in the rearview mirror, she shook her head slightly. I had to be imagining things. Was my sister actually telling me *not* to talk about something? I decided to hold my questions until later. She must have had her reasons, even though they weren't obvious to me.

We got to my house, and I led the way up front. When I got to the porch, I was surprised to see that Nathan Sizemore was still standing on the sidewalk.

"I like it," he said after a moment's pause.

"I'm glad," I said. "Trust me. It looks even better inside."

I unlocked the door, and as Maddy and I waited for him to join us, she said softly, "Save our interrogation for the ride home when he's more receptive."

"Okay," I replied.

Once Nathan joined us, I explained, "We stripped four coats of paint from the wainscoting in the living room before we got to the bare wood. It's quarter sawn oak, you know."

He looked at me for a moment, and then said, "Thanks all the same, but I don't need a tour guide. I know what I'm looking at."

"Fine. Be my guest, then. Feel free to look around all you like."

He nodded and then did as I'd suggested, wandering around the first floor without any acknowledgment that Maddy and I were still standing there. Other than a few grunts and nods of approval every now and then, the house was silent. Only when he got to the oak staircase did he hesitate long enough to look at me. "Mind?"

"Go right ahead," I said, and Maddy and I trudged up after him.

After he'd poked his head into every nook and cranny upstairs, he said, "I've seen enough."

"Would you care for some coffee?" I asked.

"Can't stand the stuff," he said.

"How about tea?"

He appeared to consider it, and then finally rendered his verdict. "Got any hot cocoa?"

"Always," I said with a laugh. We went into the kitchen, where Nathan took a seat at the table as though he'd been there a thousand times before.

As I made the cocoa, he took a checkbook out from his jacket pocket and started scribbling.

"I'm not going to charge you for it. The cocoa's on the house," I said, trying to be funny, but apparently failing miserably.

"This isn't for the drink," he said as he finished signing his name with a flourish.

After he tore it out of the book, Nathan handed

me a check for more money than I'd ever seen in my life. "What is this for?"

"I'll take it, furnishings and all," he explained as he sipped the cocoa I'd just handed him.

I dropped the check as though it were coated in anthrax. "Sorry, but my house is not for sale."

"Everything in this world is for sale, if the price is right," he said. He retrieved the check, tore it up, and then put the pieces into his pocket.

As he began to write another check, he chuckled. "I shouldn't have low-balled you the first time. My mistake."

I couldn't believe this man. Did he honestly think he was going to waltz into my home and buy it from me without even asking first? "Mr. Sizemore, I don't care how much that check is written for, I won't take it. I told you before and I meant it, so it would be in your best interest to believe me that my home is not for sale at any price."

He looked surprised. "Would you mind telling me why not?"

"My late husband, Joe, and I remodeled this place from top to bottom. Do you honestly think those kinds of memories are for sale? This is my home. More importantly, it was his as well." I felt tears come to my eyes as I spoke, but I didn't care if he saw them or not.

Nathan shook his head. "Mrs. Swift, I don't want to buy your memories. The house is all I want. With your little pizza place struggling, I figured you'd be happy for the chance to make some real money."

"I guess you were wrong, then," I said, and then

pressed my lips firmly together before I said anything I might regret.

"You don't want to see the amount? You might change your mind if you do." He was watching me closely to see how I'd react. "I know there's not a single soul in Timber Ridge who thinks I have money, but they're all wrong."

"It's not a factor, anyway. Would you like more cocoa?" I asked. "I think I'll have some." I looked at Maddy, but she just shook her head silently. My sister was clearly intrigued by what was going on, and she didn't want to interrupt for fear of breaking the conversation up.

"I don't get it," he said as he shook his head. "You and I both know that it's not worth half what I'm offering. Sentimental attachment is understandable, but there comes a time when turning money down just doesn't make sense."

He wasn't trying to be offensive, I could see that now. I really wanted him to understand my reasoning. "Maybe it doesn't make sense on one level, but in my heart, there isn't enough money in the world to make me give this place up."

Nathan put the checkbook back into his pocket and looked at Maddy. "Do you understand her?"

"About half the time, if I'm having a good day," she admitted with a grin. "The rest of the time I just play it by ear."

Nathan seemed to finally grasp what I'd been trying to tell him. With a dour smile, he said, "Okay, it's not for sale. Got it. Tell you what I'll do," he said after a moment's pause. "If I hire the right crew, can they come here to see what you've done? I'd appreciate if you'd give them pointers, too, if it wouldn't be too much trouble."

"I can do that," I said. "As a matter of fact, I'd be glad to help in any way I can."

He nodded. "That sounds like a plan. We'll negotiate your fee later."

"We'll do it now," I said firmly.

He looked surprised by my tone of voice and the direct nature of my reply, but he nodded briefly. "Tell me what you're asking, and we'll go from there."

"Listen carefully, because I'm not a woman to be trifled with. I have a figure in mind, and I won't back down from it."

He took that declaration seriously. "Let's hear it, then."

"I will accept nothing for whatever help I'm able to give you," I said, "and that's my final offer."

He looked bewildered by my requirement; that much was clear. "Why would you do that? What's in it for you?"

I gave him my broadest smile. "To see another bungalow brought back to life is all the pay I need. These houses need to be preserved, not destroyed to churn out large houses that no one needs. What do you think?"

He seemed to mull that over, and then said, "Ma'am, I'm not sure I can accept that deal."

"Then I'm afraid we're stuck," I said.

Again, Nathan turned to Maddy. "Is she always this stubborn?"

"You don't know the half of it," my sister said.

Nathan nodded, and then chewed on his lower

lip for a few seconds before speaking again. "I'm a hermit, and I know how folks talk about me in town, but if I'd known you were around, I might have made more of an effort to get to know some of the people in Timber Ridge."

"I take that as a compliment," I said.

"Good, because that's how I meant it." He looked around admiringly, and then added, "You made the right decision."

That was a real switch in attitudes. "Do you mean it's worth more than you were offering?"

"In dollars? No, there you're crazier than most folks think I am. But I can see this place is your home. I'm beginning to understand why you won't sell it." He yawned, and though the hour was still early, Nathan said, "Ladies, if you'll excuse me, I'm bushed. Can I catch a ride back home?"

"We'd be glad to take you," Maddy said before I could reply.

Once we were in the car, my sister asked from the back seat, "Did you hear about what happened at Italia's today?"

"No," he said. "I've been wrapping up a deal all day. Other than that snot-nosed lawyer I've been dealing with, you two are the first folks I've talked to all day." He paused, and then added, "The past three days, as a matter of fact. I don't exactly have a parade of folks just dropping in on me."

"There was a murder," Maddy said softly as we approached Nathan's house.

He turned in his seat to look at her, and I could see worry in his expression. "What are you talking about?"

"The owner was killed sometime last night," she said.

I pulled up in front of Nathan's house, and without a word, he unbuckled his seat belt and stumbled out of the car.

Opening my own door, I called out, "Nathan, are you okay?"

He waved a hand in the air toward me, and as I saw him go into his house, the look of weariness and anguish on his face was nearly too much to take.

"What should we do?" I asked Maddy as I stared after him.

"There's nothing we can do," she said. "If he'd wanted us to follow him in, he would have invited us. One thing's for certain. He hadn't heard the news until I told him. If I'd known how he was going to react, I would have done it a little more delicately."

"I wonder what his connection to Judson Sizemore is."

"I don't know, but it's something we need to find out. I can't imagine that shrewd old man willing to back Judson without a very good reason."

"But not tonight," I said as I stifled a yawn. "We're not going to be able to uncover anything at the moment, and I'm completely worn out."

Maddy nodded. "I'm exhausted myself. Why don't you drop me off at home so I can grab a shower and go to bed early?"

My sister was known for keeping late hours, and I had to wonder if her exhaustion was because of what we'd done at the Slice today, or whether it had been brought on by her rift with Bob Lemon. "Don't you want to go back to the Slice and get your car?"

"I forgot all about it," she said. "I shouldn't just leave it parked there all night. Something might happen to it."

As we drove back to the Slice, I said, "I can't stop thinking about how Nathan reacted back there."

Maddy paused, and then answered, "Is there any chance he might be related to Judson? After all, they share the same last name."

"It should be a possibility we consider. Why else would he back him in a business?" I asked. "A pizzeria doesn't really seem like Nathan's style."

"After meeting the man, I can't imagine why he'd do it."

"He could have had lots of reasons," I said. "For all we know, he didn't like our pizza and wanted somebody else's."

Maddy looked at me as she shook her head. "That can't be it."

"Why not?"

"Because I can't imagine anybody not liking what we make at the Slice," she said with a smile. "Maybe I'll put off going to bed and do some work on the case, instead. I need to do a little digging around on the Internet tonight and see what turns up. What are you going to do?"

I stifled another yawn as I said, "I'd planned to take a shower and go to bed."

"Very productive. What's your game plan for to-morrow, sleep in?"

"No," I said as we neared her car, and stopped.

"I'm going back to Nathan's first thing in the morning and ask him directly about why he was trying to put me out of business. There's got to be something that he's not telling us, and I mean to find out exactly what it is, and I'm not leaving until I do."

Chapter 5

"Okay, just to set things straight, your plan last night was better than mine," Maddy said as she picked me up at my house the next morning at eight.

"Why? Didn't you have any luck online?"

"I didn't think it was possible, but Nathan Sizemore has literally made himself invisible on the Internet," she said. "I could barely find any place that acknowledged that he'd ever been born."

"How was Bob able to find out so much about him, then?"

I knew I was poking an angry bear with a stick, but I really wanted to know. "Don't you think I've been asking myself that same question? The only thing I can figure out is that he's got access to some kind of extended search engines that I don't have."

"You could always ask him for help," I said.

"Gosh, Eleanor, sometimes it's like you don't even know me at all," she said with a smile.

"Granted, that was a stupid suggestion. How

about Judson Sizemore? Did you have better luck looking into his life?"

Maddy didn't answer, and after a second, I looked at her, concerned that she hadn't replied. "What's wrong?"

In a low voice, she said, "Eleanor, I don't know how to tell you this, but I didn't even check. I had so much trouble getting anything on Nathan that I completely forgot about digging into Judson's life. Some detective I turned out to be."

"Hey, don't beat yourself up about it, Maddy. We've got time."

We drove in silence for a few miles, and then my sister asked as she pulled up in front of his place, "Do you really think Nathan's going to talk to us if we just show up on his doorstep?"

"I can't think of anything better to do at this point, can you?"

"You've got a point. We don't have anything to lose," she said.

We rang the doorbell a dozen times, but there was no reply.

"He's not home," Maddy said, "and that's not going to change no matter how many times you ring that bell."

She was right, but I wasn't ready to give up yet. "Maybe he's just not in the house. Let's look around back."

Maddy touched my shoulder. "You saw how he reacted when we showed up unannounced last night. Do you really want to take the chance he'll think we're a pair of trespassers?"

"We *are* trespassing Maddy, need I remind you?" I asked.

"Okay, but that still doesn't protect us from a shotgun blast."

I laughed out of humor and more than a touch of sheer terror. "What do you want to do, Maddy, live forever? Let's go."

I led the way around the house, and she followed me, something I wasn't entirely certain would happen. In the end, no matter what, my sister always had my back, and I always had hers. It was what was so good and right about having her as family.

When we got around the side to the back of Nathan's house, it was like stepping back in time. The man hadn't wasted a cent on lawn care, mainly because there wasn't a lawn. Instead, there was a garden large enough to be a small farm, but I didn't see the usual crops of corn and beans growing. Instead, Nathan was growing sugarcane, cotton, and the oddest collection of plants I'd ever seen in my life.

"Hello? Nathan? Are you back here?" I called out.

I saw a scarecrow with two heads among the crops, and suddenly realized that one of the heads was alive. He didn't look all that pleased to see us, and I had to wonder if that shotgun was somewhere close by. "What are you doing here?"

"We just want to talk," I said. I held my empty hands in the air and added, "We're not armed."

He shook his head. "I'm not, either. You're here, so you both might as well come on over."

We walked down the path toward him, and as I looked around, I said, "I've got to tell you, I haven't seen cane and cotton growing since I was a girl."

He nodded. "It reminds me of my childhood. I spent too many hours working my daddy's farm not to appreciate how tough they are to grow."

"They're beautiful," I said, meaning it.

"Well, it's kind of you to say, and I appreciate it," he said. "What brings you back here to my place?"

"We wanted to apologize," Maddy said. That was news to me, but I decided to go along with it and see where she was heading.

"What did you do?" he asked as he arched one eyebrow.

"Last night we sprang that news on you without considering for one second how you'd react to it," I said.

"Doesn't matter either way to me," he said gruffly.

It was decision time. We could pretend to accept that at face value, or call him on it. There was really no doubt in my mind which way to go. "We know you backed the restaurant," I said. "You had a stake in what happened, whether you want to admit it or not."

The friendly warmth that had been there vanished as Nathan looked at me sharply. "What makes you say a crazy thing like that, just when I was starting to like you?"

I didn't know how to respond to that when Maddy answered for the both of us, "It's amazing how much ground is covered by Mountain Properties and Trust."

That got his attention. "Okay, you know about me; I can see that. Now tell me who I need to fire."

"What do you mean?"

He was openly angry now, and I was glad that he didn't have his shotgun with him. I was even happier that his ire wasn't directed at Maddy or me. Nathan said loudly, "Somebody's been blabbing, and I won't stand for it. I took particular care to make sure no one knew about that."

"There's no one to blame, really. We just stumbled across it," I said.

"I know better than that," he said harshly.

There was no way I was going to throw Bob Lemon under the bus just to stay in this man's good graces. "Sorry, but that's the only answer we've got. Tell us about your relationship with Judson Sizemore."

Nathan shook his head, kicked at a clod of dirt, and kept his gaze on the ground without answering.

"Why won't you tell us?" I asked softly. "It might make you feel better."

"It might, but I'm willing to bet that it won't," he said.

"We're not going to just go away," I said, without threat or implication.

"I know that," he said as he idly kicked at another clod. "I just hate spreading my business around town. This is personal, as personal as it gets."

I looked at Nathan and said, "We won't say anything to anyone that you don't want us to."

"You speak for your sister, do you?"

Maddy nodded. "Here and now, about this, she does, completely."

Nathan seemed to take that in, and then he finally nodded his agreement. "It just might be good to get it all out, at that. It's been weighing heavy on my mind, and I need to talk to somebody about it." He took a deep breath, let some of it out, and then added, "Judson was my nephew, and now my family's just about all gone."

Once Nathan started talking, it was hard to believe that he'd been so reticent with us before. Maddy and I did our best to listen without interrupting as he spoke.

Staring at the dirt at his feet, Nathan said, "My brother was one mean son of a gun, let me start with that. He tortured me as a kid, beating me up for no reason other than because he could. The summer after my eighth grade year in school, I went to stay with my uncle Bob and his family on their farm. They're all long gone now, but I'll never forget what happened while I was there. I was a scrawny little kid when I left home, but a few months of throwing hay bales over my head made me strong, and the home cooking I got didn't hurt, either. When I came back home, my brother greeted me by punching me in the gut. Instead of doubling over, I tensed myself and took it, and then I put him down with one blow. That's all it took, and he never lifted a finger toward me again. Needless to say, as soon as we could go our separate ways, we did, and I never thought twice about him until the day he died."

"You didn't have any contact with him at all?" Maddy asked.

"My momma used to keep me updated on his shenanigans back when she was still alive, but the two of us barely spoke at her funeral, and our dad was long gone. After that, I had no reason to think about him. And then he up and died." Was that a tear in the corner of Nathan's eye? I couldn't tell for sure because he brushed it away so quickly. He continued, "Now, I've long known that just because someone's family, it doesn't mean you have to love them, and there was none lost between the two of us, trust me when I tell you that. But I felt a compulsion to go to his funeral, so with mixed emotions, I drove to Chastain to pay my last respects, mostly because my momma would have wanted it that way. What I didn't expect to find were two kids in their twenties who didn't hold my past with their father against me. Turns out they hadn't been all that fond of the jerk, themselves."

"It must have been a shock when you just showed up like that." I couldn't help speaking as I tried to imagine what it must have been like for him. Maddy and I have had our differences in the past, but she was so much a part of me, I could never turn my back on her. Then again, Nathan hadn't had it all that easy, if his story was even close to what had really happened between the two brothers.

He shrugged, and then kicked at the dirt again. "It was a surprise to all of us. Their mother was already gone, so it turned out that the three of us were all that was left of our line. Oh, there was a rumor of a cousin somewhere here in town, but nobody ever came right out and claimed kinship with me, so I figured it was just one more thing folks around Timber Ridge got wrong. I came back here after we screwed him into the ground— my brother was too crooked to go in any other way—not expecting anything else from either one of his kids. Then, Judson and Gina both showed up on my doorstep nine months ago."

"What did they want?" I asked, unaware that all this drama had gone on right under our noses. Hearing him tell it was like seeing it unfold on the screen, it seemed so vivid to me.

"Believe it or not, they wanted to get to know their uncle Nathan," he said. "And before you think they came here after my money—they were as much in the dark about what I'm worth as everyone else in Timber Ridge has been—until you two poked your noses into my business."

"I'll bet they were surprised when you told them," I said.

"I never did tell them. They had no idea, and now Judson will never know." He leveled a look at us and said, "Ladies, I'd appreciate you keeping what you know about me to yourselves."

"I'm sorry, but I already told Bob Lemon," Maddy said. That wasn't strictly the truth, since it had been the other way around, but it was a clever way to get Bob's knowledge of Nathan's wealth out in the open without incriminating him.

"Don't worry about him. He's a good man, and I know he'll keep quiet about what he knows." Nathan paused, and then as he looked at Maddy, he added, "Especially if you're the one asking him."

I couldn't believe it, but my sister actually blushed at that. "You're right. You can trust him. I'll talk to him."

"I appreciate it. Anyway, back to my story. I asked the pair of them what they wanted to do with their lives, since they were both kind of adrift.

Judson said he'd always dreamed of running a real old-fashioned pizzeria, and I wanted him near me. I told him I was stone broke, but that I had a friend who invested in things like that, and I set the deal up through someone in Hickory so they'd have no idea I was involved." He turned to me as he added, "That's why he opened Italia's right on your doorstep, Eleanor. I'm sorry about that. I wasn't thinking what that would do to your business; but when The Shady Lady closed down, it seemed to work out beautifully for us."

"What did Gina want?" Maddy asked.

"Nothing more than to move here and stay with me," he said proudly. "She wasn't due to move until next week, but Judson's death has moved things up. There're lots of details to see to about her brother's arrangements, and I don't have the heart to do any of it. Besides, if we're being straight up about it, I hardly knew the boy. But that chance is gone now, and I owe someone a load of buckshot for robbing me of it."

"I'm so sorry for your loss," I said. "I know what it's like to lose family." I thought about how different I'd felt since losing Joe, and how I could still feel his presence from time to time, as though he'd never been ripped away from me.

Nathan nodded. "I appreciate that, but I'll tell you something I've never admitted to anyone before in my life. I'd give up every square foot of land I own if I could have had the same relationship with my brother growing up that you and your sister have right now, and that's the honest truth."

What could we say to that? Maddy and I didn't

always see eye to eye, but when things got tough, we were always there for each other. I knew, even more than Nathan did, what he'd missed growing up with a brother like that, and he had my sympathy.

We had just finished talking when I saw a striking brunette in her mid-twenties come around the corner. Her six-inch heels buried themselves into the soil with each step she took, and her short skirt pulled up with each attempt to free herself. She finally found a patch of solid ground and moved quickly toward us.

When she spoke, the illusion of her beauty was suddenly diminished. Gina's words were like acid as she lashed out at us, "Why are you two bothering my uncle? He's in no shape to talk to anyone."

"Gina, cool your jets," Nathan said. "These ladies are friends of mine, and I'll ask you to keep a respectful tone in your voice when you address them, do you hear me? This is Eleanor," he said as he bobbed his head toward me, "and this is Maddy."

"Sorry," she said quickly to us. "I just don't want him to have to deal with any drama right now. If you'll excuse us, we have some details to go over for the funeral."

I nodded. "We're sorry for your loss, and we understand completely. Nathan, if there's anything we can do, just let us know."

"We will," Gina said as she moved to block us off from her uncle.

Maddy and I took the hint, so we walked back to her car.

"Wow," I said, "she comes on like a hurricane,

doesn't she? Did she look to you as though she even noticed that someone killed her brother?"

"Maybe she keeps it all bottled up inside."

"Maybe," I said.

As we got into Maddy's car, she asked, "Is it terrible that I'm beginning to wonder if she's going to take over the pizzeria?"

"I've been thinking about the exact same thing," I admitted. "She doesn't look the type to me. Does she to you?"

Maddy shrugged. "Who knows? Most of the people who know me outside of Timber Ridge would be amazed that *I'm* working in a pizzeria."

"You're more than an employee, and you know it," I said as we drove.

"Co-owner?" she asked with a grin.

I had to laugh at the way she'd asked. "Not in your wildest dreams. Would you be happy with 'valuable assistant manager'?"

"I'll have to be, won't I?"

"You bet," I said with a grin of my own.

"Okay, I'll take it. Will you have business cards made up for me, or should I do it myself?"

We were both joking, but I didn't want her teasing about it with Greg and Josh. "Let's just keep this promotion between the two of us, okay? We can't afford to make waves right now."

"Sis, I would never do anything to alienate the guys."

"I know that," I said, though I wasn't entirely sure that it was true.

As we neared the downtown area, it was time for a decision. "What should we do next?"

I glanced at my watch. "I hate to break it to you,

but there's no time to talk to anyone else. I need to make two batches of dough this morning, one to use fresh, and one to freeze. Our inventory was completely wiped out yesterday, remember?"

"I'm not about to forget," she said. "My feet are still killing me."

"That's what comes from not wearing sensible shoes," I said. I was a big fan of tennis shoes, and I'd been trying to get Maddy to work in them as well, all to no avail.

"Maybe so, but I look good, and that's worth a little extra pain every now and then, to say nothing of the tips I get when I look especially nice."

"If you say so."

As we drove to the Slice, I said, "Nathan told us that his niece doesn't want to do anything but stay there with him, but Gina doesn't exactly look like the stay-at-home type, does she?"

Maddy frowned. "Now that you mention it, she does look as though she'd fit in better in Charlotte or New York than in Timber Ridge."

"I hate to break it to her, but if she's serious about being around her uncle and getting to know him, she's going to have to get used to our quaint little town."

"I give her a week," Maddy said.

"Before she gets bored out of her skull and leaves?" I asked.

"No, until she breaks down completely. You know what, Eleanor? It might be fun to watch."

"Have I ever told you that you've got a mean streak, Sis?" I asked.

"I'm not being particularly cruel. I made the

transition myself, so I'm in a position to know," Maddy said.

"We'll see," I said as we parked in back of the promenade. "She might just surprise us both."

I actually enjoyed living in our town and running the pizzeria, though I knew there were plenty of people who didn't like where they lived or what they did for a living. I had a house I loved, and I was my own boss, which made me the toughest employer I'd ever worked for, but it gave me a sense of permanency in the world that I had always craved. The other reason I stayed in Timber Ridge was much less practical. Joe and I had started A Slice of Delight together, and every time I walked through the front door, I still expected to see him there, waiting to wrap me up in one of those bear hugs he always loved giving me. Joe would have loved the weather we were having now. Autumn was by far his favorite time of year, and for the umpteenth time, I wished he was there to enjoy it with me one more time. I didn't have him beside me any longer, but I did have more memories than I could count, and a sister by my side who truly loved me.

She'd admitted to me once that she'd been looking her entire life for what I'd found, and I was grateful for every moment I'd spent with my husband.

"You're awfully quiet," Maddy said as we walked through the shortcut toward the promenade. "Thinking about Joe again?"

"Is it that obvious?" I asked.

"Just to people who know you." She looked

down the promenade as we came out onto the wide swath of brick pavers. "Tell you what. Let's go over to Paul's Pastries and see what kind of goodies he has for the season before we get started."

I thought about my expanding waistline, and then I put it far from my mind. "I'm game if you are." On an impulse, I started running toward the bakery. "Race you there. Last one pays."

Maddy began laughing as she ran, and I felt the burden of my deep thoughts desert me. It was a day for joy, a day filled with sunshine, both inside our hearts and out in the real world, and I wanted to savor every moment of it. Whenever murder visited Timber Ridge, it reminded me of just how important it was to hold onto every precious moment that came my way, to cherish it, and then to file it away to enjoy again at another time.

"Are you two drunk this early in the day?" Paul asked as we raced inside his store, laughing the entire time. The aromas coming from the back were even fattening, but I didn't let that stop me from inhaling the ambrosia deeply.

"On life, maybe," I said. "What's good today, Paul?"

The tall and lanky young man smiled at me. "That's like asking me who my favorite kid is, if I had children, that is."

I looked in the display and saw that something new had been added to his offerings. "What's that?"

He pulled one out and showed it to me. "I'm kind of proud of this. It's a pumpkin muffin with cinnamon nutmeg glaze and a few sprinkles thrown in just for fun. Would you like one?"

"We'll take two," Maddy said.

"Each, or all together?"

For some reason, the question made us both giggle, and I said, "Two total."

As I paid for our treats—despite winning the race—Paul said, "There's something I want to tell you, but I don't know how to say it without sounding like I'm heartless. I'm sorry that man had to die, but I hope it keeps you in business. Any word about what they are going to do with it?"

"Not a clue," I said, in total honesty. I truly had no idea, and it hadn't even occurred to me to ask Nathan earlier. After the discussion I'd had with Maddy on the drive over, I couldn't see Gina running it; but then again, I'd been wrong before. "Thanks for the treats."

"You're most welcome," he said.

As we made our way to the Slice, I couldn't help myself and reached in to pinch off a bit of one muffin.

"Hey, no fair," Maddy said. "If you're going to eat yours, I want mine."

I looked at my watch. "We've got a little time, and the sun feels really warm today. Why don't we go get a couple of coffees and eat these out here?"

"That sounds great. I'll be right back," she said as she started back to Paul's. Then she stopped abruptly.

"What's wrong?"

"No more sneaking bites. Agreed?"

I pulled my hand out of the bag and nodded.

"Okay, you win. But if you're not back in three minutes, all bets are off."

She hurried into the bakery, and I found a nearby bench where I could enjoy the sun.

I must have closed my eyes, because the next thing I knew, someone was blocking my light.

"That was fast, even for you," I said.

"I hadn't realized you were expecting me," a familiar voice said.

I opened my eyes to find Art Young—our well-dressed local shady character—standing there looming over me.

I started to stand as well, and Art said, "Please, I didn't mean to interrupt your leisure time. I know how little of it you manage to get."

He was a slim man, with light blond hair carefully styled, and he had an air of civility about him, despite all the rumors of his shady activities I'd heard recounted. We'd formed an odd friendship over the years, though no one else seemed to understand it, including Maddy.

"It's fine," I said as I moved over on the bench. "Join me."

Dapper as ever, Art brushed at the bench with his gloved hand before sitting down.

"I understand you've had a bit of trouble," he said. "I just this moment got back into town, so forgive me for not coming by sooner."

"It's okay. I'm not directly involved in the murder investigation," I said.

He shook his head. "I know you are not that naïve, Eleanor. When a competitor dies, the second person the authorities look at is the person with the most to gain financially."

"I'm curious. Who's the first?"

"Love interests: wives, girlfriends, mistresses. There's more passion there, and murder can be a very spur-of-the-moment event. Has our esteemed chief of police spoken with you yet?"

"Briefly," I admitted. Some of the glory of the day was fading under the reality Art was offering, but it was counsel I needed to hear.

"He'll be back soon, I have no doubt about that," he said. "Is there anything I can do?"

I was about to say no, and then changed my mind. "As a matter of fact, there is."

Art looked surprised by my response, and there was a hint of pleasure in his expression as well. "Just name it, and if it is in my power to grant, it is yours for the asking."

"Maddy and I have decided to look into the murder ourselves so neither of us gets steamrolled by the police," I admitted, something I wouldn't say out loud to many folks in Timber Ridge.

"A wise precaution," Art said.

"I've been wondering about the murder victim. There could be lots of reasons he was killed besides trying to wipe out my pizzeria."

Art started ticking off the fingers of his gloved hand. "Love, money, revenge, protection, all these things come to mind."

"We're looking into a few of those ourselves, but we don't have any contacts in the area that Judson Sizemore comes from. Do you know anyone in Chastain?" It was a town twenty minutes from Timber Ridge, the place where the Sizemores had lived. It amazed me that Nathan had been located that close to his brother and yet had still been estranged from him all those years. Then I realized that there are more distances in life than could be seen on a map.

He nodded. "I have several acquaintances there," Art admitted.

"But no friends?"

His smile was a wry one. "Eleanor, I can count my friendships on one hand, with fingers left over." He looked at me covertly, and then added softly, "I hope I can include you in that list."

"You know you can," I said, meaning it.

He smiled with an air of satisfaction. "I'm sure many people in our community wonder about that."

"Let them," I said. "I don't submit my friendships for their approval, and I don't expect them to consult me about theirs, either."

He stood, brushed the seat of his pants lightly, and then said, "That's good to hear. I'll be in touch."

"Don't go to any special trouble," I said. "Just ask around when you get the chance."

He looked down at me. "How many times have you asked for my assistance with anything?"

I thought about it for a moment, and then admitted, "I can't remember ever asking you for a favor before."

"Because you never have," he said. "Our balance sheet leans heavily in your favor, so any opportunity I can get to even things out is always welcome."

"I don't put my friendships on a scale, Art. That's not what it's about as far as I'm concerned."

"Of course not," he said quickly, clearly chastened by my comment. "Just know that I am thrilled to do this favor for you."

He looked behind me and said, "Good morning."

Maddy nodded. "Morning."

There was an awkward silence for a moment or two, and then Art left us with a wave of his hand.

"I still can't believe you are friends with that man," Maddy said as she handed me a cup of coffee.

"Do you honestly want to have that conversation again?" I asked.

"You know what? I really don't. Today is too pretty to spoil." She looked at the bag in my hand. "Now, are you going to hand one of those over, or am I going to have to take it from you?"

"Don't be so grabby," I said with a smile as I gave her a muffin. "There's plenty for both of us."

I'd taken my first bite when I heard a pair of high heels clicking up the promenade toward us.

Why did I have a sudden premonition that this wasn't going to be someone I wanted to talk to?

I turned to find Gina Sizemore approaching with a look of anger plastered on her pretty face.

It appeared that I wasn't going to get to enjoy my treat after all.

Chapter 6

"Good morning, Gina," I said as she neared us. "How are you today?" Because of the expression on her face, I decided to stand when I greeted her. It wouldn't do to be caught unable to flee, though I hoped it didn't come to that.

"Stay away from my uncle," she said flatly.

"You can't be serious," I said. "You heard what he said. He's our friend."

Her face screwed up into a deep frown, and her attractiveness took an instant nosedive, at least in my mind. "You both tricked him, and you know it. I won't have you harassing him anymore, do you understand?"

"We never harassed him," Maddy said, her voice matching Gina's state of agitation. She decided to stand as well, and the three of us were faced off like gunfighters in the Wild West.

"I heard what you were talking about when I got there. Why were you grilling him about my brother? It's none of your business, and now he's upset about your involvement in the case. He sent me here to tell you that he never wants to see either one of you again."

"We didn't kill Judson," I said a little louder than I should have.

"The police believe you both are suspects. Would you care to deny that?" There was real anger behind her glare this time.

"I have no control over what the police think," I said. "Your uncle didn't suspect us when we spoke this morning. What changed his mind so quickly?"

I had a hunch what the answer was, but I wanted to see if Gina was brazen enough to admit her part in his shift.

"Do you honestly have the nerve to ask me that? I'm in town to finalize the arrangements for burying my brother."

"You don't seem all that torn up about losing him," I said, and instantly regretted it. I'd let her anger spill over onto me, and I didn't like what the woman was bringing out in me. "I'm sorry. I shouldn't have said that, and I apologize for it."

She wasn't in any mood to receive it, though. "Forget it. I had a message to deliver, and I've done that. Be warned, I'm deadly serious."

"So are we," Maddy said.

Gina turned and left, her heels clicking away as she moved.

"Wow, that was impressive, wasn't it?" Maddy asked me after she was gone.

"What, how quickly she managed to change Nathan's mind about us, or the manner in which she just attacked us?"

"Both." She reached down, retrieved her muffin, and then took another bite.

I couldn't eat mine. Gina had sucked the last bit of joy out of it for me. "Are you ready to get started on prepping for pizza?"

Maddy had finished her muffin by then, and she pointed to mine. "Aren't you going to finish that?"

"You can have it," I said. "I just lost my appetite."

She took mine and had a healthy bite of it as we walked over to the Slice. "I wouldn't want to offend Paul, would I?"

"No, we can't have that," I said as I unlocked the door and let us in. After I had it bolted behind us, I made my way into the kitchen. I had a lot on my mind, but making pizza dough would help relieve some of the tension.

As I started measuring the flour and yeast, Maddy said, "Don't forget, we need more sauce, too."

I glanced at the clock and realized that I was going to have to work really quickly if I was going to get everything prepped in time for our opening. I might even have to take a few shortcuts to do it.

Maddy started to talk as she chopped vegetables, but I had to focus on what I was doing.

"I'm sorry," I said, "but I really have to concentrate on this. We can talk later, but right now, I need to work."

"That's fine with me," she said.

After a minute, Maddy reached over and flipped on the radio. "This is okay, though, isn't it?"

"It's fine as long as you don't turn it up any louder," I said. That was a distraction I could at least live with.

"I could always make the sauce myself," Maddy said as she finished her prep work. "I've watched you a hundred times."

I was about to decline when I realized that it would make my life easier if she pitched in. I was normally a bit of a control freak in my kitchen, but this was no time to quibble.

"Okay, but on one condition," I said.

She smiled. "You name it."

"No ad-libbing on the recipe. If it says two table-spoons of something is needed, that's what you add, no more and no less. If you can't agree to that caveat, I'll do it myself."

"I promise. I'll follow your directions to a tee," she said.

"Then knock yourself out," I said.

"Could you taste this?" Maddy asked me forty-five minutes later. I'd just finished punching the second batch of dough down, so I set it aside to rest with its mate.

I grabbed a spoon, tasted a bit of sauce, and then nodded. "Hey, that's really good."

"It is, isn't it?"

I laughed. "Don't act so surprised. I knew all along that you could do it."

"Then why did you wait so long to let me try?" she asked.

"You know me, I've got to be in charge of every-thing. I've had a hard time letting go of things since we were kids."

"Eleanor, it's okay to delegate now and then."

I smiled at my sister. "You're absolutely right. I'll try to lighten up a little."

"Can I take a stab at that pizza dough tomorrow?" she asked.

"Don't push your luck," I said, "or I'll have you make the sauce every time we need it."

"It's not nice to threaten your favorite sister," she said with a smile.

"You're my *only* sister," I reminded her.

"Then I've got to be your favorite, don't I?"

"Just don't get too carried away with that status. By definition, you're also my least favorite sibling, too."

Maddy grinned at me. "Hey, it never hurts to ask."

We had a line waiting for us when we opened the Slice, and it was going to be just me in the kitchen and Maddy out front. I was understaffed and I knew it, but most of the time we were able to handle the crowds, and it helped my bottom line not to have an extra person on the payroll when the four of us could handle the jobs we needed to get done.

Unfortunately, this wasn't going to be one of those times.

I helped Maddy seat the first twelve customers, including our loyal fan, Karen Green. "It's good to see you, Karen," I said.

"There's nowhere else I'd rather be," she said as she smiled broadly at me. "It's a beautiful day out, isn't it?"

"I couldn't say anything about how it is outside right now," I replied. "I've been in the kitchen for hours."

"You really should take time to enjoy all this," she said as she looked around the crowded pizzeria.

"That's the trouble. I either have time on my hands with nothing to celebrate, or I'm too busy working to appreciate what I've got."

"I know exactly what you mean. I either have money and no free time, or the absolute reverse."

"Then we should make a pact to enjoy it more," I said. There was something a little odd about Karen, but then again, I could say that about most of my customers, friends, and family, too, if I was willing to admit it.

"Oh, I do, believe me. Coming here gives me the greatest joy in my life."

"If we're your greatest joy, then trust me, you need to get out more," I said as I winked at her. "See you later."

"You know you can count on me," she said.

I disappeared into the kitchen, and Maddy soon brought back the first round of orders. As she gave me the slips, she asked, "What were you and Karen talking about just now?"

"This and that. I was just making time to stop and smell the roses," I answered as I got out the first dough ball and started knuckling it into the pan. "Why?"

"It's probably nothing," Maddy said, "but she gave me the oddest look when I took her order."

"She's never been conventional, has she?"

Maddy shook her head. "That's not it. It was almost as if she expected me to thank her for something."

I waved a free hand in the air. "If we try to figure

out our customers' motivations, we'll both go stark raving mad and not get a bit of work done all day."

"You're right," Maddy said.

"Can you handle the front by yourself until reinforcements arrive?"

She grinned at me. "Do I have any choice?"

"We could always hire someone else to come in and give us a hand when we need it," I said.

"Are you crazy? We're barely surviving as it is. We don't need anybody else on the payroll. I can handle this mob if you can."

"Just keep the orders coming," I said. "I'll bring them out as they're ready, so that will save you some steps."

"See? We already have a system worked out. See you soon," she said as she disappeared back out into the dining room.

I kept glancing at the clock as things hit a lull, but it seemed to move so slowly that I didn't think Greg would ever show up. The kitchen door finally opened, but instead of Greg, Bob Lemon walked in.

"You've got the wrong sister," I said as I slid a pizza onto the conveyor. "I know you passed Maddy on your way in."

"Is she ever going to let me off the hook for what I said?"

I shrugged. "With Maddy, you can never tell."

Bob shook his head sadly. "If you don't know from being her sister all your life, I don't have a prayer."

I considered his options, thinking about the

past men in Maddy's life, and how she'd reacted to them when they'd transgressed, at least in her mind. In the end, there was just one thing the forgiven all had in common. After due consideration, I finally said, "Bob, the only plan I have involves a great deal of begging and groveling on your part. Are you up for it?"

"That depends," he said. "I'm still not entirely certain that I was wrong in saying what I did to her."

My laughter must have alarmed him, because before I could contain myself, he asked, "Eleanor, did I just say something funny?"

"With that attitude, you've got your work cut out for you. When did right and wrong ever figure into arguments between men and women? Seriously, think about it. You're a smart man. I know you'll see it if you just try hard enough."

He nodded reluctantly. "Okay, I see the logic in what you're saying. What should I do, bring her candy and flowers?"

"Come on, think outside the box. That's so conventional, and we both know my sister isn't that easy," I said.

"So, you're saying I should go more along the lines of something like filet mignon and a new car?"

I just shook my head, wondering how this savvy and successful attorney could be so wrong. "You're nowhere close. The only thing I can think of that will get you back in my sister's good graces is an honest and sincere apology. She's not interested in vehicles and pricey steaks."

"I'd rather buy her a car," he said reluctantly.

Maybe he was finally getting it. "Don't you think she knows that? Hey, you asked me for my opinion. It's up to you whether you take my advice or not. I'm washing my hands of the whole thing."

"I just wish that I could, myself. Well, here goes nothing."

He was heading for the door when I yelled, "Stop. She doesn't have time for an apology right now. In case you hadn't noticed, we're buried in customers at the moment. The only way you can help is to grab an apron and pitch in." Things had picked up again quickly.

Bob shocked me by grabbing one of the aprons hanging on a hook by the door.

It was time to give him a graceful way to back out. The attorney didn't owe *me* an apology for anything. "I was just kidding."

"I'm not," he said as he doffed his suit jacket and put the apron on. "I've got an hour I can give you. Should I take orders out front with Maddy, or work back here with you? I'm handy with a knife, if you need anything chopped."

"I think the best thing you can do is keep out of her way right now," I said. I looked around for something he could do, and spotted the dirty dishes waiting for me in the sink. "If you're serious, you can wash those. That would be a big help."

"Ah, that's something I'm well qualified to do, trust me. I worked my way through law school washing dishes at a steakhouse chain. I'm a real wiz at it."

"Then knock yourself out."

I turned back to the next pizza I was making,

and as soon as I had it on the conveyor, I grabbed a finished one and cut it for delivery.

"I'll be right back," I said.

Bob just nodded, intent on filling the sink with warm, soapy water.

I delivered the pie to Maddy, who frowned as she accepted it. "Where did he go? Don't tell me he snuck out the back. What a coward."

"No, Bob's still here. As a matter of fact, he's back there washing dishes right now," I said.

She looked at me as though I'd just claimed to be the new queen of England. "What's he really doing, Eleanor?"

I wasn't about to get involved any deeper than I already was. "If you don't believe me, go look for yourself. You can work the kitchen while you're back there, and I'll finish waiting on tables until Greg gets here."

"I have half a mind to take you up on it."

I took my apron off and tossed it to her. "Find the other half, then. I've made a decision. We're trading."

"Yes, ma'am," she said as she gave me her own apron.

Before Maddy could leave, I asked, "Who hasn't paid yet?"

"Tables three and seven. Four gets the pepperoni, one is waiting for their check, which is in your apron pocket, and nine needs refills on their sodas."

I processed all of that, and then I got to work. I was better in the kitchen, but I needed practice up front nearly as much as Maddy needed it in back. We changed off every now and then to keep things fresh, but neither one of us wanted to make a habit of it. We were both out of our comfort zones with this alternate arrangement, and neither of us was afraid to admit it.

I was waiting for the next pizza to show up, but when it wasn't forthcoming, I decided to go see what was holding it up. To my surprise, I found my sister and the attorney together in a warm embrace.

Bob grinned at me and said, "She forgave me."

"I couldn't help myself," Maddy explained. "He looked so cute in that apron, up to his elbows in suds."

"Yes, we're all adorable here," I said as I untied her apron. "Now we're changing back." I gave her the apron, took mine back, and cut the pizza that was waiting on the far side of the conveyor. As I did, I had to reach in and pull two more out of the oven to keep them from burning since they were stacking up.

"Maddy, as a chef . . . ? I think you're better suited at being a waitress."

"Hey, this was your idea," she said. Before Maddy delivered the first pizza, she turned to Bob and said, "You don't have to finish those, you know."

"Bite your tongue," I said. "He offered his aid, and I'm going to take him up on it. Go on, he'll be here when you come back."

Maddy took the pizza, gave Bob a wink and a big grin, and then left.

"Sorry about that, Eleanor," he said.

"Don't apologize. Wash."

He did as I asked, and when things slowed

down, I said, "I can think of another way you could help."

"Would you like me to sweep the floor? I'm afraid I'd be out of my league making pizzas."

"Trust me, you're not getting anywhere near my oven. I'm talking about helping us investigate Judson Sizemore's murder."

Bob frowned at me. "I understand you've already gotten someone to assist you there."

"Hey, you've worked for Art Young before, so don't give me any holier-than-thou attitude."

He shrugged. "Just because I've worked for the man doesn't mean that we're friends."

"If it did, I'd like to think that I wouldn't judge you based on someone else's rumored actions that I couldn't confirm or refute, even if I cared about them in the first place."

Bob put the platter he'd been washing back in the sink. "Don't kid yourself, Eleanor. He's not as charming as you seem to think he is."

That did it. I was tired of his attitude, even if he *was* washing dishes for me. "What does it matter how charming I think he is? He's my friend, and I asked him for help. You should think about the fact that he gave his assistance without hesitation, which is more than I can say for you."

Bob nodded slowly. "It appears that I'm determined to be in one of your doghouses, doesn't it?"

"It seems that way to me at the moment," I said.

"Let's start over. What can I do for you?"

"Nothing," I said, suddenly cooling to the idea of getting him to help us. "I've got it covered."

"Eleanor, I've already apologized. What more do you want from me?"

I gave him my coldest look. "I'm sorry; I must have missed that. When exactly did you apologize?"

He thought about it for a few moments, and then nodded. "You're right, of course. I shouldn't have said anything about a friend of yours, no matter what my personal opinion of the man might be."

"I suppose there is a request for forgiveness buried somewhere in there," I said. "For a man who's supposed to be good with words, you are alarmingly lacking at times, did you know that?"

"In front of a judge and jury, I'm fine. It's just when I'm dealing with you and your sister that I seem to cause myself the greatest number of problems. I honestly am sorry, if it matters."

"Of course it does," I said. "Your apology is accepted."

"Then how may I help you?"

I thought about punishing him a little more, since I was overly sensitive about anyone attacking my friends. Then I realized that with Maddy as a girlfriend, he got enough grief without me adding to it. "I don't know anything about Judson Sizemore or his sister, Gina. Would it be possible for you to ask around in Chastain and see what you can find out about either one of them?"

"I can do that," he said. "When do you need the information?"

"As soon as possible," I replied.

"Then I'll leave the rest of the dishes to you, and I'll get right on it, as long as I have your blessing, that is."

"If you can help with this, I'll be happy to finish up the dishes myself."

He took his apron off, and then said, "Then I'll be going. I'll let you know what I uncover as soon as I learn anything about them."

"I'd appreciate that. Thank you, Bob."

"It's my pleasure."

After he was gone, I was starting to feel better about our chances in the murder investigation. With Bob Lemon working one side of the street and Art Young working the other, I felt like we had the opportunity to get a real handle on why Judson Sizemore had been killed in his pizzeria.

That good feeling quickly faded away when the door opened again ten minutes later, but instead of Greg, I saw someone I had no interest in dealing with at the moment.

"What can I do for you, Chief?" I asked Kevin Hurley as he came back into my kitchen. I'd had no idea that it would be such a popular spot. If I had, I might have tried to fit in a comfy chair or two alongside my pizza oven.

"We need to have an extended conversation," he told me.

"About what? I can teach you how to make pizza, but you'd have to pay attention, and I wouldn't mind if you took notes."

"I know how to make pizza," he said. "I've got a number by the phone to call one in whenever I want."

"Then I'm afraid I can't teach you much else."

"Would you be quiet long enough for me to talk, Eleanor?"

"Yes, sir," I said. "Sorry, sir."

He just shook his head. "Do you always have to do things the hard way when it comes to dealing with me?"

He had a point. I never made things easy on him, even when it worked in my favor. "I'm sure that it appears that way sometimes, doesn't it? Okay, I'll try to be a little more cooperative from here on out."

The police chief bit his lip, most likely to keep from making a crack about my promise. "We need to talk more in depth about Judson Sizemore."

My ears burned a little, since I'd been talking about the man all day. "Go on, I'm listening."

"Remember, I'm here to ask questions, not disseminate information," he said.

"I have to hear the question before I answer it, don't I? What do you want to know? If I've got an answer, you'll get it without any sass."

He glanced in the little notebook he always carried around in his breast pocket, and then he asked me, "Is it true that you threatened him two days ago?"

"I wouldn't exactly call it a threat," I said. "He rebuffed every attempt I made at a cordial relationship, even though we were going to be competitors. I just told him that I'd tried being nice, but since that hadn't worked with him, I'd have to try another course of action."

Kevin shook his head. "Yeah, you're right. I can't imagine him taking that as a threat."

"Me, either," I said. "I'm glad we agree on that."

The police chief frowned at me. "Eleanor, I was being sarcastic."

"Were you? Sometimes it's so difficult to tell. Okay, I promised you a straight answer. I didn't threaten him, at least not in my mind."

"When was the last time you saw him?"

"You were there," I said. "It was when you helped me get him out of the Slice when he was here handing out flyers for his pizzeria."

"And you didn't see him after that. Is that correct?"

"Kev . . . I mean Chief, I did not see him after we had that conversation in my pizzeria."

"All right," he said as he jotted something down in his notebook. "Eleanor, I've got to be honest with you. It would be a lot better for you if you had an alibi when the victim was murdered."

"I'm not about to apologize for sleeping alone," I said.

He shut his notebook. "I'm not asking you to do that, and you know it."

"Just so we're clear."

"I heard David Quinton was back in town."

Where was this going? Were we still discussing the murder case now? "True. We had lunch together, but he's leaving again soon."

"Sorry to hear that."

"For me?" I asked.

"For everybody. I always liked David."

"So did I."

After a few more seconds, he left me alone in the kitchen, wondering what the end of that conversation had been all about.

The door swung open a second later and Greg walked in.

"Where have you been?" I lashed out at him, not meaning to take my anger out on him, but not able to stop myself.

He just laughed. "Well, Mom, it's like this. I was planning to come straight home, but Betty Jo wanted to get a malted, and gee, you know how swell I think she is. Lighten up, boss, I'm three minutes early."

I let out a deep sigh. "I'm sorry, I didn't mean to take it out on you."

"Chief Hurley must have really rattled your cage."

I wasn't about to discuss that with him. "If you're ready to work, we can use you."

"Just point me to a customer, and I'm on it," he said.

"Ask Maddy," I said.

"I'd love to, but she's not out there. As a matter of fact, I was kind of hoping you could tell me where she went."

Chapter 7

"She's not out there?" I asked. I couldn't believe my sister would just abandon her post like that.

"Not as far as I could tell. I figured she was back here with you picking up someone's order."

"Well, she's not."

As I raced out the kitchen door, a thousand scenarios went through my mind. Where could Maddy be? Had something happened to her? I had to believe that it would take something urgent to make her leave her post,

"I'll help you look for her," I said as I scanned the dining room.

She wasn't there, and I was getting really concerned. I stormed out of the Slice, not caring if my customers walked away with the contents of the entire place if they were in the mood to. Being paid for my pizza was not even on my mind.

Maddy was all that mattered at that moment.

I found her just outside the door. As a matter of fact, I nearly ran her over as I rushed out.

"Where have you been?" I asked as I hugged her.

"Our illustrious chief of police was interrogating me, and I didn't think you'd want our customers to see it. Why, were you worried about me?"

"Of course I was," I said. A twinge of anger came up. "Now get back inside before I have to fire you."

She grinned at me. "You can't fire me. You love me, remember?"

"Trust me, I can and I will if you ever disappear from the Slice like that again."

As we walked inside, I saw Margaret Wilmoth standing at the register. She said, "I would have left my money if I'd had the exact change."

"Sorry about that," I said. "How was everything?"

"Delicious, as always. Is everything all right, Eleanor?" Margaret had been a guidance counselor at my high school, and I'd always been a big fan of hers. She and Billie Davis, another counselor who'd worked there, were two of the reasons most kids in jeopardy of dropping out had stayed in school.

"I'm fine," I said. "Thanks for coming."

"I wouldn't miss it for anything in the world."

After she was gone, I turned to Maddy and asked, "Do we have everything under control now?"

She nodded as she sniffed the air. "We do on my end. Is it me, or is something burning in the kitchen?"

* * *

I raced back into the kitchen, certain that the place would be in flames, but I didn't find anything even close to igniting.

It took my heart ten minutes to slow down enough for me to decide that calling 911 might be a bit premature.

Our lunch break finally arrived, and I was so exhausted from the mass of customers we'd had that I was tempted to find a booth out front and take a nap, though it would have been the worst time in the world to do it.

For some reason, my sister was perky and ready to go.

"How do you do it, Maddy? I know you worked just as hard as I did this morning, but you still look fresh."

She grinned. "I recommend Mountain Dew. It's my caffeine beverage of choice."

"Maybe I should have some myself," I said.

"It's up to you, but I think it's great stuff."

"I'd better not. After all, I don't want to get hooked."

She smiled at me. "There are worse things in the world, trust me, and you can pick one up just about anywhere."

"I've been thinking about something," I said. "I'm not ready to give up on Nathan just because Gina wants us to. How do we even know that she's telling us the truth about her uncle's intentions?"

"It's like we're psychic or something," Maddy said. "I was just about to suggest we pay him another visit."

We got to Nathan's place, and I started for the

porch when Maddy stopped me. "We've got a better chance of getting him alone if we go out to the garden, don't you think?"

"It makes sense to me."

As we walked around the house, I kept looking in the windows, hoping not to see Gina Sizemore there. The woman had been in Nathan's life for less than a year, and she was already trying to control his every movement. It made it tough to talk to him, but I wasn't about to be stopped that easily. I hated the idea that Nathan could believe that I had anything to do with his nephew's death. But I couldn't convince him of that if I didn't get the opportunity to speak with him.

We got around the back, and Maddy's instincts were on the money. Nathan was there harvesting snap peas and, better yet, Gina was nowhere to be seen.

"Nathan, could we speak with you?" I asked as we approached him.

He looked up at us, and then went back to his harvesting. The tender green pods were exploding with peas, and they looked so good, I wanted a few for myself. Nathan's face had been serene as he'd been picking vegetables, but the second he spotted us, a cloud crossed his face.

"I'm not talking to you, Eleanor."

"How about me?" Maddy asked.

"Neither one of you," he said firmly. "You're trespassing on private property, and you both need to leave."

"Give us just three seconds to speak with you and then we'll leave you alone," I said. "Nathan, we didn't have anything to do with what happened to Judson. You've got to believe us."

"There's no reason I should," he said harshly. "You wanted him dead, and from what I've heard, you told him as much yourself."

"Who told you that, Gina? If she did, you should realize that she's lying to you, at least about us."

"That's enough," a voice I recognized said from the back porch. I hadn't even heard her come out. I looked up to see Gina holding her uncle's shotgun, and it was pointed right at both of us. "You heard the man. You're not welcome here."

"We just came to talk," I said.

Maddy grabbed my arm. "Nobody here is interested in what we've got to say. Let's go, Eleanor."

"Listen to your sister while you still have the chance," Gina said. "Now move."

She held the gun like an old friend, and I knew that Maddy was right. We didn't really have any choice in the matter. It was time to go.

"Okay, we're leaving," I said. Before I could let it go, I turned back to Nathan and said, "Listen, if you change your mind and decide that you want to talk to us, you know where to find us."

"That's not going to happen," Gina said as she stepped off the porch and moved toward us.

I'd pushed our luck as far as I could. Maddy and I left at a fast pace, but at least we hadn't run away from the scene.

Maddy and I didn't speak again until we were back in the car and driving away from Nathan's house.

Finally, Maddy looked at me and grinned. "That went well, didn't it?"

I honestly had no idea what she was talking about. "What do you mean? We didn't learn anything, and we just ended up making matters worse."

Maddy smiled. "I don't think so. We found out how far we could push Gina, and how much control she has over her uncle. Can you believe that he didn't make a move to protect us when she threatened us with that shotgun?"

"There's something we need to keep in mind. Nathan just lost his nephew, and Gina lost her brother," I said. "In some parts of the country, it could be said that they reacted in a reasonable manner."

"Something's going on there," Maddy said.

"Do you have any idea what, exactly?"

"Not yet, but give me time. I will."

"I have no doubt about that," I said. "What should we do now?"

I glanced at my watch and saw that we had a little less than thirty minutes left on our lunch break. "We could go back to the Slice and take a nap before we have to reopen," I said.

"We could, but I honestly can't imagine us doing that, can you?" she asked. "Our investigation time is limited, so we can't squander the free time we've got."

"So, where do you suggest we go?" I asked.

"That, I'm not certain about. I've got an idea. Why don't we drive around until we can come up with something?"

"Sounds good to me," I said.

As Maddy drove past the promenade, I glanced over at the Slice as I always did, and I was surprised to see a man standing out front. One quick look in the parking lot and I spotted the long, black car I'd come to recognize over the years.

Art Young was standing there patiently waiting for us to return.

"Maddy, pull in."

"Why?"

She saw Art then, and then noticed his car. "Can't he wait until we get back?"

"That would be rude. He might have news for us," I said.

Maddy pulled into an open space, and then said, "Fine, but I'm not going over there with you. I'll be at Paul's again looking at his pastries. Come find me when you're finished."

"He's not here this time of day," I explained to her. Paul had some horrible hours, including coming to work in the middle of the night and leaving not long after most folks took their lunch hours.

"Look again," Maddy said with a smile. Paul was indeed still open, later than was his normal custom.

I wondered what he was doing there that late, but I couldn't let it concern me at the moment. "Okay, I'll meet you over there as soon as I finish up with Art."

As we got out of Maddy's car, she said, "Boy, are you ever getting the short end of that stick. I'll think of you when I eat a cinnamon bun."

"Good. While you're doing that, I'll be thinking about your waistline."

"Eleanor, that's just mean. How am I supposed to enjoy a wondrous treat if I'm thinking about how it's going to end up looking on me?"

I laughed. "Knowing you, I'm sure you'll find a way to justify it before you hit the front door."

"I'm good about things like that," she said.

Maddy veered off toward Paul's bakery, and I headed toward Art Young.

"Are you waiting for me?" I asked as I neared him.

"You didn't have to rush over here. It's a beautiful day, so I didn't mind waiting for you. I have news, and I thought you'd be eager to hear it."

"I am," I said. "Would you like to come inside? I can make you lunch, and you can eat while you're telling me about it."

He appeared to consider it, and then said, "The offer is tempting, even if I have already eaten. Another time, perhaps. Would you mind if we have our conversation on one of these benches?"

"Are you kidding? I spend my day in the kitchen, and there's no window in the back of my building. It sounds delightful to me."

We found a bench, and as soon as we sat down, Art took out a small leather notebook and flipped it open. "Judson Sizemore liked to gamble, and he was extremely bad at it. He owed an associate of mine in Chastain over a hundred thousand dollars, and from what I was able to learn, he was quite tardy in paying any of it back."

"Would someone kill him over that? Everyone realizes it would be hard to collect anything from a dead man."

"Yes, but sometimes these things escalate. There's also talk that he owed a private individual about the same amount, though how he managed to talk anyone into giving him money is beyond me after everything I've heard about him."

"So there could be a set of motives there," I said as I listened to this darkness about Judson while sitting in the warm sunshine.

"Possibly. Also, I understand that he recently broke off his engagement to a woman in Chastain named Lacy White. Apparently, Ms. White has a temper, and if my sources are right, she's been arrested for assault on two other boyfriends in the past when they ended things. If she reacted that way to broken romances, how might she take having an engagement end?"

"Not good, I'm guessing. Do you have any idea how I can find her?"

He glanced at his notebook again. "She works at Carole's, a women's clothing store in Chastain. It's at five-sixty-two East Morning Street. Also, there's a man Lacy's close to named Jack who might be trouble. I don't have a last name for him yet, but I'm working on it. He also has ties to Gina Sizemore." Art closed his notebook, and then added, "I'm afraid that's all I've been able to find out so far."

"That's excellent," I said. On an impulse, I leaned forward and kissed his cheek. "Thanks for helping."

He looked pleased by the public display of affection, no matter how minor it was. "All you need do is ask."

Standing up, Art nodded toward me. "Now, I'm afraid I must go. I have an appointment in Charlotte, and if we hurry, I'll just be able to make it after all."

"Thanks again," I said as he headed to his car. I nodded to his driver, a big man I'd spoken to before. I waved at him, but if he saw me, he didn't give any indication that he knew me. Laughing softly to myself, I walked to Paul's bakery. At least now Maddy and I had somewhere to go.

I walked into Paul's again and took a deep breath, basking in the aroma of freshly baked bread and pastry treats. The scent of baked goods was so powerful—even though most of them were already gone—I could already feel myself gaining weight just by being there.

Maddy was at a table sitting with Paul. She was eating a cinnamon bun the size of a dinner plate, and there was another one, untouched, beside her.

I pointed to the treats and said, "You're not eating both of those, are you?"

"That all depended on how long you took," she said.

"Hi, Paul," I said as I sat and joined them. "How are you?"

"I'm delightful," he said. "It's past closing time, and I'm just about ready to go home, so it's all good news for me."

"Don't worry. We won't keep you," I said.

"Stay," he said with a smile. "I'll flip the OPEN sign to CLOSED, and we can chat a little. I've been talking to Maddy about the Halloween Blowout. I can't wait."

"I nearly forgot all about it," I admitted. It was my favorite event at my most special time of year, and the pallor of Judson's murder had nearly wiped it from my mind.

"How could you do that? It's in three days, Eleanor. You'all are participating again, aren't you?"

"Absolutely," I said as I reached for the cinnamon bun. "We're making little ghost pizzas with mozzarella cheese this year. How about you?"

He grinned. "That's why I'm here now. I've been trying some things out in the back. Would you like to see what I've been able to come up with so far?"

"Absolutely," I said.

He jumped up, went back into his kitchen, and then returned a minute later.

"What do you think?"

He presented a tray filled with all kinds of kid-friendly spooky confections. There were white glazed ghosts, black frosted bats, and yellow iced moons laid out for our inspection.

"You've outdone yourself," I said. "The kids are going to love it."

"Thanks," he said, and then added with a wicked grin, "Now, would you like to see what I've got for the grown-ups?"

Maddy finished a bite of her cinnamon bun and replied before I had the chance. "Bring them on."

He put the tray on the counter, and then came back with another, also adorned with decorated goodies. On this tray, I found a large brown stake, a zombie's face, and a broomstick, all iced in bright neon colors.

"What makes these for grown-ups?" I asked.

He pointed to the zombie. "This one's overfilled with a cherry and raspberry filling, so when you bite into it, it oozes out all over the place. I got the idea from a donut shop called Voodoo Doughnuts in Portland, Oregon. The stake is glazed with rum icing, and the broomstick is made with a beer batter I've been playing with." He frowned as he added, "It's not that great at the moment, but I've still got time to perfect it."

"You'll be the hit of the Blowout," Maddy said. "I'd like to order a dozen of the stakes and zombie heads myself."

"You've got it. In fact, you could both do me a favor, if you wouldn't mind."

"Anything for you, Paul," I said. "All you have to do is ask."

"Then I'm asking. I need a taste tester, and it's not something I can ask just anyone. Could I drop off samples tomorrow when I leave to get your reactions to them? You can taste them after you lock up, and leave me a note on my bakery door with your ratings. What do you say?"

"Why not?" Maddy replied. "On second thought, cancel that previous order. Why pay if I'm getting to sample them for free?"

He grinned. "I like the way you think. Tell you what. I'll throw in a dozen each as your payment, anyway."

I smiled at him. "You don't have to bribe us, Paul."

"Are you kidding? I'd love to be able to barter with you. You'd really be helping me out here."

Maddy patted my hand. "Eleanor, let me handle this. I'll do the negotiating for us," she said with a smile, and then turned to Paul. "We're happy to help."

"I knew I could count on you," he said. "What have you two been up to since this morning?" Paul asked as he took the trays away.

I didn't even hesitate to tell him what we were doing. "We're trying to figure out who killed Judson Sizemore."

He nodded. "I figured you had to be."

I wanted to tell him more but I'd promised the police chief that I wouldn't. "It was something related to his business," I said.

That was enough for Paul. "Has our esteemed chief of police been after the two of you about it?"

"He seems to think we've got motive, though it's becoming clearer and clearer that we're not the only ones. I wouldn't put it past that sister of his, to be honest with you," Maddy said.

"Her name's not Gina, is it?" he asked, half-joking.

"As a matter of fact, it is," I answered. "How did you know that?"

"That's not funny, Eleanor."

Maddy shook her head. "She's serious. I'm the funny one, remember? Do you know Gina Sizemore?"

"You could say that," Paul said as the energy seemed to go out of him. "I was going to marry her someday."

"What?" I nearly choked on my cinnamon bun. I never expected Paul to say something like that. "You're joking."

"I wish I were. Gina broke my heart in college, and to tell you the truth, I'm still not completely over it. I never heard Judson's last name until just now. I knew Gina had a brother, but she never talked about him."

"I can't get over the fact that you two were together," I said, still not able to believe it. Our gentle, sweet Paul with that barracuda was just too much to take.

At least he looked sheepish as he admitted, "I know. Opposites attract. She was everything I wasn't—brash and flirty—with an appeal that was hard to resist. I didn't have a chance once she set her sights on me."

"What happened?" Maddy asked.

"She found out that I wanted to be a baker and not an attorney, and she couldn't dump me fast enough after she heard the news."

"That's pretty shallow of her, isn't it?" I asked. I didn't know what was wrong with some women, ruining good men who deserved better. I'd had my share of friends who had been treated badly by men, and I was a firm believer in equality, especially when it came to broken hearts.

Paul shrugged. "Gina has always had expensive tastes. When she realized that I wouldn't be able to support her in the style she wanted to become accustomed to, she dumped me on the spot. I'm not sure I ever got over it, because it was so sudden. One second we were in love, and the next she was going out with one of my classmates. It was almost too brutal to take."

"What it all boils down to is that it's her loss," I said.

Maddy agreed. "What a fool that woman is." She finished her last bite, and then asked, "Paul, can I ask you something, since you knew her pretty well back then?"

"Go ahead. I'll be glad to help if I can."

"Do you think she is capable of murder?"

That rocked him back, though I'd been expecting Maddy to ask him the question. He seemed to think about it for thirty seconds, and then he said, "Gina? I just can't see her doing something like that."

It was my turn to step into the conversation. "Not even if she found herself backed into a corner?"

Paul thought a little longer about it, and when he answered, his voice was heavy with sadness. "I wish I could say no for sure, but it's hard to imagine how her mind works these days. If she was put under the right amount of stress, I'd have to say that it's possible she might kill to get what she thought she deserved, especially if it concerned money. Why do you ask? Her brother wasn't rich, was he?"

"No, but her uncle is." I just at that second realized that I'd promised Nathan to keep my mouth shut about his money. Then again, he hadn't done anything to merit that respect.

"Who is her uncle?"

I was still debating about how to respond to that when Maddy volunteered, "Nathan Sizemore is loaded, and no one here in town knows it. We're supposed to keep that information secret, so do us a favor and keep it to yourself."

Paul just shook his head in disbelief. "I'm not sure how much more of this I can take. My head feels like it's going to explode. Where did Nathan come up with more than a hundred bucks at any one time in his life?"

"He owns all kinds of land," Maddy said.

"I didn't even realize that Gina was related to Nathan," Paul admitted. "I wonder what else she kept from me when we were together."

"Don't beat yourself up about it," I said. "She didn't know she was his niece herself until her father's funeral."

Paul scratched his chin. "If she's known for that long, what took her so long to show up in Timber Ridge? I can't imagine her staying away from a rich uncle a second longer than she had to. Like I said, in college, the girl was all about the cash."

"That's another question we're going to try to find out," I said. "Care to give us a hand with our investigation?" It could be risky asking, especially where his heart was concerned, but Maddy and I couldn't afford to skip anyone who might be able to help us.

To his credit, Paul knew his own mind. In an instant, he replied, "Ladies, you know how much I care for you both, but I'd rather walk barefoot through a dry swimming pool full of rattlesnakes than get anywhere near that girl again. Sorry, I just can't do it. It's a chance I'm not willing to take."

"We understand completely," I said. "We've got to run, but feel free to drop off your concoctions anytime."

"It's a deal," he said.

Once we were outside, I said to Maddy, "Can you believe that? Is there any odder couple you can imagine than Paul and Gina?"

"I don't know, I didn't appear to be a fit with at least two of my ex-husbands, but we managed to get along just fine."

"Until the divorces, you mean," I said.

"Yes, there's always that. But if there's one thing I've learned on my repeated trips to the altar, the heart gets what it craves, and there's no explaining it sometimes."

Poor Paul. I knew he was no choirboy, but I also understood that at the core, he was a good and decent man. His past relationship with Gina might explain why he had so much trouble finding a girlfriend now that he lived back in Timber Ridge. "I shouldn't have asked him for help, but I figured he'd be honest with us if he couldn't do it."

Maddy nodded. "We have enough reinforcements as it is, anyway. What did Art Young have to say?"

I brought her up to speed about what I'd learned as we walked over to the pizzeria, and then Maddy glanced at her watch. "There's no way we're going to get to Chastain and back and have time to interview Lacy White."

"Then there's only one thing we can do," I said as I opened the door to the pizzeria.

"We're not going to blow off a lead like that, are we?"

"Not a chance," I said as I walked to the back and grabbed a blank sheet of paper from the copier. With a thick black pen, I wrote, *back at 4:30* and handed it to Maddy. "Do you want to tape that to the front window?"

"I will, but I still can't believe it. You're actually willing to lose income for this investigation?"

I nodded. I didn't think I had much choice, given the way things were going. The faster Maddy and I could find the real killer, the quicker our lives would get back to normal. "Just think how much it will cost us if Kevin Hurley locks one of us up for murder. I don't even want to think about what the lawyers' fees would be." And the past few days had been so busy, I figured we could spare a couple hours.

"You've got a point." As she taped the sign in the window, Maddy asked, "What should we do about Greg and Josh?"

I thought about calling them, but I knew both young men hated getting cell phone calls from me, especially ones that were work related. "They'll see the sign like everyone else. We can explain it to them when we get back."

"That's the spirit. Let's go."

As we drove to Chastain, I couldn't help thinking about Paul and Gina, and how her greed had broken them up. I knew that kind of thing happened more than I realized, but I still couldn't imagine throwing away such a fine young man as Paul simply because his earning potential wasn't up to her expectations. Gina would bear closer scrutiny when we had the chance. The fact that she'd held that shotgun on us with such ease began to worry me more and more as well.

But at the moment, we had a more important lead to pursue. If what Art Young had told me about Lacy White was true, and I had no reason to believe otherwise, then Judson could have brought his doom upon himself. Maddy and I would have to push her to see if we could get that temper to flare up enough for her to speak a little too freely. If we managed that, we might just be able to learn the truth.

I wasn't looking forward to the confrontation, but I knew that my sister reveled in it.

For the millionth time, and for the thousandth reason, I was glad to have her by my side.

Chapter 8

"This is lovely," I said to our interview subject, a sales clerk at Carole's whose nametag read "Lacy." The shop's official name was Carole's House of Fine Clothing, but it was no surprise that folks abbreviated it. Maddy and I had gone in with a plan to try to catch Judson's former fiancée off-guard, and after considerable debate, we'd decided that I'd be the shopper and she'd listen in, stepping in only if the conversation became confrontational. It wasn't that I didn't trust my sister to handle the delicate questions we needed to ask, but she had a tendency to come on a little too strong at times, and we might need her to close in for the kill if I couldn't get Lacy angry enough on my own.

I held a dress up to my body and then turned to her for an opinion—not that I could afford the thing on the pittance I paid myself at the Slice.

"It would look dreadful on you, I'm afraid," the elegantly dressed young blonde said. It was amazing how much disapproval she managed to get into her words. I suddenly felt embarrassed for even daring to be there.

Lacy studied me for a few moments, and then finally said, "I'm afraid there are only a few things in this shop that would fit you, and, to be frank, their colors are completely wrong for your skin tones. Perhaps you'd have more luck at the mall."

I smiled at her and said as sweetly as I could manage, "Wow, you really are obnoxious, aren't you?" So much for my pretext of being the level-headed one of the family.

"I tell the truth," she said with a derisive snap. "If you can't deal with that, perhaps you'd be better off leaving the store."

"Do you want to know something? I'm beginning to understand why Judson Sizemore dumped you," I said.

The woman suddenly lunged at me with a coat hanger in her hand, and I was glad that Maddy was there to stop her.

"Slow down there," my sister said as she cut her off. "You don't want to do that."

"And why is that?" Lacy asked.

"Trust me. We have friends you don't want to make unhappy," Maddy said. That certainly wasn't part of our plan. What was she doing threatening this woman?

Lacy backed off with that comment. "I didn't mean anything by it. It was such a shock hearing about what happened to Judson."

"I bet it was," I said. "When's the last time you were in Timber Ridge?"

"What possible business is it of yours?" she asked me.

"You can tell us, or you can tell the state police," Maddy said.

"Those are your friends?" she said with a laugh. "I'm not afraid of the police."

Maddy chuckled softly. "Neither are we, but if things go south, we may use them as a backup."

"I've heard enough from you. You both need to leave."

I knew where Maddy was headed, but I wasn't about to let her use Art's name to intimidate this woman. If anyone was going to do that, it needed to be me. "Do you have any idea who has been asking questions about you, Lacy? Surely someone's reported back to you that there have been inquiries made."

"I had a call earlier," she said as she looked at me. "They said it was nothing to worry about."

"There's where you're wrong. The man who is helping us isn't known for putting up with foolishness from anyone."

"I'm not saying anything until I know who wants to know."

"Do you mean us?" I asked.

"Of course not. I'm talking about the heavy-hitter backing you up."

I just laughed. "He wouldn't appreciate me using his name like that, but think about who called you. Do you know anyone they might be afraid of?"

Lacy took it all in for a moment. No one had said she was stupid. "I don't know anything about Judson's death. I haven't been in that town since I was in college, and that's the truth."

"Where were you the night of the murder?"

She didn't want to answer, I could see it in her eyes, but she did just the same. "I was at my apartment. I had a cold, so I left here early and I didn't come in at all that day. I was shocked to hear about it on the radio, but I didn't kill him."

I didn't know whether to believe her or not. There was something about the way she spoke that made me doubt every word out of her mouth. She could have told me it was hot in July, and I would have asked to see a thermometer before I believed her.

"Is that all?" she asked, finally getting some of her spirit back. This would be a hard woman to browbeat for very long without a very real weapon in our hands. "I have work to do."

"That's it, for now," Maddy said.

As we left, I stopped at the shop door before I exited. "I hope for your sake that you're telling us the truth."

She made no reply, and Maddy and I walked out of the shop. There was a man hovering nearby, pretending to read a news-paper, but it was obvious he was watching us.

"Well, it's good to know that you're the calm one," Maddy said softly outside. "Nice subtle hint there."

"I saw where you were going with your line of questioning, so I decided to step in. If anyone was going to use our connection to Art, it needed to be me. Besides, I wanted to have a little fun myself and try to make her squirm. Don't tell me that you would have just stood there and taken the way she was treating me." I looked back for the man with the newspaper, but he was gone. Could that have been the mysterious Jack that Art told me about?

"Me? She would have been wearing that hanger as a choker if she'd said it to my face. I was honestly impressed with your restraint."

"At least we did one thing—we established that she has a temper," I said as we made our way back to Maddy's car.

"You almost had proof of that up close," she said. "Her story doesn't give her much of an alibi, does it? With that convenient 'cold' she had, no one can say when, or even if, she was home. Where does that leave us?"

"I'd say she's a genuine suspect, so that's progress." I glanced at my watch. "I'm afraid that's all we're going to be able to do right now. We need to get back to Timber Ridge and open the restaurant."

"We might as well," Maddy said. "I hate to admit it, but Art Young came through for you today."

"He's not all bad," I answered.

"I'll withhold judgment on that," she said.

As we started back to Timber Ridge, Maddy's cell phone rang. I wasn't crazy about her talking and driving, and she knew it.

After a moment, she said, "Tell Eleanor."

Maddy handed me the telephone, and I heard Bob Lemon on the other end.

"Where are you?" Bob demanded.

"We're in Maddy's car. Is this a new game we're playing? I just love games. Now it's my turn. Where are you?"

"I'm in front of the Slice with two very worried young men," he said, finding no humor in what I'd said at all. "You've got to tell someone when you're not going to be here. We were all worried about you."

"I appreciate that," I said, "but it's misplaced. Maddy and I have been getting into trouble for years together, and I don't see any indication of it stopping anytime soon. Besides, we left a sign on the door."

"It must have fallen off, because I don't see it. There's someone dangerous out there, Eleanor. You can't take it too lightly."

I'd had enough of that. I felt like David Quinton had finally learned his lesson, but Bob Lemon clearly hadn't. "Trust me, we're not," I said with an edge in my voice. "That's why we're investigating Judson's murder. So, unless you have important information for us about that, I suggest you hang up before you say anything else you might very well live to regret."

"I'll tell you the rest when you get here," he said.

"Fine," I replied, and then hung up.

I put the telephone back in Maddy's purse, and she glanced over at me for a second. "Wow, you missed your calling, Eleanor. You should have been in the diplomatic corps."

"He was trying to protect us," I said.

"We both know he has a reason," Maddy said calmly. "You need to take it easy on him."

"That's funny. I never thought you'd put up with that kind of behavior."

Maddy bit her lip, and I knew she wanted to say

something, although it was clear that she wasn't certain she should. I decided to help her with it. "Go on, say what's on your mind."

"What are you afraid of, Sis?"

That wasn't what I'd been expecting. "I'm sorry?"

"You reacted the same way when David Quinton started caring too much about you, and when Bob shows the least concern for our welfare, you bite his head off. Can't you let any man get close to you again? Do you think that's what Joe would have wanted?"

I was so stunned by her words that for one of the few times in my life, I was literally speechless. Maddy looked over at me, but I couldn't meet her gaze. My thoughts were going a thousand miles a second. Is that how I was acting? Had I reacted that way every time David had expressed concern over my well-being? My sister had held a mirror up to my behavior, and I didn't like what I saw.

We drove the rest of the way in silence, and when Maddy parked in back of the pizzeria, she said softly, "I didn't mean to be so hard on you. I'm really sorry."

"Don't apologize," I said. "I needed to hear it."

"Then you agree with me?" she asked with a grin.

"Let's just say you've given me food for thought."

We got out and moved to the shortcut. "Let me give you one more piece of advice. When you see Bob, you need to apologize."

"Funny, I gave him that exact advice last night concerning you."

Her smile broadened. "And see how well that worked out?"

We walked around to the front to find the three of them waiting for us.

Ignoring Greg and Josh for the moment, I hugged Bob as I said, "I'm sorry for my behavior. It's sweet of you to care about us, and I appreciate your concern."

He nodded and pulled back away from me. "I didn't mean to upset you."

"We're fine," I said.

I turned to Greg and Josh and added, "We should have warned you we were skipping out, but we got a hot lead, and we decided to follow up on it while we had the chance. If it makes you feel any better, there's a note on the floor on the other side of this door that says we'll be back at four-thirty."

"It's all good," Greg said. "Did you have any luck?"

"We added someone to our list of suspects," Maddy said.

"Then it was worth it." He slapped his hands together and rubbed them. "Now, I don't know about you ladies, but I say we start making some pizza."

"That sounds like a plan," I said. I hesitated after unlocking the door. "Bob, would you like something? It's on the house. You can think of it as a peace offering."

"Thanks, but I'm waiting for a telephone call back at my office. I might stop by later, if that's all right with you."

"You're welcome here anytime," I said.

After he left, I walked into the Slice and flipped the CLOSED sign to OPEN as I picked the handwritten sign up off the floor. As I suspected, the tape hadn't held on the cold, moist glass. Maddy and I might have missed out on a little business while we'd been gone, and if we had, I was sorry for that, but what we'd confirmed was much more valuable than the money we'd lost. It felt good having at least one viable suspect—besides the two of us— make the list.

I wasn't expecting to see Bob Lemon back so soon, but half an hour after he left us, he came into the kitchen.

"Did you decide to take me up on that free meal?" I asked.

"Maybe later. My phone call came through, so I rushed right over here as soon as it was over."

"Should we wait for Maddy?" I asked. I knew how my sister hated being scooped, especially when it came to news from her boyfriend.

"She gave me her blessing to go on and tell you," Bob said.

"Then go on," I replied.

"Gina Sizemore is in quite a bit of financial trouble," he said. "She has outstanding debt on her credit cards that you won't believe."

"How much are we talking about here?" I asked. It wasn't hard to see a motive if Nathan had been murdered, but unless her brother, Judson, had an insurance policy that listed her as sole beneficiary, it was tough to blame her for the murder.

"From what I discovered, she's amassed over a hundred thousand dollars in debt, and she's just been paying the minimum balance for years. Until this month, that is."

"What changed?"

"If I were guessing, I'd have to say that Nathan stepped in and started helping her out," Bob said.

"He paid off that kind of debt, just like that?"

"No, that's the odd part. There haven't been any charges on her accounts since the first, and only five percent of the debt has been paid as of today."

"That's really strange," I said as I took a finished pizza from the line and cut it before sliding it into a waiting box. "Why would Nathan pay off such a small percentage of her debt? You'd think it would be either all or nothing."

"I'm guessing that he's doing it to teach her a lesson," Bob said. "Can you imagine how angry she must be that he wouldn't clear it all off the books as soon as she found out he could handle it without any financial hardship on him at all?"

"It still doesn't explain why she would kill her brother."

Bob nodded. "You're going to have to think a little more deviously than you're used to," he said. "With Judson out of the way, what do you think becomes of Nathan's money if something happens to him now?"

"I imagine that Gina would get all of it," I said, suddenly aware of the positioning Gina might have made by committing the murder. It would take a cold-blooded woman to kill her own brother, much harder than murdering an uncle. "Are you saying that half of Nathan's estate wouldn't be enough for her?"

"It's possible. Greed knows no boundaries with some people."

"We have to warn Nathan," I said.

"And tell him what, that his last living relative wants him dead, based on no more proof than information he already has? It's not time to do that yet."

"Then what should we do?"

"The best thing I can think to do is to let her know that we're on to her," Bob said.

"Hang on. What do you mean, 'we'?"

"I've decided to help you," he said proudly.

"You just did."

"I mean, take a more active role in your investigation."

I wasn't about to let him risk his law practice, not to mention his life, because of us. "Thanks, but no thanks."

He studied me carefully. "This isn't about before, is it?"

"No, I promise that it's not," I answered with a sigh. "Maddy and I don't have nearly as much to lose as you do."

"That's not true. Your *lives* come to mind."

"I mean besides that," I said with a grin. "We can both still make pizzas, even if we have criminal records. You have a successful law practice to protect. Don't worry about the two of us. We'll be fine."

"I certainly hope so. There's one more thing you need to know, and then I have to go. I'm going to be late for a court appearance as it is."

"Tell me quickly, then."

"Gina has a rather unsavory boyfriend hanging around somewhere in the shadows," Bob said. "From what I've learned, he's a bad seed."

"Do you have a name?" I asked. Art had told me about someone named Jack associated with both Gina and Lacy, but he hadn't had a last name. I suspected it had been the man with the newspaper who'd been watching Lacy at the clothing boutique, but I had no proof of it.

"Not yet, but I'm still looking," he said.

"Let me know when you find out. And thanks, Bob. Maddy and I both appreciate what you're doing for us."

"It could be more," he said.

"Or not," I replied. "I just love these word games, don't you?"

After he left, I took the pizza I'd boxed out front. As I looked for our customer, I couldn't help wondering about Gina, and her real feelings toward her uncle. Regardless of what Bob had just said, I still felt that someone should warn Nathan that he might have invited a viper into his home, but with the way she had been blocking our access at every turn, it couldn't be us. I'd have to think of another way to warn him that keeping her close might be the worst thing he could do, at least if he wanted to survive until Halloween, let alone Christmas.

I walked out to talk to Maddy and found Karen Green sitting at a table with books spread out on top of it.

I detoured over and asked her, "What are you reading?"

She grinned brightly at me. "I had so much fun taking a genealogy course in the adult education program at the college last semester that I decided to take two classes this time."

"That sounds like fun. What are you taking?"

She held up a book for me to read.

I studied the title and the book's description, and then said, "Wow. Basic Law looks tough."

"It's nothing compared to my other class. I decided to take an auto repair class in case I get stranded somewhere. So far, I'm not sure if I've learned anything."

"That's how I've spent half my life," I said. "I admire you for improving yourself. Can I get you anything?"

"Thanks, Maddy just took my order."

"Then I'll let you get back to work."

I approached my sister and told her about Karen's ambitious schedule. When I finished, I asked her, "Do you have any orders for me? I'm caught up in back."

She smiled as she handed me two order slips. "I was just coming back there to give you these. How did it go with Bob?"

"He wants to help us," I said.

"How sweet."

"No, you don't understand. He wants to join our little investigation team and start digging."

She shook her head. "That's not going to happen for so many reasons. I hope you told him that."

"In so many words," I said.

"Then he needs to hear it in those exact words."
I touched her arm lightly. "Don't."

"Don't what?"

"Do not use this as an excuse to pick another fight with that man."

She frowned at me. "I don't know what you're talking about."

"Madeline, I mean it." I rarely used my sister's full name, just as she didn't call me Ellie, unless it was for something important. "I thought you wanted to get married again someday."

She shrugged. "I'm not so sure about that anymore. After all, I've walked down the aisle so many times, I'm starting to wear a path in the carpet."

"That's entirely up to you, but don't take your reticence out on Bob. He's only been trying to help."

"Point taken," she said. "Now, are you going to make those pizzas, or am I going to have to?"

"You can do it," I said as I handed the slips back to her.

"I was just kidding," Maddy said, quickly back-pedaling.

"Come on. We could both use a break in our routine. We'll switch up for the rest of the evening."

Maddy reluctantly took the slips and headed back into the kitchen, and I grabbed Karen's drink and refilled everyone else's glasses. This was going to be a piece of cake.

I hoped.

Ten minutes until closing, everyone was happily eating, and I was doing a bit of spot cleaning up front. Greg had gone home early to study for a major exam, and Josh was watching the clock like it was about to tell the future instead of the time. Staying closed a little longer for lunch had made for a short evening—or was it because I hadn't been in the kitchen all that time? It did seem to go by quicker interacting with customers instead of just my staff, but I would be ready the next day to recapture my solitude. I could swear I was getting a bit hoarse from all the talking I'd done.

I glanced again at Josh, whose gaze had never left the clock.

"Got a big date tonight?" I asked.

He shrugged. "If I get out of here in time, I do."

"Never let it be said that I stood in the way of young love," I said.

"Does that mean I can go?"

"It does," I said.

I could barely finish before he was out the door.

Things were slow, and I considered closing early, when the chief of police came in, a cloud across his face.

"I know I should have made him stay, but he had big plans, and I didn't have the heart to keep him here," I said.

"What are you talking about?"

"I just let Josh go early for a big date. Isn't that why you look so upset?"

He shook his head. "Believe me, my son's love life is the least of my problems at the moment."

I pulled him aside out of earshot of my customers. "Don't tell me. I'm probably at the top of that list, aren't I?"

He rubbed his face, looking tired and worried beyond his years. I certainly gave the man my share of grief, but I never really thought about the toll his job must take on him. It was an unusual position to be in, feeling sympathetic for him, but I couldn't help myself.

He ran a hand through his hair and then asked me, "Have you been doing something you shouldn't have?"

"I can't even begin to answer that question," I said. "How in the world could I ever know?"

"I don't have time for these word games of yours, Eleanor, no matter how much fun you find them."

"You implied that you had big problems. What's going on? Is it about Judson Sizemore's murder?"

"No, but it's kind of related. You heard about what happened with Nathan today, didn't you?"

"What are you talking about?" I asked.

"Are you serious? For once, I actually have the information before you do."

"Don't make me wait," I said as I stared at him. "What happened to him?"

I thought I might choke him, while the chief of police just stood there looking at me. If he thought he was going to get away with jerking me around like that, he was sadly mistaken.

Chapter 9

"You know I'm going to find out sooner or later, so you might as well tell me now," I said.

"You've got me there. Fine, I can't imagine what it will hurt telling you about it. The only thing that amazes me is that one of your customers hasn't mentioned it to you already: Nathan had an accident with his lawn mower. He was cleaning up some leaves on his property with it this evening, and apparently it went out of control and nearly drove him into the river in back of his place. That would be bad enough for most folks, but Nathan never learned how to swim, and it's pretty deep along his property line. He managed to jump off just in time, but his mower isn't going to make it."

"Did someone tamper with the brakes?" I asked. The instant I heard what had happened, I began seeing it as an attempted murder.

"What? Your imagination's running a little too wild even for you, Eleanor. Have you seen that bank he has to mow? It would make a mountain goat nervous."

"No," I admitted, "I've only seen the front of his garden."

Kevin looked surprised. "I'm shocked you've seen even that much. He's pretty private about his land."

Apparently our chief of police knew the secret land baron better than the rest of us did. "Have you seen it, then?"

"No," he admitted. "I got the call from his niece, Gina. She was worried about him when she didn't hear from him, so she asked me to drop in and check on him."

That sounded suspicious to me. "If she was so concerned, why didn't she go herself?"

"She was in Chastain when she called me. She phoned the house because he was supposed to call her about something, and when he didn't answer, she got worried. It's perfectly understandable, Eleanor."

"Maybe, but don't you think it's odd that this happened so soon after Judson's murder?"

He laughed, but there wasn't an ounce of joy in it. "Now you're seeing conspiracies where they don't exist."

I wasn't all that fond of being mocked, especially in my own pizzeria. "Since you clearly had no intention of telling me about Nathan, what brings you here?"

"I was hoping to get a pizza to go. I'm working late tonight, and I got hungry. I called and got Maddy, so it should be ready."

"I'll get it for you," I said.

I went back into the kitchen to find my sister with her hands buried in detergent doing dishes, something she hated.

"Getting an early start on leaving?" I asked.

She shook the bubbles from her hands as she pulled them out of the water. "No offense, but I can't wait to get out of here. Whatever I did to deserve this, trust me when I say that I'm sorry, and as soon as I figure it out, it will never happen again."

"I keep telling you, it's not punishment," I said as I looked at the to-go warming shelf and saw Kevin's pizza there.

"It's sure not a reward," she said.

When Maddy saw me pick up the lone box, she asked, "Did our esteemed chief of police finally make it in?"

"He's there now. Nathan Sizemore had an accident this evening," I said.

"What?" she asked, nearly dropping the soapy glass in her hand. "What happened to him? Is he all right?"

"He's fine, but his mower ended up in the water at the rear of his property."

Maddy frowned as she finished washing the glass in her hand and put it in the other sink to rinse. "Do you think it was really an accident?"

"I don't know. It's hard to imagine that it's just a coincidence."

"They do happen, you know," Maddy said as she started rinsing things.

"I still don't have to like them," I replied.

The kitchen door opened and Kevin walked in. "Let's go, ladies. I don't have all night."

"You don't need it. Here you go."

He handed me his money, and I said, "Hang on, I'll get your change."

"Put whatever's left in the tip jar," he said. "From what you pay my son, he can use his cut of every extra penny you get."

"Hey, he loves being here," I said defensively.

"I know. I don't get it, but I can't talk him out of it. Good night."

"'Night," I said.

I looked at Maddy. She looked exhausted, and I knew how tired I was as well. "Let's close up. I'm tired of people right now, and I just want to go home and take a long hot soak in the tub."

She managed a faint smile. "It's not so easy out there, is it?"

"I never said that it was," I replied.

Maddy offered a slight sigh. "Then I can be honest with you when I say that I'd rather go hungry and never shop again if it meant I didn't have to work in the kitchen for another second."

"Wow, don't hold back, Sis. Tell me how you really feel," I said with a smile. I knew it was hard work, but I enjoyed it.

"I can go into more depth and detail if you'd like me to," she said.

"I think I've got it," I said. "Why don't you go lock up, and I'll finish up back here? Think of it as an early parole for good behavior."

"Are you kidding?" she asked as she rinsed a plate. "I've almost finished up. The dining room is all yours."

"That's only fair," I said.

I announced we were closing, and our last two customers left without complaint.

As I was sweeping the floor, Maddy came out.

I looked up and said, "I thought you were going to finish in the kitchen."

"I am," she said. "I just came by for the rest of the dirty dishes." Maddy walked over and flipped the sign to CLOSED, something I'd neglected to do. "As soon as I'm finished, I'll come out and give you a hand."

"I'll be finished before you will."

"In your dreams, Sis," she said.

"I'll race you," I challenged her with a laugh.

"You're on. You're going to get slaughtered, you know that, don't you?"

"We'll see," I said as I started cleaning at a much more harried pace. It was childish, immature, and lots of fun to try to beat Maddy, and it came as no great surprise that I lost the competition.

As we walked to Maddy's car in back when we were finished, the air was getting a real bite to it that had been missing so far. October was coming to a close, and it was ending on a much cooler note than it had started on.

Maddy pulled her jacket closer to her. "If it keeps this up, the kids are going to have to trick-or-treat in their jackets."

"Remember the time it snowed, and Mom made us wear our snowsuits over our costumes? That had to be the worst Halloween ever."

"At least we got lots of candy," Maddy said as we walked through the shortcut.

"Because not many other kids were insane enough to go out in eight inches of snow just for a little sugar."

"Were we crazy, or savvy?"

"I vote for crazy."

I could see her smile in the glow from the street-light. "Yeah, you're probably right, but we were rarely bored as kids. A little crazy is never a bad thing."

"That's part of our charm, don't you think?" I said. "That reminds me. We've got to get things ready for the Halloween Blowout."

"Funny, it feels as though we just had one," she said as she opened her car door.

"What can I say? Time flies when you're getting old," I said with a laugh.

"Hey, at least I'm not as old as you are," she said, her laughter carried away by the wind.

As she dropped me off at my place, I said, "See you tomorrow, Maddy."

"Not if I see you first," she said.

As I walked up to my front door, I realized that I fussed about the cool temperatures sometimes, but, in truth, the chilled air always invigorated me. Joe had been a great deal more warm-blooded than me, and he'd always had a blanket on when the thermometer plummeted, since I was always reluctant to turn the heat up past 67 degrees. It was no surprise that the weather change made me miss him. Just about anything could pull that trig-ger, from the way the leaves changed colors to coming across an old book we'd both loved to read. The edge of my despair had softened since he'd died, but there was still something there when I thought about him, a large portion of thankfulness that he'd been in my life for so long, and a hint of sadness that all I had of him now were memories. Maddy was right, and I knew it. He wouldn't have wanted me spending the rest of my life looking back. If my late husband had believed in one thing, it was that life was meant to be lived to the fullest, and I was finally beginning to realize in my heart as well as my head that was exactly what he would have wanted me to do.

It was just so much easier to talk about than to accomplish.

I was surprised to see David Quinton's car parked on the street in front of my place when I looked out the window. A little of the gloom I'd been feeling seemed to lift from my shoulders when I saw him there.

He got out of his vehicle as I stepped outside. "I hope you don't mind me just showing up like this. I went by the Slice to see you, but you were closed, so I thought I'd come by here. If you want, we can talk tomorrow."

"No, this is fine," I said as a gust of wind sent shivers through me. "Want to come in for some hot chocolate?"

"You know what? I really would," he said and smiled, as he followed me inside.

Most of my weariness melted when I saw that smile. It was amazing how much of the somberness had left him since he'd moved to Raleigh. David was suddenly fun to be around, something I hadn't felt before.

As I took his jacket and hung it in the hall closet, I said, "You seem absolutely giddy these days."

"Do I?" he asked. "It must be the air. I love the chill here. Timber Ridge has to be at least five degrees cooler than Raleigh."

"How do you like it so far?"

He shrugged. "The work's challenging, and I'm around a lot of nice people, but I'm a mountain kind of guy, and if the foothills here in Timber Ridge are as close as I can get, that's something I can live with."

"Well, I'm glad to see you again," I said as I moved into the kitchen. David followed and took a stool at the counter. It was natural to have him with me, and I found myself enjoying his presence more than I had before. I had to wonder if that was entirely due to his change of address or more because of his new disposition.

"Likewise," he said with a smile. As I started the milk on the stovetop and gathered my special blend of cocoas and sugar, he added, "It looks like I'm going to be here a little longer than I'd expected."

Was that a hint of happiness in his voice as he said it, or was I reading something into it that wasn't there? "What's going on?"

"It appears that my old boss was playing fast and loose with some basic accounting principles, and it's going to take some work to straighten things out and hire his replacement."

"You're firing him?" I asked.

David shrugged. "Well, I could have him arrested, so on the whole, I think it's a better alternative for everyone involved. He's agreed to pay back the money that 'disappeared,' and in return, we've promised him that we won't prosecute. If he reneges on the agreement, he's going to jail, so I don't think that's going to be an issue with him."

"I'm sorry about that, but it will be nice having you around town a little longer."

He nodded. "I'm pretty happy about the assignment myself. I'm actually going to be able to go to the Halloween Blowout. I don't have much time to come up with an outfit for it, but I'll find something."

It was tradition for many of the adults in town to dress up for the festivities, but David had never done it before. "Are you really going to wear a costume?"

"Absolutely. I'm thinking of being either a pirate or a gangster." He scratched his chin, and then added, "Hey, I just had a thought. Maybe I'll be both. I could wear a pirate outfit and add a black fedora."

"I love it. Your parrot can have a tiny little machine gun," I said laughing, getting into the spirit of it.

He nodded. "It would present quite the image, wouldn't it? What are you going to wear?"

"To be honest with you, I wasn't planning to dress up this year."

He frowned. "That's insane. I love your costumes. You can't let me or the rest of the town down."

David had a point. I usually came up with something good, and several folks had asked me if I'd decided what I was going to be yet. I hadn't felt moved to do it before, but now I was in the mood to add to the event's festivities with something of my own. "Why not? If you're going to dress up, then I will, too."

"But not as a gangster–pirate," he said with an air of mock seriousness about him. "That's mine."

"Never that," I agreed. "But don't worry, I'll come up with something."

"I can't wait," he said. His voice softened for a moment as he asked, "Any chance you could save me a dance?"

There was a dance held on the promenade, filled with folks from around town wearing the craziest getups. I loved to watch, but I'd never really participated since Joe's death. "I don't know if I'll be able to. I'll probably be busy selling little ghost pizzas."

I expected an argument from him, but he just shrugged as he said, "If you have time, I'll be around." There was no hard sell like the old days, just an offer to dance, if and when I was interested. Nice.

David took a deep breath, and then asked me, "It smells heavenly. Is there any chance that it's ready yet?"

I stirred it again gently and looked down into the richness. "It looks good."

I poured the hot cocoa into two stout mugs, and David surprised me by saying, "I know this is going to sound counter-productive, but do you have any interest in drinking these outside? I just love the way the wind blows the leaves around on the ground when it's dark, and there's nearly a full moon tonight."

"I'd love to," I said.

We put our jackets back on, grabbed our mugs, and then went out to the porch. Each of us took a rocker, and we chatted and sipped as we looked around the neighborhood. It was a quiet and special time, and I found myself relaxing even more in the comfort of the mood and the easiness of the conversation.

I was startled later when David stood and handed me his mug. "That was the most fun I've had in ages, but I've got people to fire tomorrow and money to confiscate."

"It sounds like a busy day," I said as I stayed seated.

"Are you going in?"

"No, I think I'll stay out here a little longer. Thanks for coming by."

"The pleasure was all mine," he said, bowing at the waist, and then adding, "Rrrrrrr, good night, Eleanor. You're quite a dame, you know that, don't you?"

"In fact, I do, but I never get tired of hearing it," I said.

After David was gone, I sat out there a little longer, but the night had lost some of its magic without his presence, so I wrapped my jacket closer, collected our mugs, and went back inside. It was too bright and much too warm in there, but I knew I'd get used to it soon enough. It was funny how things worked out sometimes. I'd been happy to see David leave Timber Ridge, knowing that I could never give him what he wanted, but only by leaving did he become more interesting to me.

It was no surprise that most men found women hard to understand, since we didn't always know why we did the things we did, ourselves. As far as I was concerned, that was one of the things that kept life interesting.

My telephone jarred me out of bed at three A.M., and as I reached for it blindly, I wondered who would be calling me at that hour.

"Keep nosing around where you don't belong and you're going to pay for it," someone said in a gravelly whisper before hanging up.

It appeared that I'd made an impression on someone in my questioning.

But it would have been nice to know who.

I called Maddy immediately, and was surprised to get a busy signal. It was on the edge of possibility that she could have made the call as a twisted joke, but I had a hard time believing it. I hung up, and was about to try again when my telephone rang.

As soon as I heard that it was her, I asked, "You got a threatening call just now, too, didn't you?"

My sister seemed surprised by the statement. "Are you saying that you didn't just call me?"

"And threaten you? No, that wasn't me."

Maddy said, "If you thought it was funny, you're wrong."

"Maddy, wake up," I said loudly.

"I'm awake," she protested.

"Then think about it. In your wildest dreams, can you ever imagine that I'd find something like that amusing? You maybe, but me? Never."

She took a deep breath, and then let it out. "You're right. I might do it on a whim, but you never would. Wow, I can't believe someone actually threatened us."

"It's great news, isn't it?" I asked her.

"I'm not so sure about that," she said.

"Think about it. We managed to get someone so riled up in the past few days that they thought they had to try to scare us off."

She hesitated, and then said, "But maybe not the murderer."

"I told you before, I don't believe in coincidences."

"That might not be what this is. We've been digging into a lot of people's lives, only one who is likely a killer. But that doesn't mean other folks don't have secrets of their own to hide."

She had a point, I knew that, but I wasn't about to embrace it. "I refuse to accept that," I said. "I'm looking at this as good news."

"Wow, then I'd hate to hear what thrills you. Eleanor, should we call someone about this and tell them what happened?"

I thought about it, and then answered, "In this day of disposable cell phones, I doubt anyone would be stupid enough to call us from their home phone. If we tell Kevin Hurley, then we have to admit that we've been digging into Judson Sizemore's murder, and that's a conversation I don't want to have. If we tell Bob, he'll just worry about us, and it won't do any good."

"Then we keep this to ourselves, at least for now," Maddy said.

"And we keep digging," I added.

"See you in a few hours," she said.

"If you can get back to sleep."

"Trust me, I'll be out before you're off the line."

I doubted I'd be that lucky, but I had to try. I couldn't face the day without at least making some kind of attempt to get more rest. To my surprise, I was able to nod off again without too much trouble. Whoever had called us had been threatening enough, but they didn't know my sister or me. We don't scare easily, even when it makes perfect sense for us to be terrified.

All it was going to do was intensify our search for Judson Sizemore's murderer.

"We need to talk and clear a few things up," Lacy White said to Maddy and me the next morning as she barged into the pizzeria. We'd just opened for business, so at least we didn't have any customers yet, but I knew that could change at any moment.

"What's on your mind?" I asked as Maddy started inching toward the baseball bat we kept at the register for protection. It wasn't that we didn't believe in guns—I had some of Joe's locked up safely in a gun cabinet at home—but we didn't want any on the premises.

I was hoping that my sister's actions would go unnoticed, but Lacy didn't miss Maddy's movement. "Where exactly are you going? If you have a gun behind the register, you're not going to need it. I'm here to straighten some things out, not start any trouble."

Maddy looked at me for input on what she

should do, and I nodded slightly to her that it would be okay to wait and see what Lacy had to say. Maddy and I had developed a way of communicating that felt as though we were psychic at times.

She stopped in her tracks, and I asked, "Why the sudden change of heart, Lacy? Yesterday you weren't inclined to give me the time of day, let alone talk openly with me about what I wanted to know."

"Let's just say I found out who your special friend is, and found out it would be in my best interest to cooperate," she said. It was clear that she wasn't all that happy about speaking with us, but she was there; that's all that mattered.

"So talk," Maddy said.

"Judson and I were in the process of patching things up when he was murdered. I slipped once, he found out, and I begged him for forgiveness. He agreed to see me again, and before we could work it all out, someone killed him. Believe me, I want to catch the murderer just as much as you do."

I wanted to believe her, but she didn't make it easy. If Lacy was telling the truth, she was doing a truly unconvincing job of it. "Who did you sleep with?"

She looked at me as though I'd just slapped her. "Is that really something that you need to know? It wasn't my finest hour."

"It wasn't Jack, was it?" It was a total guess, but I'd said it mainly to gauge her reaction to hearing the man's name.

It was a shot in the dark, but it looked to hit home. "How did you find out about Jack?"

"We hear lots of things," I said. "Was it him?"

"We're just friends," Lacy said. It wasn't exactly a denial, but I doubted she'd answer my question honestly, so I let it drop.

There was something else I wanted to pursue, so I said, "Funny, we never heard that you and Judson were reconciling."

"We wanted to keep it under wraps until the Halloween Blowout," she said. "Judson thought it would be sweet if we went to the festival here as Romeo and Juliet. I already rented our costumes. They're sitting on my bed, but we'll never get to wear them now."

"They both died, you know," Maddy said softly.

"Nothing's going to happen to me," she said. "Listen, I've told you both everything I know. Is that all?"

"Not quite," I said. "There's just one more thing. Where were you really at the time of the murder?"

"Jack and I were in Charlotte that night, but it's not what you think."

Maddy stared at her and asked, "How do you presume to know what either one of us is thinking?"

"I just meant that we're friends, and that's it. We've never been anything more, no matter what your sources told you."

"What were you doing together in Charlotte, then?" I asked.

I could tell she wanted to tell me to go to the devil, but Art's influence must have been reaching out to her. "I had a doctor's appointment late that day, and Jack was nice enough to drive me. Judson volunteered, but with the pizzeria about to open, I knew he couldn't spare the time, so I insisted he stay right where he was. Jack and I decided to go to a club while we were in town, and we didn't get back until nearly dawn the next day."

"So, by the time you got back into town, he was already dead," Maddy said.

I didn't expect Lacy's tears, but that's what we got. "Don't you think I realize that? If Judson had taken me himself like he'd wanted to, he'd still be alive today."

"I don't know how you could possibly assume that," I said. "If it's your time to go, I believe that there's nothing you can do about it."

"Do you really think that's true?" she asked, and I could swear I saw a hint of relief in her eyes as she asked it.

Maddy answered for me. "She does. I don't."

That brought her back to reality. "Are we finished here?" Lacy asked me as our first customer of the day came in.

"I don't have anything else for you right now," I said, clearly hedging my bets.

"Then do me a favor," Lacy said. "Call your 'friend' and tell him I'm cooperating, will you?" There was almost a pleading quality to her voice now.

"Has someone threatened you?" I asked. I hated the thought of that being done on my behalf, even to Lacy.

"No, there were no threats, just some advice that I should cooperate with you. I have, haven't I?"

"So far, you've done just fine."

"Then you'll call?" she asked.

"Right now," I replied, and she was gone.

In another instant, Lacy was finally out of sight, so I said, "Hang on a second. I'll be right back."

"You're not going anywhere without me," Maddy said.

"We have a customer, remember?"

"She can wait," Maddy answered.

"Stay."

My sister did as I asked, much to my surprise.

I went out in time to see Lacy getting into a car parked on the promenade's parking strip. There was a scruffy-looking young man waiting for her, and as they drove away, I knew that it was the same man I'd seen waiting outside Carole's the day before.

Chapter 10

"Was she alone?" my sister asked me as I walked back into the Slice.

I smiled. "Not a chance. It appears that her friend Jack doesn't trust her out of his sight. I've got a feeling that you were right, by the way."

"I just love hearing you say that. Just so I'll know, about what, in particular?"

"It's the same man I saw in front of Carole's keeping an eye on Lacy. Chastain's not that big. He's got to be the same man Gina's been involved with."

"It just makes sense." Maddy shook her head. "I can't believe you let her off the hook like that. You really had her squirming for a second there. That girl was afraid, there's no doubt about it."

"I was under the impression that you don't approve of my friendship with Art Young. Doesn't it strike you as odd that you're willing to use his influence anyway if it helps us with our investigation?"

Maddy laughed softly. "What can I say, I'm a mess of contradictions. I'm just saying, she would have told you anything just then."

"We can discuss that later. Right now, we have a customer," I said as I pointed to the older woman sitting alone squinting at the menu.

"She's still deciding, but I get it," Maddy said as she took the hint and approached the woman while I went into the kitchen.

I'd purposely done it so I could be alone. The second I was back in my familiar turf, I grabbed the phone and dialed Art Young's private number. He picked up on the first ring.

"Eleanor, what a pleasure."

I let it rip. "Did you say something to Lacy White about me?"

Art paused, and then said, "I'm fine, thank you for asking. And you?"

I took a deep breath before I trusted myself to speak again. I knew Art indulged me in my temper, but I had no reason to believe that he would keep letting my abruptness with him pass indefinitely. "Sorry, I'm a little flustered at the moment. I hope you are well. I just had a conversation with Lacy, and she was a completely different woman. She asked me to call you and tell you that she is cooperating."

I couldn't believe it, but he actually sounded shocked as he said, "She called me by name?"

I thought back to our conversation. "No, not exactly. She kept referring to you as my friend, so I just figured that it had to be you."

"And we are friends, correct?"

"That's true," I said. "I just don't want anyone threatening anyone else on my behalf. Do you understand?"

His voice was so soft I almost missed the next thing he said. "Eleanor, we both need to be careful about what we say next."

I was jumping to conclusions and blowing things out of proportion like an idiot, and it had to stop right now before I damaged a friendship I really did enjoy having.

In a much more contrite voice, I said, "You're absolutely right, Art. I sincerely apologize."

His tone much smoother now, Art said, "It's gladly accepted. Think nothing else of it." After a moment's pause, he added in a softer voice, "However, you might not be entirely wrong. There's a chance that my instructions may have been misinterpreted. I asked an associate to pass a message along to Ms. White that it would be nice if she were helpful to you. I meant no inferences to be taken by it, and I implied no ramifications if she refused her assistance."

"I understand how communications can get muddled sometimes," I said, not realizing that I was beginning to model my speech after his. "I just wanted to clear this up before it had a chance of escalating."

"It's good that you called, then," he said. "Now, if there's nothing else that's immediate, I must go."

"Of course. Thank you again for your help. I truly do appreciate it. Are we good?"

"We're excellent. Goodbye, Eleanor."

After I hung up, I started to wonder if I'd done

the right thing calling Art on how he'd treated
Lacy. She wasn't a favorite of mine, but she didn't
merit threats, either. Then again, I was certain that
if I came anywhere close to having that same kind
of conversation with Art Young again, the out-
come would not be to my satisfaction.

Perhaps I should have told him about the telephone calls Maddy and I had received early this
morning, but I knew in an instant that I'd made
the right decision to keep it to myself. Putting my
friend with shady contacts in charge of what
amounted to a police investigation was so funny
that I couldn't keep myself from laughing out loud.

Maddy chose that moment to come into the
kitchen with her order. "What's so funny? Tell me
and we'll both laugh about it," she said as she
looked around the otherwise empty kitchen.

"I just had a thought," I said.

"Well, if you get another one, call me. I'd hate
to miss it, since they come along so infrequently."

Maddy accepted my whimsy like no one else in
the world did. I pointed to the pad in her hand
and asked, "Is that order for me to make, or would
you like to take a swing at it yourself?"

She shoved the pad toward me so fast it might
have been radioactive. "No thank you. What did
he have to say?"

"What are you talking about?"

Maddy grinned at me. "Come on, Sis, I know
you called Art Young the second you walked in
here. Tell me I'm wrong."

"You're wrong," I said, fighting to keep a straight
face.

"And you're nothing but a big fat liar," she said with a grin.

I made it a point not to play poker with my sister, with good reason. "Okay, you got me. He didn't mean any threats were to be conveyed to anyone, but he may have been misunderstood by an associate."

"Don't you just hate when that happens?" she said.

"Okay, I don't want to hear any guff from you. Let me make this order, and you can go back up front."

"Yes, ma'am. I can tell you in complete honesty that I wouldn't have it any other way."

As I made the woman's small pizza, I wondered about Jack, and what angles he was playing in all of this. Could he be a pawn of one of the women, or was it possible he was manipulating them both? I would love to talk to him, but not without having reinforcements behind me, and I didn't mean my sister. I'd take Art Young with me if I could, but I wasn't in any position to ask him for favors at the moment. Our illustrious chief of police would be good to have watching my back, but I couldn't ask him, either. That left Bob Lemon and possibly David Quinton, but it wouldn't be fair to put either of those two in that position.

For now, questioning Jack would just have to wait.

"We need one medium Chicago-style deep dish pizza," Maddy said an hour later when she walked into the kitchen.

"Do we? I could use a fairy godmother myself, and trust me, if I ever find one, I'm not asking her to make that pizza. Don't you remember the last time I tried to make one in my conveyor oven?"

"It wasn't pretty," Maddy agreed, "but I've got a guy out there who's homesick for the Windy City, and he wants you to try hard enough to give you this, whether you succeed or not." She held a crisp new fifty-dollar bill up in the air. "You've just got to try again, Eleanor."

"Fine, I'll do what I can."

"Excellent. I'll go give him the good news," Maddy said as she left the kitchen.

I got out my recipe book, an old binder I'd had since high school, and flipped to a recipe I'd tried before. Making an authentic Chicago-style pizza was out of the question with my conveyor oven; at least, if there was a way to produce one, I hadn't found it yet. Instead, I had something that was as close to it as I'd been able to come up with so far. I added yeast to warm water, and as that was proofing, I mixed flour, sugar, and salt in a bowl. After adding the yeast to the mix, I used my hands to blend it together, adding the necessary oil along the way. When it still wasn't developing into the shape I wanted, I added a little more water in order to form it into a rough ball.

That was where I'd made my first mistake in the past. I'd done some research, and it appeared that I'd been kneading the dough too long. One site on the Internet I'd found claimed that two minutes was all the dough needed in order to form the biscuit-like crust, so I resisted the urge to go past that and stopped when the timer went off. I would have liked three or four hours to let it rise, but I didn't have that much time, so an hour was going to have to do.

While that was set aside and I started planning out my toppings, Maddy came back. "Any idea how long this is going to take?"

"Tell him it's going to be awhile. I'm making the dough from scratch. If he wants to come back in ninety minutes, it should be ready by then."

Maddy smiled. "That's perfect. He's got a meeting, but he'll be back in two hours, if you need that much time."

I looked at my watch. "Tell him that would be perfect."

"Will do. In the meantime, I've got more orders for you."

"No more deep dish pizzas, though," I said.

"Don't worry, we both know there's not a lot of demand for that in our part of the South. I've got two regular crusts, and one thin crust."

"Those I can do in my sleep," I said.

I tried my best to ignore the deep dish dough, but I still glanced at it from time to time. I'd added a little more yeast than I should have, to speed up the process, but obviously I hadn't added enough. Ninety minutes later, the dough had just barely risen above where it had been before. I lightly floured the counter where I hand-kneaded dough, and plopped the whole thing down. I used my new European-style rolling pin until I had a crust that would be oversized for a ten-inch deep dish pan. Forming it on the bottom and up the sides, I trimmed the edges at the top and started applying the filling. I sprinkled mozzarella onto the dough, added some sausage and mushrooms, and then ladled on some sauce. I repeated that one more time, and then finally distributed a healthy layer of grated parmesan cheese over the top. I held my breath as I slid it onto the conveyor. I'd tried to keep it light, but it was still twice the weight of a regular pizza.

As it came out of the other side of the conveyor, I looked at it with some alarm. It was clearly nowhere near ready.

I had two options. I could give my customer a refund and count this as a learning experience, or I could try running it through the oven again. Having nothing to lose, I decided to do just that.

When it came out the second time, the top was a little too done for my taste, but at least the exposed edges of the crust were golden brown. It was by no means the prettiest pizza I'd ever made, but he wasn't paying me for appearance. At least I hoped that wasn't part of the deal.

Wearing hot pads on each hand, I lifted the pizza from the conveyor and decided to deliver it myself. Maddy's eyebrows shot up when I walked out, but she pointed me to the table where a man in a business suit was waiting eagerly for what I had to offer.

As I stood by his table, I said, "I'm making no promises on this. If it's not to your liking, I'd be happy to give you a full refund, but if I do, know that I'll never try to make one of these again."

I put it down in front of him, and he just stared at it.

"Is something wrong?" I asked. I must have been right. The entire pizza had probably been over-cooked.

"A knife would be nice," he said with a pleasant smile, "and I wouldn't say no to a fork, either."

"Sorry," I said with a nervous laugh. After I retrieved tableware for him, he made a grand show of cutting into the pizza and serving himself a slice. I moved away from his table, but stayed close enough in case he didn't like it. He took a single bite, and then put his fork down.

"I'm sorry," I said as I approached him, ready to return his fifty-dollar bill. "I know it's not what you were expecting."

"Are you kidding? I never dreamed you'd come this close," he said with a broad smile. "Nice job."

I couldn't believe the wave of relief I experienced. "I'm so glad you like it."

Janice Blake touched my arm as I headed back to the kitchen. "What exactly was that you just served that man?"

"It was a special order," I said. I wasn't about to encourage anyone else to order a deep dish. It was too unnerving to have them on my menu. "I hope you didn't want one. They take a great deal of time to prepare."

"Heavens, no," she said. "I was just wondering what it was doing in a pizza parlor. I can't imagine eating a slice of that."

"Don't worry. Your thin crust should be out in a minute."

Funny, but I thought it had looked delicious once he'd cut into it. If it hadn't been so much work, I might have made more, but there was no way it was going on my menu.

Twenty minutes later, Maddy came back with another order. She lingered as I prepared a fourteen-inch pepperoni and sausage, and as I slid it onto the conveyor, she said, "You just made that man's day."

"I can't believe he liked it."

"Have a little faith in yourself. I thought it looked great."

"I got lucky," I said.

My sister smiled at me. "Sometimes it's better to be lucky than it is to be good."

"If you say so. How are we doing out there?"

Maddy shrugged. "This should be it, and then we'll be ready for our own lunch break. Any chance you can make one of those monsters for us?"

"Not without at least two hours' notice," I said.

"Okay, I'm not willing to wait that long for anything but turkey, and that's just at Thanksgiving. Why don't you slide an extra pizza through for us so we can eat before we go out detecting."

As I reached for a ball of dough, I said, "Okay, but I wasn't aware that we were doing any investigating this afternoon."

"Come on, Eleanor. We've stirred some folks up, but we're not that much closer to finding out who killed Judson than we were when we started."

"I agree. I'm just not sure where to look."

Maddy thought about it, and then said, "We need to go back to Chastain. I don't know about you, but I'd like to find out more about this Jack fellow. He seems to be showing up everywhere, doesn't he?"

"I admit that I'm curious myself," I said, "but I thought we might be able to use some reinforcements."

"I don't think that's going to be necessary," Maddy said.

Had my sister completely lost her mind? "Why do you say that? This could be one scary dude."

"Think about it, Eleanor. Who do you think warned Lacy that she should speak with us? I'm willing to bet that the message came from Jack himself. We should be fine, as long as he knows that you're Art's friend."

"I'm not sure I should say that," I said. "I said some things to Art that I shouldn't have, and I don't think I'm his favorite person in the world at the moment."

Maddy shrugged. "Sometimes friends disagree, but the question is—is there any way that Jack will know that?"

I thought about it, and realized that my sister was right. "No, he won't have a clue. Besides, Art wasn't that upset with me. He still wants to protect me from harm."

"Then we'll go in with the attitude that Jack will be afraid to touch us."

I remembered how nervous Lacy had been, and wondered if this man Jack would have the same re-action. He might not look intimidated, but he'd known that Art Young, or any of his friends, weren't to be trifled with. "Okay, you've convinced me. It sounds like we've got a plan."

* * *

Before we left for Chastain, I put up another sign, making sure that the tape was securely attached to the window frame this time. If anyone wanted a pizza, they were just going to have to wait until we got back.

Maddy and I were walking out the door when Greg showed up.

"What are you doing here at this time of day?" I asked him. "We were just headed out."

"I figured as much," Greg said as he looked at the sign. "Where are you off to this time?"

Maddy answered, "We're going to Chastain to talk to another possible suspect."

He nodded. "No surprise there. Do either one of you mind if I tag along?"

"Greg, you shouldn't get involved in this," I said. He had a bright future ahead of him, and I didn't want to be responsible for any black marks on his record because of something I did.

"And yet oddly enough, I am," he answered. "Besides, I might do you both some good."

"How's that? You don't honestly think that we need a man to protect us, do you?" Maddy's voice had a serious edge to it. I knew Greg was on tenuous ground, and I hoped he realized it as well.

His reaction surprised me as he laughed heartily. "Are you kidding me? If something happens, I'm counting on you two to keep me out of trouble."

"Then why should we bring you with us?" Maddy asked, clearly starting to soften her stance.

"Because," Greg said with a grin, "I happen to

know quite a few folks in Chastain. They might ignore you, but I have a feeling I can get them to talk. What do you say? Is it worth it taking me with you now?"

"Why not?" Maddy asked, and then turned to me. "That is, if it's okay with you."

"It couldn't hurt," I said.

As we piled into Maddy's car, I asked Greg, "How do you happen to know so many people in Chastain?"

"I've got family there," he said as we drove. "My third cousin knows everybody in town, and what's more important, they all know him."

"Will he be around this afternoon?" I asked.

"Trust me, he's always nearby. I think the farthest he's ever been away from home is Asheville."

"Not exactly a world traveler, is he?" Maddy asked.

"He claims he's not missing much, and I'm not entirely certain that he's wrong," Greg said from the back seat. "So, do you two mind if I ask you who exactly we are investigating?"

We brought him up to speed on Lacy, Gina, and Jack, and our theories about their relationships.

He whistled softly under his breath. "The guy must think he's bulletproof. I've never had the nerve to string two women along at the same time in my life."

"Trust me, it's not from a lack of courage that you haven't done it," I said. "It's more like common courtesy."

"Call it what you will," he said. "Do you have a last name for this guy?"

"Sorry, we don't," I said. "Is that going to be a problem?"

"It shouldn't be. Chastain isn't all that big. Don't worry, we'll find him."

As we neared Chastain, Maddy asked Greg, "Where should I go?"

"There's an auto shop just outside of town limits. Pull in there."

Maddy did as she was directed, and as she pulled to a stop, Greg said, "It might be better if you both wait here."

"Guess again, sport," Maddy said as she opened her door and got out.

"Eleanor," Greg said with a hint of pleading in his voice.

I looked at Greg and shrugged. "You can't tell me that you're surprised she won't listen to you."

"No, but I was hoping. To be honest with you, I'm not sure Newt will talk in front of you or Maddy."

I stopped. "His parents actually named him *Newt?*"

"It's short for Newton, which he hates even more. He's a little rough around the edges, but he's a good guy. Is there any chance Maddy will let me handle this? If she goes barreling in there, he won't say a word. I can promise you that."

Maddy took that moment to rap on the glass from outside the car. "Are you ladies coming, or not?"

"I'll talk to her," I said.

Once Greg and I were outside, I said, "Maddy, this is Greg's cousin. He's going to ask the questions, okay?"

"Okay," she said.

"Maddy, I mean it."

"I agreed, didn't I? Let's go. We don't exactly have loads of time here."

"Then you should let me handle it myself," Greg said.

"Sorry, but you're still a junior grade detective, and Eleanor and I have to be present during all interrogations."

Greg looked at me for confirmation that my sister would rein it in, but I had my own doubts. I couldn't show him that, though, so I did my best to nod my encouragement.

"Don't look so worried," Maddy said. "I'll be good."

Greg realized that there was nothing he could do about it, so he took a deep breath, and then walked into an open garage door of the shop with us tagging along behind him.

"Newt? You around?"

A sandy-haired young man with grease on one cheek and wearing a faded baseball cap backward on his head rolled out from under a Jaguar. "Wally, you old dog. What are you doing here?"

I looked at Maddy and mouthed, "Wally?"

She shook her head. I was going to have to ask Greg about that later. As nicknames went, it was a little odd, to say the least.

"I need some scoop," Greg said.

Newt nodded, and then looked at my sister and me. Greg understood immediately. "These are my friends, Eleanor and Maddy," he said.

I was touched that he'd called us friends, and not his boss and coworker. I sincerely hoped he thought of us that way, because it was certainly the way we thought of him.

"Ladies," Newt said as he literally tipped his hat to us.

"Nice to meet you," I said.

To her credit, Maddy didn't say a word; she just smiled and nodded.

"What's going on, Wally?" Newt asked as he looked at Greg again. I would never be able to get used to that nickname, and it was all I could do not to ask him about it at that instant.

Greg cracked his knuckles and said, "There's a guy named Jack somewhere around town. He's been going out with Gina Sizemore, and he's friends with Lacy White. Any chance you know him?"

Newt nodded. "That's Jack Hanks. He's rotten, if you ask me. Lacy's nuts for hanging out with him, and Gina's even crazier for ever dating the dude. The guy's no good."

"What's wrong with him, exactly?" Greg asked.

Newt scratched his chin, adding a spot of grease to the marks already there. "There's no proof, but folks around here know just the same that he's the one who held up Jackson's grocery store three months ago. He gambles, and he loses more than he can afford, so the money has to come from somewhere."

"Does he have a job?"

"Not that anyone can see." Newt laughed a little as he added, "He tried to strong-arm me into hiring him once."

"How'd you handle him?" Greg asked.

Newt grinned. "I told him that it might be a lit-

tle too dangerous working around here for him."
With that, he hit a lever, and a Honda Civic that
had been up on a lift dropped instantly. It would
have crushed anyone under it. "Accidents happen.
Anyway, he got the hint right away."

Greg smiled at that. "I bet he did. Any idea
where I can find him right now?"

Newt nodded. "Sure, he's at the pool hall. You
want some company? I wouldn't mind taking a
break, and if you could use another hand, I'm
your man."

Greg shook his head. "No, I've got it, but thanks
for offering."

"Are you sure?" His voice got a little more serious as he advised, "I wouldn't mess with him
alone, Wally."

"There's not going to be any trouble. I'm just
going to ask him some questions," Greg said.

"He's not going to tell you a thing," Newt said
matter-of-factly. "I can promise you that. What do
you want to know? Maybe I can find out for you
from here so you don't go to any more trouble
than you have to."

Greg shrugged and turned to us. "Ladies? It's
your decision."

I had taken a liking to Greg's cousin, and if he
was willing to help us, it was foolish not to take him
up on his offer. I said, "We need to find out if he's
dating both Lacy and Gina, and if they know about
each other."

Maddy added, "And see if there are any rumors
about any of the three of them around town."

"Rumors are one thing we've got plenty of," he
said. "It's the national pastime around here."

"I'd still appreciate it if you'd ask," she said.

Newt nodded. "Stay right here. I'll be right back."

After he disappeared into his office, I turned to Greg and said, "It was a good idea bringing you. Thanks, Wally."

He shook his head. "How did I know I'd catch grief about that?"

"Hey, we just want to know if we should start calling you that ourselves," Maddy said.

"My name's Greg, and you both know it." He looked from Maddy to me, and then said, "I know you two aren't going to let this go, so I'll tell you. But trust me when I say if either one of you calls me Wally again, I'm walking out and never stepping another foot inside the Slice. I couldn't be more serious. Are we clear?"

Maddy and I both nodded solemnly. We knew this was no idle threat. It would be nearly impossible replacing Greg, and we couldn't run the Slice without him. Well, that wasn't strictly true. We could most likely manage it somehow, but it wouldn't be nearly as much fun.

"You have our word," I said.

Greg nodded, and then began to explain. "When I was a kid, I used to screw up more than my fair share of the time. Newt's dad thought that was hilarious, and for some reason, he decided that Wally fit me better than Greg. Since then, I've been Wally to this whole branch of the family, whether I like it or not. I can swallow it from them, but not from the two of you."

"Got it," I said. It would be even easier not calling him Wally knowing that he didn't like it.

Newt came back out to join us a few minutes later, but the jovial air he'd had about him before was now gone.

"What is it?" Greg asked.

"I'm not sure I should tell you," Newt replied.

Maddy chose that moment to break her promise to Greg. "Sorry, but it doesn't work that way. We're staying right here until we hear what you found out, or we're going to track Jack down ourselves and ask him our questions face to face. Newt, we have a job to do, and we're not going to let anything keep us from doing it. You can either help us, or get out of the way. It's your choice."

Chapter 11

Newt ignored Maddy and looked at Greg as he asked, "Is your friend always this spunky?"

"Believe it or not, she's holding back at the moment," Greg answered with a smile. "You can tell us, Newt."

He chewed that over in his mind, and then the mechanic finally nodded. "I'm pretty sure that wasn't an idle threat she just made, so I'll tell you what I found out. There's just one thing. I'd appreciate it if you didn't tell anyone how you heard."

"It's a deal," Greg said.

He turned to us. "Does that go for you two?" It was no surprise that he focused the question mostly toward my sister.

"We promise," Maddy and I said in almost perfect unison.

After a moment's consideration, Newt nodded. "Jack's been going around town half-drunk the past two or three days claiming that his favorite girl is coming into a load of cash, and soon. He's promising to pay off his debts, and most folks think he's either crazy or lying."

"Did he say which girl he was talking about?" I asked him.

"No, but he didn't have to. It has to be Gina. Everyone knows Lacy barely has two dimes to rub together, with no prospects for any more coming in."

"I don't know about that," Maddy said. "She dresses really well."

"That's the discount Carole's gives her for running the place. I doubt she could afford anything but blue jeans and T-shirts without that."

"Was it two days, or three?" I asked, suddenly doing a little math.

Newt scratched his chin again as he thought about it. "I can't say. Honest to goodness, I've had my head buried in cars for the past week, so I haven't gotten out much. Does it matter?"

I explained to everyone there, "If it's three days, then it happened before the murder. That could mean that Lacy found out about Judson's potential inheritance, and she planned to get some money out of him. If it was two days, it might be Gina, since she'd be the last living relative of Nathan's left."

Newt whistled. "So old Jack could be hedging his bets both ways. That doesn't exactly surprise me."

"Me, either," Maddy said. "Were you able to find out anything else?"

He shook his head. "I had to be careful who I asked. I don't have any desire to have him show interest in me, do you know what I mean? There's a lot of gasoline around here, and it would be awfully easy to start a fire."

"Do you think he'd actually do that?" Greg asked. "I didn't mean to get you in any kind of jam."

"Don't worry about it, Wally. I can handle Jack Hanks."

"We appreciate it," Maddy said.

I could do one better than that. "If you're ever in Timber Ridge and feel like a pizza, come by A Slice of Delight. I'll make you any pizza on the menu, on the house."

Newt grinned at me. "I love pizza. I might just take you up on that."

"We hope you do," I said.

Greg and his cousin shook hands, and then the three of us headed back to Maddy's car.

"It appears that both these women are keeping some questionable company," my sister said.

"What if one of them is using the other two?" I asked. "If Lacy or Gina is pulling everyone else's strings, it could mean that Jack's just a pawn in all of this."

"But not an innocent one," Greg said. "I've never seen Newt act that way before. I believe he's more than a little worried about Jack."

"I hope we didn't cause him trouble," I said.

"We can't worry about that. Newt's a big boy, and he can take care of himself," Greg said. He looked at his watch as we all got back into Maddy's car. "Is there anyone else you need to speak with, or should we just head back to the Slice for the evening shift?" Before either one of us could say anything in reply, he added, "And don't tell me you want to see Jack Hanks right now, not after what Newt just told us. If you want to tackle him, you're going to need more reinforcements than me. Understood?"

I nodded. We'd uncovered what we'd wanted to find out. "I think that we should go back to the Slice."

For once, Maddy didn't disagree with me.

Josh was waiting for us at the front door when we got back to the Slice. Since Maddy and I were the only ones with keys to the place, he and Greg had to come or go with our knowledge.

"I'm sorry we're late," I said as I unlocked the door.

He grinned at me. "Are you kidding? I just got here myself."

"So much for me paying your wages when I was gone," I said with a smile as we all filed in and grabbed our aprons.

Josh grinned at me as he said, "You might reconsider when you find out what I just learned."

"Josh, you know how your dad feels about you helping me investigate." Chief Hurley had made it very clear to both of us that, while it was barely acceptable for Josh to work at the pizzeria, it was out of the question for me to involve him in any of my investigations, and so far, I'd pretty much been able to keep up my end of the bargain.

"I know, but I didn't go looking for this. I just

happened to be in the right place at the right time." He pretended to be bored with the conversation as he added, "But that's okay. If you don't want to know, I can just keep it to myself."

"We both know better than that," I said with a grin. "Go on and tell us. I know it's killing you. What did you find out?"

"Judson Sizemore had a girlfriend," he said proudly.

Greg slapped him on the back. "I hate to burst your bubble, but we already know that. As a matter of fact, he was engaged to Lacy White, but he broke it off just before he was murdered, no matter what she says to the contrary."

"Who's Lacy White?" Josh asked.

"Boy, you really are out of the loop."

Josh said, "I don't know what you're talking about, but I just saw a woman named Nancy Thorpe confront Nathan out in front of the hardware store. She claims that she's carrying Judson's child from a relationship they had two months ago."

"You've got to be kidding," I said. "When did all of this happen?"

"Didn't you just hear him?" Maddy asked. "It sounds like it was right around two months ago."

"Stop being cute, Maddy. I'm talking about the confrontation this woman had with Nathan," I said.

"It wasn't more than half an hour ago," Josh explained. "I was in there picking something up for my mom when this woman approached Nathan and some girl."

"That would be Gina," Maddy said. "How did she take the news when she heard this Thorpe woman's claim?"

"She called the woman a lying witch," Josh said with a grin. "She caused quite a scene."

"What's really important is how Nathan reacted," I said.

Josh explained, "It's funny, but he seemed to take her statement at face value. Nathan even invited her to come stay with him, and she accepted so fast it wouldn't have surprised me if she had her bags packed in the car."

"I would have loved to have seen Gina's face when all of this happened," Maddy said.

"How about Lacy's expression?" I asked. "Do you think she knew that Judson was playing around on her? She doesn't seem like the type to just take something like that like a good sport."

"It appears that it doesn't seem to matter what anyone thinks about it except Nathan," Greg said.

"Hang on a second. If it's true that this woman is carrying Judson's baby, it brings a whole new set of motives into play for his murder," I said. "Lacy could have killed Judson when she found out about the baby."

"Or Nancy could have done it if Judson refused to have anything to do with her or their baby."

"Jack could have done it," Greg said.

"Why is that?" I asked.

"A new heir would have messed with his plans. If Judson turned out to have an heir of his own coming, Lacy would be out of luck, and Gina's stake could be cut yet again. Who's to say that Nathan wouldn't skip Judson and Gina altogether and leave everything to the next generation?"

"That could still happen," I pointed out.

"Yes, but this way, Jack's already lost one claim through Lacy. If Gina's inheritance was going to be cut off, that would leave him with nothing."

"So we have four suspects," Josh said, getting into it.

"Actually, I think we have five," I said.

"Who did we miss?" Greg asked.

"Nathan Sizemore himself," I answered.

Greg looked at me as though I'd lost my mind. "Nathan? Why would he kill his own nephew?"

"I don't know. Maybe he found out something that he couldn't live with. Or they could have had a fight in the pizzeria. What if Judson hit him up for more money, and when Nathan said no, he started a fight? There could be a dozen reasons. All I'm saying is that he belongs on our list. He's involved in this murder just about every way you look at it."

"Fine, we'll include him, too," Josh said.

"We, not you," I said firmly.

I could see his face begin to cloud up, much as his father's had when we'd all been younger, and I knew to head it off while I still could. "Thanks, Josh, but that's as far as you're going to go with this. You can speculate with us, but I don't want you to do a thing to investigate the murder, or anyone associated with it. Do we understand each other? I know your job here isn't much, but if your parents ever suspect that you're helping me do something behind their backs, neither one of them will let you anywhere near the Slice ever again."

"Yeah, you're right," he said softly. "But that doesn't mean I can't brainstorm with you all, does it?"

"The more I think about it, I don't even know if that's a good idea," I said.

Maddy stepped up. "Give the guy something, Sis. At least throw him a bone."

"Fine, but the fact that he's involved at all doesn't leave this room, and Josh, you can't join in if anyone else is around. Agreed?"

"That's fine with me," he said. "Now let's catch ourselves a killer."

"Not so fast, hotshot," Maddy said. "We have customers to wait on first."

I looked outside and saw some folks approach the pizzeria. "Let's get to work, everyone. There will be time for investigating later."

A little while later, Maddy came back to the kitchen to pick up an order and as she did, she asked me, "Did you know David Quinton was coming by this evening?"

"David's here? Send him back."

She laughed at me. "My, don't you have a healthy ego. What makes you think he's here for you, and not for our pizza?"

It was true. I'd automatically assumed he'd be there for me, but that line of reasoning had gotten me into trouble before. Still, I found myself hoping, just a little, that I was the reason for his visit.

"Couldn't it be a little of both? Are you telling me he didn't even ask about me?"

"Of course he did," she said, having entirely too much fun with the fact that David was back in town. "He asked me if he could come back here and say hello to you, but I told him that I'd have to check with you first."

I rolled my eyes at her as I said, "Sometimes you're impossible. You know that, don't you?"

"Hey, if I can keep it to *sometimes*, then I'm ahead of the game, wouldn't you agree?"

"I suppose so," I said as I brushed past her.

"David," I said when I found him standing outside the kitchen door. "Come on back, if you'd like."

"That would be great," he said, "but only if I'm not going to be getting in the way. I don't like people watching me work, so if you'd rather I stayed out here, it's fine. We could always chat later."

Maddy slipped between us carrying the pizza I'd just finished. "Just agree, David. That's the only way she's going to get any work done, and we have hungry customers out here clamoring for food."

I looked around and saw two couples who hadn't been served yet, and they were in deep conversation, apparently not aware that they were wasting away.

"Oh, yes," I said with a gesture, "the hungry hordes."

"Then I'd better hang out with you while you cook for them," David said with a smile. Had he always had those dimples? I could swear that I'd never seen them, but dimples don't just mysteriously appear one day. Maybe it was because I'd rarely seen him smile so openly before. Now he appeared to be grinning most of the time.

"Take a seat," I said pointing to a stool by the prep table in the kitchen. It was probably a health code violation, but I knew that the inspector was out of town on his honeymoon, so I decided to push the boundaries a little.

"How's the case coming?" he asked as I kneaded dough into a pan. I'd enjoyed the challenge of trying to make a deep dish pizza earlier, but there was something really comforting about going back to my old and familiar style of pizza-making.

"What case is that?" I asked.

"Come on," he said with a laugh. "I know you and Maddy aren't about to let a murder happen in your own backyard without digging into it. Do you have any leads so far?"

"A few," I admitted cautiously. In the past, David had a real problem with our amateur investigations, and he hadn't been shy about sharing his concerns with me. We were getting along so well right now that I didn't feel like backsliding into our old ways again.

"I know better than that," he said. "I'm guessing our loyal chief of police has been putting pressure on you two as suspects, given the fact that Judson Sizemore was opening a pizzeria within sight of this place. I wouldn't blame either one of you if you decided to start digging into the case yourselves."

"Have you been following the case?"

"Who hasn't? From the talk I've heard around town, it appears that the majority of folks in Timber Ridge think you are both innocent."

"Just the majority? I was hoping it would be unanimous."

He smiled as he said, "You're kidding, right? I've actually heard a few folks say that it was just a matter of time before one of you did something like this. Don't worry, I defended your honor."

"As if it would do any good," I said. I kneaded the dough a little harder than I needed to, and it tore in the bottom of the pan. Wetting my fingertips, I worked it back to form a new seam, and then spread sauce over the dough to hide it.

"Hey, the people who care about you know that you could never be a murderer," he said softly.

"I know, but I just can't stand people who won't give us the benefit of the doubt. We've both lived here our entire lives, if you don't count Maddy's brief detours into matrimony. You'd think they'd know us better than that."

"If I've learned one thing since I left town, it's that you can't make people feel the way you want them to, no matter how much you wish it. So tell me, who are your prime suspects?"

"Do you really want to know, or are you just being polite?"

"Trust me a little, Eleanor. I'm honestly interested," he said.

As I finished spreading the cheese on the pizza I'd been working on and slid it onto the conveyor belt heading for the oven's heart, I explained. "We have several so far. At the top of our list is Gina Sizemore. She's Judson's sister."

"Why would she kill him? He's family."

I nodded. "That's precisely the reason why. We believe that she might not want to share Nathan

Sizemore's wealth if something happens to him." I studied his reaction to the news, and David hadn't even flinched. "You knew he was loaded, didn't you?"

David grinned as he nodded. "I didn't know for a fact, but, in all honesty, I suspected as much."

"How did you know? No one else in town had any idea."

"Believe me, I came across the information by accident. I was researching the title to some land I was thinking about buying before I left town," David said. "The funny thing is that Nathan's company kept showing up on the deeds I was interested in."

"That was supposed to be a really closely guarded secret. How did you know that the company belonged to him?"

David shrugged. "You're not the only one in Timber Ridge with connections. Anyway, I suspected Nathan was wealthy, at least as far as land was concerned. Funny, you could never tell by the way he lives."

I grinned. "A few days ago, he offered to buy my house, and all of its furnishings with a check," I said, though I wasn't sure why I felt the need to share it.

"How many pieces did you tear it into?"

"How can you be so sure that I did? His offer was for double the fair market value," I added.

"I'm not buying it. Eleanor, you wouldn't sell that place if he offered you your own state. That house means too much to you, and it should. You and your husband worked hard to make it happen. I can't imagine you ever leaving it."

"No, I can't either," I said, but then added with a grin, "though holding that check in my hand was a close call."

"It wasn't that close. I'm sure of it. So, who else has made your list?"

"Let's see, there's Lacy White, Judson's former and—if she is to be believed—future fiancée. And we've got a man named Jack Hanks who appears to be working behind the scenes on both Lacy and Gina. Then there's Nancy Thorpe. She's new on the investigation, and she claims to be carrying Judson's baby. From the sound of it, Nathan believes her."

"Is that it?"

"Well, we've been considering the idea that Judson and Nathan might have had a fight over something the night in question. That would mean that Nathan killed him, but I can't see that happening."

"Anyone else make your list?"

"No, that's really about it. Why?"

David shrugged. "Don't mind me. It's your investigation."

"Come on, talk to me." I knew he had an idea, and I wasn't about to disregard it unless I heard it first and thought he was off-base.

"I was just wondering if there were any more relatives who might be in line to inherit. That would put Gina in danger before anything happens to Nathan."

I remembered something I'd heard recently. "You might be right. Nathan told me he's got a cousin in town, but he's not even sure who it is. Apparently it's some kind of family secret."

"So you have another suspect, Cousin X."

I nodded. "I'll put him on the list. It's getting hard to go outside without tripping over a suspect, the way they're piling up," I said. "We seem to be adding to our total, not taking away from it."

"Don't worry. I'm certain you two will uncover the truth."

I made the last pizza order Maddy had given me as I asked, "What gives you so much faith in us all of a sudden?"

"Eleanor, it isn't so abrupt. After all, this isn't the first time you two have gone after a bad guy. Whoever it is, I'm betting that he doesn't stand a chance."

"Or she," I said, reminding him that at least, so far, the majority of our suspects were women.

"Oh, yes, I can well imagine a woman being angry enough to commit murder. As a group, you seem to have a greater capacity for love, and hate, than most men are capable of."

"You make that sound like a bad thing."

He shook his head. "I believe that the ability to feel is one of man's greatest achievements," he said solemnly. David must have sensed his own serious tone. "To be honest with you, I'm a little peckish watching those pizzas fly out of here. Is there any chance you could make something for me?"

"All you need to do is ask," I said.

He nodded. "I was hoping you'd say that. I've been craving one of your garbage pizzas since I left town. The only problem is, you won't make a small one, and there's no way I could eat a medium by myself."

"You have two options then," I said. "You can ask me to break my own rules and make you one, which is a possibility—but by no means certain— or you can snack on something to hold you until I get off, and then I can make a medium we can share on my front porch this evening. I had a lot of fun last night."

"So did I." David scratched his chin as if he was having a difficult time deciding what to do. After an elaborate act of consideration, he finally said, "Eleanor, if it's all the same to you, I choose option two."

"That sounds great. I'm looking forward to it."

"So am I," David said as he pushed off his stool.

"Where are you going?"

"You suggested it yourself. I've got to get something to hold me over," he said. "I really am hungry." With an added smile that brightened the room a little, David said, "Don't worry, I won't fill up. See you soon, Eleanor."

"'Bye, David." I found myself laughing as he left, wondering about the change in him that appeared to have brought out a change in me as well. I found myself humming as I worked, unaware that our plans had suddenly given me a lighter step.

Unfortunately, it didn't take all that long for my good mood to be ruined.

The kitchen door opened, and I half hoped that David was returning.

When our chief of police walked in, the disappointment on my face must have been noticeable.

"Wow, I've had warmer greetings when I was serving arrest warrants," he said.

"Sorry. I was expecting someone else."

A little of the old Kevin Hurley slipped through his hard exterior when he said softly, "He's a lucky guy."

I wasn't sure that he even realized that he'd said it aloud, and I wasn't about to ask him about it. "What can I do for you, Chief?"

"I told Josh I needed a pizza to go," he said. "Don't tell me he forgot to tell you about it."

He had, but I wasn't about to admit that to the young man's father. "I was just starting it. Pepperoni and ham, right?"

"That's what I like," he said. "How long is this going to take? I was hoping it would be ready to pick up."

"Good things come to he who waits," I said with a smile.

"Okay, but that doesn't answer my question, does it?"

"Eight minutes," I said. "You're at the head of the line."

"Mind if I wait here?" he asked.

"Be my guest," I said as I threw his pizza together in record time.

As I worked, he sighed loudly and I couldn't help noticing it.

"Troubles?" I asked

"Like you wouldn't believe," he admitted.

"If you want to talk about it, I'm right here." Our relationship had been full of contradictions since the first day we'd met in high school, but I knew that Kevin didn't have an easy life, though much of that was his own fault. He'd married

Marybeth because she'd been pregnant with Josh, and they'd never had a smooth path since.

He looked tempted by the idea, but then suddenly changed his mind. "Sorry, I can't do it, no matter how much I'd like to."

His cell phone rang, and I heard one side of a heated conversation. I could imagine his caller as I listened to Kevin's responses.

"No, not yet. Because I'm not ready to, and I don't need the help. Trust me, the state police aren't going to be able to do anything that I can't. I'm sorry you feel that way." After he hung up, he said, "Goodbye."

"It sounds like Nathan's getting impatient with you."

"You have no idea," he said, and then caught himself. "How did you know that was Nathan Sizemore?"

"It's not rocket science, trust me," I said. "Have you considered calling them in for backup?"

"I'm giving myself until November fifth," he said. "After that, they're welcome to the whole mess."

"Why the delay?"

He frowned at me as he answered, "You know as well as I do why I'm waiting. If I ask for help before the Halloween Blowout, that's all folks are going to be talking about. I can't afford that, not so close to election day."

"That's right, you're running again," I said. His signage was nearly nonexistent, as was his one opponent in the race, a man named Jerry Klein who was known around town to lie even when the truth suited him better. "Do you honestly think Jerry has a chance against you?"

"Don't ever underestimate what will sway the voters," he said. "Sure, I'd love to make an arrest before Election Day, but not asking for help from the state police is the next best thing in my book."

"Would you feel that way if Judson was a Timber Ridge native?"

He bristled at the suggestion. "Everyone gets equal treatment and protection in my jurisdiction."

"I didn't mean anything by it," I tried to say, but he started to walk out in anger.

"Have Josh call me when my pizza's ready," he said as he started for the door.

"Come on, Kevin."

He just shook his head as he left. I had to wonder if what I'd said had struck home with him. There might be two levels of justice in Timber Ridge, and he might not even be aware of it. I tried to imagine if the victim had been Shelly Steele or Amanda Lancaster, people well known and beloved in our little community. Having the victim come from out of town had to have colored his point of view a little, whether he was aware of it or not.

Three minutes later, the chief's pizza came out of the oven, and I boxed it and cut it immediately. Carrying it out front, I hoped I could catch him outside before he got too far, so I could apologize again.

I never expected to find him still in the Slice, and being openly berated by a woman I'd never seen before in my life.

Chapter 12

"You need to find his killer," the woman shouted. She was pretty in an understated kind of way, with a figure that was even curvier than mine. At the moment, all eyes were on her. I could see that my customers had lost all interest in their food in favor of the floor show she was providing.

Our illustrious chief of police looked trapped. "We're doing everything we can, ma'am."

"Well, clearly it's not enough," she said loudly.

I approached them and handed Kevin his pizza. "Here's your order, Chief."

He looked almost happy to see me as he shoved some money in my direction and said, "Thanks."

"I'm not finished with you," the woman shouted.

"Sorry. I have to run." And that's just what he did, sprinting out of the dining room at full speed.

I half expected the woman to follow but, instead, she slumped down in an empty booth and began to cry softly.

Maddy started to join me, but I waved her away.

Even though I knew that my sister wasn't crazy about the idea, she got my motion and took my place in the kitchen so I could talk to this woman. I knew Greg and Josh would pick up the slack out front without being asked, so I had some time to spare her.

"I'm sorry for your loss, Nancy," I said softly as her crying began to ease.

She looked at me, clearly startled. "How do you know my name?"

"It's not hard to figure out," I said, happy that I'd guessed correctly. "You must be under a lot of stress right now."

"You can't even imagine it. Nathan is being so nice, but that Gina is a real shrew to be around. She doesn't believe the baby is Judson's, and she's the reason he broke it off with me in the first place. She told him that I was beneath him, someone unworthy of his love. Can you imagine anyone saying something so harsh?"

I had no problem envisioning it. "It must be tough being around her."

"She's constantly taking shots at me," Nancy said. "I loved Judson, and I know in my heart that he loved me."

"But I heard he was engaged to someone else," I said softly.

She looked at me as though I'd slapped her. "Lacy White? What a fraud. Judson never loved her. Sure, she's nice to look at, but there's nothing inside. That has to count for something, right?"

"It means everything to me," I said, "but some men are hard to figure out."

Nancy bit her lip. "He would have come back to

me, especially when he found out that I was pregnant. I just know it. Someone robbed me of my chance for happiness, and this sheriff isn't doing anything to find the killer."

"He's not a sheriff; he's the chief of police," I corrected gently.

"I don't care if he's the grand high marshal," she said with a bit of irritation in her voice. "I just want him to do his job."

"Do you have any ideas who might have killed Judson?" I asked Nancy. It might be good to get her take on the murder while I had her there, and if I was preying on someone when she was vulnerable, I was doing it for a cause that she claimed to be championing, herself.

"I can't imagine anyone killing my Judson," she said, softly beginning to whimper again. "He never hurt anyone in his life."

I doubted that, but it wasn't the most opportune time to point that out. "I'm sure you must miss him."

"It's as though my heart has been ripped out," she said.

"Can I get you something to eat?" I asked.

"I couldn't even look at food. I've lost my appetite entirely."

"But you're eating for two now," I reminded her.

That brought another wave of fresh tears. Nice touch, Eleanor. Make the pregnant lady cry, though I couldn't see any signs that she was with child, at least not yet. With her frame and size, it would be months before she started to show enough for people to notice. I decided to keep that little tidbit to myself.

She started to stand, and I did as well, as I asked, "Can I have one of my waiters see you home?"

"No, I need the exercise, and the cold air might be good for me." She stopped before she left and added, "Thank you for your kindness. Besides Nathan, you've been the sweetest person I've met in Timber Ridge."

I'd been pumping her for information, but evidently she hadn't noticed. "Take care of yourself," I said.

After she was gone, Josh joined me. "I don't care what you think, but I don't like that woman."

"Because she was yelling at your dad in public?"

He dismissed that with a wave of his hand. "No, it's the way she walked in here gunning for him. I have my own problems with the man, you know that as well as anybody else does, but she never even gave him a chance to explain himself."

I was surprised to see Josh defending his father, knowing how many difficulties the two had experienced over the years, but it was refreshing to witness. Maybe Josh was finally growing up and learning to separate the man from the office.

It would be good for both of them if they could work it out, and sooner would be better than later.

Things were mostly quiet for the rest of the night, and fifteen minutes before we were due to close, I sent Greg and Josh home, much to their mutual delight.

I was in back preparing the pizza David and I were going to share when Maddy walked in.

"The front's clean," she said, and then she noticed what I was doing. "Sis, you read my mind. Put extra cheese on it, would you? I'm starving."

"Sorry, but this one is to go," I said as I finished adding the toppings. "I'm taking it home with me."

Maddy pouted for a second. "You seriously aren't going to share that with me? Come on, have a heart."

"It's for David," I said, waiting for the onslaught of whoops of joy from my sister. I had braced myself for it, and was surprised when she appeared to take it in stride, as though I'd announced that I'd just changed long-distance carriers.

"Don't you want to know what's going on?" I asked her.

"No, I think it's nice," she said.

"We're going to share it on my front porch as soon as I leave here," I said, pushing her even further.

"Yes, I got that. Have a good time."

As I slid it onto the conveyor belt, I asked, "Maddy, did I do something wrong?"

"No, not that I know of," she said.

"Then why are you acting this way?"

"What way is that?" I knew that I wasn't mistaking the cool tone in her voice.

"Sis, look at me." I took her hands in mine so she couldn't avoid me. "What's going on?"

She just shook her head, but I wasn't about to let go.

Finally, Maddy said, "I'm happy for you, Eleanor, believe me. I just don't want to see you get hurt."

That thought had never occurred to me. "Seriously? Do you believe for one second that David Quinton would ever cause me pain?"

"I don't know. Is he moving back to Timber Ridge?" she asked.

"No, not that I know of. He's extended his stay here, but that's just until he finds a replacement for the branch manager here in town."

"Then he's going to hurt you when he goes back to Raleigh. You've had more than your share of pain. Think about how it's going to feel when he leaves after you've finally started to chip the ice off your heart. I'll be here to help you get over it, you know you can always count on me, but that doesn't mean I'm looking forward to seeing you get hurt, and the more you see him, the greater chance there will be of that happening."

I didn't understand her reaction at all. I knew my sister cared about me, but sometimes the way she showed it drove me crazy. "Maddy, I thought you wanted me to see him."

She nodded, and I saw a tear creep down her cheek. "When he lived in Timber Ridge, he would have been perfect for you. But a long-distance relationship is not going to work. You're married to this pizzeria, and he's got an important job there. It's not like you two are going to see each other on a regular basis."

I released her hands and touched the tear on my sister's cheek. "Maddy, even if he leaves tonight, I don't regret spending time with him. I'm not exactly sure how he's done it, but I honestly believe that he's helping me to finally heal my heart. Something you keep saying to me is actually beginning to hit home," I said with a smile. "Joe wouldn't want me to live the way I have been since he died. He believed life was for the living, and I haven't exactly been respecting that belief, have I? I'm not saying that I'm ready to fall in love again, but I do know that I can't keep shutting the possibility of it ever happening again out of my life. If I get a little bruised and battered finding my way back, it's a price I'm willing to pay."

She hugged me, and I could swear that I actually felt the love my sister had radiate toward me. "I just want you to be happy."

"The same goes for me," I said. I was surprised to find that both of us were crying.

When we pulled away, we wiped each other's tears, and then we grinned at each other.

"Wow, that felt good," I said.

"I've been needing a good cry for weeks, but I never had a reason." She looked at the conveyor and saw my pizza come out. "I'll do that for you." As Maddy slid the pizza into a box and cut it, I turned off the oven.

"Don't do that yet," she said.

"Are you planning on making a snack, after all?"

She handed me the pizza and said, "Something better than that. Go on, Sis, I can finish closing up here."

"Are you sure?" Most of the dishes were done, so I knew there wasn't that much work left to do.

"I've got it," she said as she pushed me toward the kitchen door. "Have a good evening, and give David a hug for me."

"How about if I just tell him you said hi?" I said.

She laughed. "Do whatever you want to, as long as you just go."

I let myself out, and then locked the door behind me. It meant so much to have my sister care about me with the depth that she did. A lot of people I knew had never experienced that kind of devotion and loyalty, and I knew that no matter what happened with the rest of my life, I'd always be able to count on her.

David was waiting on the porch for me as I parked and walked up the steps. He'd set up a card table near the rockers, and the top of it was laid with paper and plastic dishware from the grocery store.

"You just couldn't wait to see me, could you?" I asked him.

"Sure, that's it," he said grinning as he took the box out of my hands. "I never got my snack, so I'm starving."

He took a slice from the box and put it on a paper plate.

"I love the table layout," I said as I grabbed a slice for myself.

"I decided to provide the plates and cutlery, not to mention glasses and refreshments." He showed me the plastic champagne glasses, and filled them each with Coke.

"I hope you approve," he said as he handed one to me.

I pretended to smell the soda as though it were fine wine, and then I took a sip. "This is an excellent year, with a light bouncy taste followed up with the slightest hint of caffeine."

"I'm glad you approve," he said as he took his first bite of pizza. "That was worth waiting for," he said as he finished eating it.

"The company, or the food?"

"Why can't it be both?" he asked. "Oh, wait. I almost forgot." He reached into a jacket pocket and pulled out a small luminary candle. "I thought we could dine by candlelight tonight."

"Then you're going to need more candles than that," I said smiling as I took another bite.

He reached into more pockets as he said, "Funny you should say that."

As he pulled out candle after candle, I started laughing. "What happened? Did you find a sale in town?"

"What can I say? I'm just a romantic at heart." After the candles were all lit and spaced out on the porch railing and the table, we settled into our rocking chairs and enjoyed the pizza and soda.

When we were finished, I was surprised to see that the box was empty. "We were hungry."

"I'm glad to see that I wasn't the only one starving. Sorry for those wolflike feeding sounds I made."

"Are you kidding? I consider them the highest compliment." It was easy sharing these moments with him, and I found myself amazed at how relaxed I felt.

"Then I shouldn't have held back."

As David collected the plates, empty plastic glasses, and spent box, I said, "I'll get those later."

"No, ma'am. You've been waiting on folks all

day. I even brought my own trash bag. How's that for being prepared?"

"It's just about perfect."

After he'd collected everything, he tied the trash bag shut and tossed it toward his car. After he folded the card table up and put it in his trunk, David asked me, "Can you spend a little time out here, or do you need to go in?"

I glanced at my watch. On a normal night, I would have been fast asleep in bed by now, but I wasn't even tired at the moment. "I'll stay out here as long as you will."

"I think it feels wonderful," David said, "but if you get chilly, I've got blankets in the trunk."

"Wow, you really did come prepared," I said with a laugh.

"I just didn't want there to be any reason for you to go in," he admitted. As we rocked in an odd kind of unison, he asked, "Can you believe that Halloween is just two days away?"

"I know. Usually Maddy and I are excited about it, but we barely remembered to put our decorations up the other day."

"Murder must have taken some of the joy out of it," David said.

"True, and before that, we found out that Judson was going to open Italia's, so we haven't been in a very festive mood lately."

"I wonder what's going to happen to the place now?" he asked idly.

"Who knows? Someone will probably lease the building and turn it into a store of one kind or another."

"Buggy whips and bow ties, maybe?" David asked, the laughter full in his voice.

"How about a clothing store for pets?"

"Don't laugh. There's one of those in Raleigh."

"You're joking."

"Not a chance. They've even got an Internet website where they sell their wares. I'll give you the link if you want to see it."

I rocked a little more, and then said, "There are a lot more opportunities in Raleigh than there are in Timber Ridge, aren't there?"

"I suppose that all depends on what you're looking for," he said so softly I barely caught it.

"What are you looking for, David?" I asked.

He took so long to answer me that I wasn't sure he'd heard my question, but finally, David said, "Once upon a time I thought I knew, but lately that seems to keep changing on me."

"Don't worry, you'll figure it out," I said, happy and yet a little disappointed that he hadn't said me.

"I suppose you're right," he said. After a few minutes, he stretched in his chair, and then stood. "I hate to break this up, but I've got a dozen interviews scheduled for tomorrow to find a new manager."

"Is there any chance you'll have time for dinner again tomorrow night?" I asked hopefully, amazed by how quickly I'd grown to look forward to our meals together.

"I'd love to, but two of the candidates can't make it until late, so I've got interviews scheduled a great deal later than I wanted."

As I stood, he added, "Tell you what I'll do. If one of them cancels on me at the last minute, I'll give you a call, if you'd like."

"I'd like that very much."

He looked at me for a few lingering seconds, kissed my cheek lightly, and then said, "Good night, Eleanor."

"Good night," I said.

The mood was special and heartfelt, a moment to remember, until he tripped over the garbage bag on the sidewalk.

Instead of being upset, he just laughed it off. "And that's why they call me Mr. Smooth."

"Clearly they haven't seen your act up close," I said.

"See ya," he said as he collected the bag and stowed it in the trunk.

"Right back at you."

After David was gone, I went inside. It felt cold in there, cooler than it should have been, but when I checked the thermostat, it was exactly where I'd left it that morning. I wasn't sure if it was a sign that I missed David, or if I was just chilly, but I cranked it up a few degrees before I went to bed and dreamed of picnics on the porch, surprising dimples, and, most important of all, a heart that was finally beginning to thaw.

The next morning, Maddy was at the pizzeria before I made it in, though I was twenty minutes early myself.

I found her in the kitchen working at the prep table.

"Good morning," I said as I grabbed my apron. "You're here early."

"I couldn't sleep, so I decided to get a jump on things."

"What happened to you and your crafts and your mystery novels? They used to fill your time."

She shrugged. "It's not what it used to be. My favorite mystery writer quit writing craft-based cozies awhile back, and I've kind of lost the desire to do anything more at the moment."

"I wonder why he stopped. Did he just get tired of writing them?"

She shook her head as she waved her knife around in the air. "Trust me, I wanted to know the exact same thing, so I wrote him an email."

"I'm sure he doesn't have anything better to do with his time than to correspond with you, Maddy."

"That shows you how much you know. Actually, he answered me right away. It appears that he was happy to keep writing them, but his publisher decided not to do any more, so he's kind of out in the cold at the moment."

"I hate when that happens," I said as I started measuring out flour, water, yeast, olive oil, and salt for my basic crust recipe. "He should write some of those food-oriented mysteries. I hear they do really well."

"He's a real wizard with crafts, but I don't know if he can cook or bake, so that might be a disadvantage for him," she said, laughing.

"Come on, it's all fiction, right?"

"You'd think so. At least I hope so. That's a lot of murder we're talking about."

I paused before I turned on the mixer. "Can you

imagine how many bodies Agatha Christie alone was responsible for?"

"I don't have a clue, but I'm willing to bet there's a website on the Internet that's got every last one of them listed."

"Somebody's got too much time on their hands." I flipped the mixer on to stir the dry ingredients while I waited on the yeast to proof.

"Ask a question, get an answer."

"Hey, I was just curious. I didn't expect a full-blown lecture," I said with a smile.

She just chuckled as she shook her head. "I figured you'd learn someday, but it hasn't happened yet."

"Give me time," I said. "I'll get there sooner or later."

I thought I heard something out front, so I flipped the mixer off. That action was followed by a sudden silence.

"Did you hear that?" I asked Maddy.

"Hear what?"

I listened more, shook my head, and then turned the mixer back on. Just as I did, the pounding started again.

As soon as I turned it off, the pounding stopped.

"Are you saying you didn't hear that, either?"

"Maybe the mixer's going bad," she said. "If there's something wrong with the motor, it might cause the whole thing to thump."

At that moment, the pounding resumed.

"Thank goodness it's not the mixer," I said as I wiped my hands on my apron.

"Don't answer it," Maddy said. "We're not opening for another few hours, so they can wait like everyone else."

"What if it's important?" I asked as I moved toward the kitchen door that led to the dining room.

"What if it's not?"

It was too late to stop me, though. I had a thing about letting telephones and door knocks go unanswered.

When I looked outside, I saw Gina Sizemore, and from the expression on her face, I was willing to bet that she didn't have good news for me.

Chapter 13

"We don't open for a few more hours," I said through the door as I approached Gina. I made no move to unlock it. I hoped she wasn't under the impression that I was going to let her inside.

"I'm not here for pizza. I figured you had a right to know what I'm doing. Trust me, you're going to want to hear this." She looked annoyed that I had shown no interest in letting her inside where it was warm. "Do we really have to keep talking through this door?"

She certainly had my attention. Against my better judgment, I unlocked the door, but Gina stayed out on the sidewalk. "I'll make this quick. I've decided to open Italia's in honor of Judson. We're going to be holding our grand opening tomorrow night."

I was shocked by the news. Was I going to lose the Slice after all? "You're doing it at the Halloween Blowout? Are you kidding me?"

She smiled brightly at me. "What better time to

announce ourselves to the community than when everyone's gathered together on the promenade."

"I thought the pizzeria was your brother's dream," I said as I took the new flyer she presented me with.

"It was. That's why I'm doing it. It's the best way I can think of to carry on in his honor. He would have wanted it that way."

I looked at her for a second before I asked, "Are you telling me that's not going to creep you out at all?"

"What are you talking about?"

I couldn't believe that she hadn't even considered the ramifications of what she was about to do. "You're going to make pizzas on the exact same spot where your brother was murdered. You'll see it every day when you go to work, have to look at it the entire time you're there, and then it will be the last thing you see when you leave."

"I can deal with it," she said, though at least some of the sunshine had faded from her expression. "I've made up my mind, so there's no use trying to change it." She started to go, and then turned and looked at me. "You and your staff are welcome to come, but I'd appreciate it if you didn't enter any of the drawings we'll be having. I want to reserve those for my new customers. We're giving away some exciting stuff. Have a great day," she said as she walked toward Paul's Pastries with her handful of announcements. I wondered how my friend was going to take the news that his former girlfriend was going to be running a business so close to his own. And, in a perfect world, I probably should have warned him that she was on her way, but in all honesty, I had problems of my own.

Maddy came up front with a puzzled expression on her face. "Your timer went off, so I turned off the mixer." She looked closer at me, and then added, "Eleanor, is something wrong? You look as though you've just seen a ghost."

"Maybe I did," I said as I handed her the flyer. "If not of a person, then of a business that's probably going to slaughter us."

Maddy was clearly upset when she read the flyer. "Of all the nerve of that woman. Are you kidding me? She can't be serious."

"I don't see it as a joke," I said.

"So she's saying she can walk back in there and not think of her brother's body on the floor every time she turns around?"

I nodded. "I asked her the same thing, and she didn't seem all that concerned about it."

"She's either lying, or she's delusional, then."

I couldn't disagree with anything my sister said, but I didn't see how saying it would help us. "Either way, we have to face this threat again."

"Don't worry, Sis, we'll handle it. Judson may have been a problem, but I'm guessing the pizzeria won't be Gina's idea of a good time. She'll probably keep it open a few months, and then shut it down and move onto something else."

The future wasn't as rosy as my sister seemed to think, and I hated to bring her mood down, but there was something she hadn't taken into account. "That wouldn't be a problem if I thought we could last two months with no business to speak of."

There was another pounding on the door, and I

glanced out and saw Karen Green standing there with a flyer in her hand.

I didn't want to let her in, but Maddy said, "You'd better go ahead and let her vent, or we're going to have to buy another front door. That woman has some serious anger built up inside."

"Can you believe this?" Karen said angrily the second I opened the door. "We can't let her get away with this, Eleanor. It's just not right."

"Karen, do me a favor and take a second to catch your breath before you pass out on me."

She nodded, and then took a few deep breaths until I could see the color start to leave her cheeks. After she'd managed to calm down a little, I said, "That's better. Now listen to me. Don't worry about this. We're going to be fine, okay?"

"You sound so confident," Karen said hesitantly.

"I am," I lied. "Everything is going to work itself out."

She let out another deep breath, and then finally said, "I'm so sorry about that. I just got so peeved when she had the audacity to hand me one of these. As if I'd ever go anywhere else for my pizza but A Slice of Delight."

"Thanks, we appreciate your support," I said. "Now, if you'll excuse me, I've got to get back to work, or no one's having pizza today."

She grinned at me. "Then you'd better get to it. I'll be back when you open, don't you worry about me."

"That's good, because I'm counting on you," I said as I locked the door again.

Maddy was in the kitchen, smiling broadly, when

I rejoined her. "Karen really gets worked up about things, doesn't she?"

"Sometimes I wish I had half her passion," I said.

As I added the yeast mixture to the blended flour and salt, Maddy said, "Speaking of passion, how was yours last night?"

"Excuse me?"

"Come on, don't hold out on me. How did things go with David?"

"We had a wonderful time," I admitted.

"Eleanor, we both know you can do better than that. I want details."

It was nice to see the smile on her face, but I wasn't about to tell her more than I wanted to. "I brought the pizza home, but then you already knew that. He brought Coke, paper plates, and plastic champagne glasses. Oh, and candles, the oddest mishmash of tapers you've ever seen in your life."

"It sounds adorable," my sister said.

"You know what? It was."

Maddy smiled. "Are you getting together again tonight?"

"I suggested it, but he can't."

"Why not?" She honestly looked more disappointed than I had been when I'd gotten the news.

"He's got some late interviews he couldn't move," I admitted. Then, just to keep Maddy guessing, I said, "He did ask me the other night to save him a dance at the Halloween Blowout."

"What did you say?" Maddy asked.

"I told him if I had time, I'd try to squeeze him

in." I couldn't keep my laughter contained any longer and let some of it slip out.

She laughed along with me. "Good for you. I'm proud of you, Sis."

"Yes, I'm just the perfect picture of good mental health, aren't I?" The timer went off again, and I pulled the beater out so the dough could proof.

Maddy said, "My part's already finished, so while we wait on your dough, why don't we do a little sleuthing?"

"What did you have in mind? I can't leave this dough, and you know it."

Maddy shook her head. "Eleanor, nothing's going to happen to it. The least we can do is walk over to Paul's to see how he reacted to Gina's news."

"Would that be detecting, or just being nosy?" I asked as I washed my hands and dried them on a towel by the sink.

"Why can't it be both? Are you game?"

I looked at the dough and realized Maddy was right. There was nothing I could do for nearly an hour. I set the timer on my watch, and then smiled at her. "Why not? Let's go."

"All right, that's the spirit," she said with obvious delight.

We locked up the pizzeria and started toward Paul's Pastries. He was inside, but instead of his usual smile, the poor man looked as glum and unhappy as I'd ever seen him.

"Maybe this isn't such a great idea after all," I said as I touched Maddy's shoulder lightly and pointed toward Paul.

She just shook her head and kept going. "It looks as though he could use a friend right now, and if one is good, just think how great two will be?"

Before I could stop her, she walked on into the bakery, and I had no choice but to follow her.

Paul looked expectantly toward the door as we walked inside, but his face fell a little when he saw that it was us.

I just hoped Maddy didn't comment on his reaction to our presence.

"You look as though Hurricane Gina just hit you," Maddy said.

Paul nodded sadly. "I thought I was over her, but evidently I was wrong. Can you believe she's going to do this?"

"What 'this' are you talking about?" I asked.

"She's going to go ahead and open Italia's," Paul said. "What did you think I meant?"

"Exactly that," I said. "Don't worry, we'll be all right."

"I'm not absolutely certain you're the only ones I'm concerned about right now," he admitted. "If I reacted this way to just seeing her again this morning, imagine how difficult it will be having to see her every day." He took a deep breath, and then added, "If it comes to that, I may have to shut the bakery down and move somewhere else."

"You can't do that," Maddy wailed.

"We need you," I said. It was disastrous news realizing that we might lose Paul forever. I'd like to think that our reaction was from the thought of losing a dear friend, and not just the loss of all those delightful treats, and the sandwich rolls for the pizzeria he provided.

Paul looked startled by our reaction. "It's nothing to be concerned about yet. I'll probably stay in town, at least for a little while," Paul said.

"But if you go, who's going to bake me my treats?" Maddy asked.

Paul looked at her to see if she was serious, and when he saw her smile, he managed a faint one of his own. "You're too much, you know that, don't you?"

Maddy put a hand on her hip. "Why does everyone keep telling me that?"

"Seriously, though, we don't want to lose you, Paul," I said. "At least that much is sure."

He lowered his head and then said, "I don't know what I'm going to do right now, and that's the truth."

"Promise me one thing," I said.

He looked up at me, saw that I was serious, so he nodded. "I will if I can. What do you want?"

"Think about it long and hard before you do anything rash, and come talk to me before you make any final decision."

Paul frowned, bit his lower lip, hesitated for a few moments, and then finally said, "You're asking a lot of me."

"I know. I wouldn't presume to do it if we weren't such good friends. I'd hate to lose you, Paul."

"And I'd hate to lose the two of you," he admitted. "I can't tell you how many times you've come by here and made my day."

"It wouldn't surprise me in the least," Maddy said with a big smile. "Would you be startled to hear that we feel the same way about you?"

At that comment, Paul nodded, and then gave us a little brighter smile than he had before. "Okay, I've had enough. I hate it when you two gang up on me."

"That's a smart move. It pays not to go against us," Maddy said.

"Let's leave the poor man alone," I said. "Paul, I shouldn't have to even say this, but you know that we're just down the promenade if you need us."

"Thanks. I might just come by later, if you're sure you don't mind."

I smiled broadly at him. "You're always welcome at the Slice. If you do come by, you can redeem one of those 'free pizza' coupons you've been saving up."

He looked confused. "I never got any coupons."

I laughed. "I never got around to making them, but you've earned them just the same. All you have to do is ask."

"Thanks, ladies. You're both good for my spirits."

We left the bakery, and I was surprised to hear someone calling our names once we were out on the promenade. I'd half expected Gina to be lurking in the shadows, but it was her unwilling roommate, Nancy Thorpe, who was hailing us.

"I'm glad I caught you," she said as she ran toward us. There was no sign that her pregnancy was slowing her down any, but then again, I didn't see her every minute of the day, either.

When she caught up with us, I asked her, "What can we do for you, Nancy?"

"You were so nice to me yesterday," she said,

"that I wanted to come by and thank you. Could I take you out to lunch?"

"We're kind of tied up here until two," I said.

"That doesn't work for me. I eat at eleven, and then again at four," she admitted as she patted her belly, which was still fairly flat.

"Perhaps another time, then," I said as her cell phone rang.

I motioned to Maddy, and we started walking away, when Nancy called out to us, "Hang on a second, this won't take long at all." Then, into the phone, she said, "Okay, I'm with them now. I'll ask them."

She held the telephone to her shoulder. "Nathan needs to see you both at two-fifteen, and he won't take no for an answer."

I thought about all the reasons we had to refuse him, especially since he was again financing our latest competitor, but as I was trying to word my response, Maddy surprised me by jumping in and saying, "Tell him we'd be delighted."

"Wonderful," she said, and then as she spoke into her phone again, she walked off, completely forgetting us.

"Have you lost your mind?" I asked my sister as I unlocked our door.

"Have you? I could see it in your eyes. You were about to say no, weren't you, Eleanor?"

As I led us inside and locked the door behind us, I said, "You'd better believe it. I have no desire to see Nathan Sizemore at the moment."

"Sis, look at the big picture. We've been wanting a chance to talk to the man again, and Nancy drops an opportunity right in our laps. We can't say no."

"Even with everything that's going on?"

"Especially because of it," she said. "This is an opportunity that we can't afford to miss."

I could see Maddy's point, but that still didn't mean I wasn't upset with everything that had gone on since Judson had first announced the opening of his pizzeria. Nathan Sizemore was behind it all, if only with his money, and I wasn't happy about seeing him again, but I knew that didn't mean that Maddy was wrong.

"Okay, we'll go," I said.

"That's the spirit. Now, the only thing left to decide is whether we're going to kill him with kindness, or confront him the second we walk through the door."

I thought about it for a few seconds. "As much as I'd love to blast him, I think we should wait and hear what he has to say," I said. "We can play it by ear from there."

"Agreed," Maddy said.

As I got the dough out of the covered bowl and started to work it on the countertop, she said, "While you're doing that, I'm going to make up a list of questions for him. There's no sense going in there unprepared."

"I agree," I said. After a moment's thought, I added, "I think we should take him a pizza, maybe one of those deep dish ones I made, just to show Gina what she's up against."

"Maybe you should take him a regular garbage one, instead," Maddy said softly.

"Are you saying you don't like my new pizza?"

She shook her head. "I'm not insane. I would never say that. All I'm saying is that it might be risky taking something you haven't thoroughly tested."

She had a point there. "Then I'll make a few before we go, and we can see how they taste," I said. "I actually have time now to let the dough rise, so we should be fine on that count."

When Maddy couldn't find any flaws with that argument, I got my old recipe book out again and leafed back to the deep dish section. Maybe I'd take one of each kind of pizza I made: a thin crust, a regular one, and a deep dish.

That, more than anything I could say, would show him that we meant business.

After the dough was ready, I made up the first batch of deep dish pizzas. "Maddy, ask anybody who comes in if they'd like to try a slice of deep dish," I said as the pizzas started piling up in back. I'd made enough dough early on to make a dozen pizzas, and so far I had eight made.

"You've officially lost your mind, Eleanor," she said as she looked at the pizzas stacked in the kitchen. The first five had been questionable in one way or another, and I'd decided not to serve them, but the last three were looking good.

"Come on, think of it as a public relations campaign for good will. We're going to need every last customer we can get when Gina starts showing off that flashy new pizza oven and a chef who can spin dough in the air."

"Okay, you might not be so crazy after all," she said.

Another deep dish came out of the oven on its second trip through when Maddy came back in.

"Do you have any more orders for me?" I asked.

"Are you kidding? Did you honestly think people were going to buy pizza when we're giving it away? Give me a hand, will you?"

I nodded as I cut the last pizza. "Come on. This will be fun."

I started carrying pizzas out front, and Maddy and I delivered slices until everyone there had sampled some. There were nods and smiles all around, and I embraced the warmth of my customers.

Karen took hers with a smile. "Wow, you really have the gift," she told me as I served her.

"It's just pizza," I said.

"Don't ever say that. What you do transcends that."

Her earnestness was a little too much for me. "How are your classes going at the college?" I asked.

"I'm learning something new every day," she said with a grin. "It's amazing how fascinating the world can be."

"Any ideas on what classes you'll be taking next semester?"

She smiled at me as she said, "Money management and investment sounds like fun."

"If you say so," I said as I moved to another table.

By the time we were out of pizza, several customers asked about ordering entire pies.

Maddy approached me back in the kitchen with a handful of orders. "You've created a monster out there. I hope you like making these things, because I've got a feeling they're going on the menu for good."

"Whatever keeps folks eating here is fine with me," I said. Not that long ago, I'd been intimidated by the thick and gooey pizzas, but now that I'd mastered them, they were actually fun to make. I looked at the list of orders and realized that I might just have enough dough left and still have a new style of pizza to take to Nathan's, but it was going to be close.

"Don't take any more deep dish orders," I told Maddy before I started working on the first one in line.

My sister frowned at me. "Do you think that's wise? You've got them wanting it, and now you're not going to deliver?"

I smiled at her. "In a way, their rarity will probably make them more desirable, don't you think? If our customers can't get them every day, they might order more when they know they're available on a limited basis."

Maddy shook her head as she heard my rationale. "I long ago gave up trying to figure out your reasoning."

I lowered my voice. "Besides, the real reason is that I don't have much dough left. Play along with me, okay?"

She nodded. "Got it. Sis, are you still intent on taking three pizzas to Nathan's house?"

"Why? Do you think it's a bad idea?"

Maddy laughed. "Believe it or not, I've come

around to your way of thinking. That's exactly the right move to make with him, bold and audacious."

I went back to cranking out deep dish pizzas again. I owed my mystery customer from yesterday a debt. This new menu item might be enough to see us through some tough times ahead, and even if it didn't, it had reignited my desire to keep the Slice open regardless of what was going on outside the pizzeria's doors. Opening A Slice of Delight had been Joe's idea, but I'd grown to love it over the years as something of my very own. It was just one more debt I owed Joe's memory in a long line of things I was thankful for.

As our lunchtime closing neared, I made my last deep dish, and then added a thin crust and a regular pizza to the conveyor. I wanted everything to be fresh, hot, and ready to roll when we left.

Unfortunately, what I wasn't counting on was another visit from our chief of police.

Chapter 14

"Kevin, I'd love to chat, but there's someplace I need to be soon," I said as he came back into my kitchen.

He looked at the oven and saw the deep dish pizza appear on its first pass through the oven. "It looks like you're still busy."

"Those are to go," I said. "I'm leaving in eight minutes."

"Then you have time to talk after all."

I could tell he wasn't about to leave until we had this conversation. "Fine. We can talk while I clean up." I threw him a dish towel and smiled. "Would you like to dry?"

"Sure," he said, surprising me.

"I was just kidding," I said.

"I wasn't."

I started washing dishes, and after I rinsed them, I handed them to our chief of police, which he dutifully dried and stacked.

"You're doing it again, aren't you?" he said with an edge to his voice.

"Sorry, did I leave some soap on that one?"

"Eleanor, you know full well what I'm talking about. You just can't keep your nose out of this case. Are you ever going to learn how dangerous that can be?"

I didn't like the sound of that. "You're not threatening me, are you?"

He snorted. "Of course not. But someone killed Judson Sizemore, and you're taking too many risks with your life to try to find out who did it."

That was an interesting twist on things. "So, you don't think I did it anymore, is that what you're saying?"

He shook his head. "Would I be standing here helping you with the dishes if I did? I've known you my entire life. I can't imagine you killing him, at least not over pizza."

"Don't kid yourself. I take it pretty seriously," I said as I handed him another plate to dry.

"Are you really trying to talk me into believing you did it?" he asked as he dried it and added it to the growing stack.

"No, I'm just saying this isn't some kind of hobby for me. It's become my life."

"I know that," he said. "But it wouldn't make you a murderer."

"What would?" I asked him.

"I can think of a few reasons. If someone threatened Maddy or Greg or even Josh, I could see you doing it."

I nodded. "You're right. They're my family." It was an odd thing to say to Josh's father, but he understood exactly what I meant.

Kevin smiled as he said, "Trust me, my kid would

walk through fire for you, and we both know it. That's one reason I'd hate to see you get hurt."

"Then why don't we compare notes about the case? I might have uncovered some things you don't know about yet," I said. It was a crazy thing to say, and I knew it the second it left my mouth, but unfortunately, I couldn't take it back.

He shook his head and dropped the dish towel on the counter. "You never know when to stop, do you?"

"I've had that problem in the past," I said.

So much for the good mood that had existed between us, however briefly. As Kevin left, I wondered what had brought him to my kitchen in the first place. Had there been something he'd wanted to tell me, or was he fishing for something else? My comment had been out of line, and I'd known it, so now I would probably never find out why he'd visited.

At least the dishes were nearly done.

As the pizzas were ready, I moved them to boxes, and then to warming sleeves. Maddy came back just as I had them stacked and ready to go.

"What did our illustrious chief of police want?" she asked.

"He came by to help me do dishes," I said.

Maddy frowned at me. "Be that way. Eleanor, if you don't want to tell me, just say so."

I told her what had happened, and she whistled softly. "Sometimes you've got the guts of a cat burglar."

"That's what it takes in this world, don't you think?"

"If you say so." She picked up the stack of pizzas

and asked, "Are you ready to go see why Nathan summoned us to his home?"

I took a deep breath, pulled off my apron, and then dropped it onto the stool. "I suppose I'm as ready as I'll ever be."

"Then let's go."

When Maddy pulled up in front of Nathan's house, it was clear that he'd decided to begin his renovation without my guidance. There was a crew of three men working on the front of the house, removing vines and prepping the entire place for painting. A carpenter was working on replacing one of the rotting porch posts, and I could already start to see the bones of the place show themselves. No matter how I felt about Nathan, it was good seeing that he was making a start at restoring his bungalow.

We made our way through the workers, and Maddy rang the bell as I held the pizzas.

Gina answered the door, but she seemed reluctant to let us inside. "What have you got there?" she asked as she pointed to the bright red sleeves.

"We thought you might be hungry," I said.

"We already had lunch," she said. In a lowered voice, she added, "This was my uncle's idea, not mine."

"I suspected as much," I said.

Maddy said loudly, "Why aren't you inviting us in, Gina?"

She shot my sister a nasty look as Nathan appeared at the door. I was shocked by the difference

I saw in him. Where he'd been vigorous and full of life earlier, it appeared as though the past few days had aged him years. His face was pale and gaunt, and there was a nervous tic to his forced smile that made me wonder what had happened to him since he'd invited Gina and Nancy into his life.

"Come in," he said.

"We brought lunch," I said brightly.

He managed a weak smile. "Thanks all the same, but I've been a bit under the weather lately. I don't have much of an appetite these days."

Maddy and I stepped inside, and I could see that the changes were taking place there as well. There were painters working in the living room stripping the woodworking, and I was happy to see that they were trying to restore the quarter sawn oak to its original splendor. At some point in the house's lifetime, some idiot had decided to paint it, and as the garish yellow shade was stripped away, the true beauty of the wood underneath it was beginning to come out.

"I like what you're doing with the place," I said as I looked around.

"You know how it is, more than most. It's a work in progress," Nathan said. "Why don't we go out onto the back porch? No work's started there yet, so we'll have some peace and quiet."

We moved through the house to the back, and it was no wonder that Nathan had been losing sleep. I knew from experience how difficult it was to live on-site when a remodel was taking place. Dust seemed to get everywhere, and there was a constant level of noise that quickly became unsettling.

Nancy was already outside waiting for us. There was a nice sundeck on the back of the porch, with enough seating for all of us.

She smiled apologetically at us as she said, "I needed some peace and quiet, for the baby, you know."

Gina glared at her as though she were covered in boils, but Nathan's smile brightened somewhat when he looked at her. "It's perfectly understandable, my dear," he said as he patted her shoulder paternally. She sat tall, and Nathan took his place beside her, with Gina barely finding enough room on the other side of her uncle.

Maddy and I took the remaining chairs facing the three of them, and Nathan began to talk.

"First of all, thank you both for coming. I know it's been difficult, but I've decided to put the past behind us and clear the air."

"Then you don't actually believe that we killed Judson anymore?" Maddy asked him.

Nathan shook his head. "No, of course not. I never did, not really. Sometimes it just helps to blame someone for the troubles you endure in your life, you know?"

"We appreciate that," I said. "It means a great deal to both of us. Was that all?"

"No, there's another reason I've asked you here," Nathan said.

"What is it?"

"I want to apologize again for this situation with Italia's. I know it's not fair to you both, and I want to say that I'm sorry."

"Sorry enough not to open the restaurant up after all?" Maddy asked.

As Gina glared at my sister, Nathan said, "No, I'm afraid that's out of the question. Gina needs the work to take her mind off her grief, so as far as I'm concerned, it's a done deal."

At least I was right about one thing; it was clear from her reaction that Gina had no desire to run that pizzeria. Her expression told the truth no matter how much she tried to hide it.

Nathan took a deep breath, and then he said, "I don't know if you've heard about my recent accident, but it's changed my entire perspective on things."

"I'm so happy that you weren't hurt," I said, meaning every word of it. Despite everything, I liked Nathan, and I hated seeing him like this.

"It could have been tragic," he agreed. "It's made me reevaluate some of the decisions I've made in the past, and I've decided to rectify as many of my sins as I can, while there's still time."

"Nathan, you're still a young man," I said, though it was clearly a lie to all of us sitting there.

"Not in any way, shape, or form," he said with a smile, "but I appreciate you saying it." He took a heavy breath, and then said, "Putting things in order before I go is the most important thing in the world to me right now."

"Have you decided on what you're going to do yet?" Maddy asked innocently.

"That's no concern of yours," Gina snapped.

Nathan patted her knee. "Now, Gina, be civil. We invited these folks here, remember?"

"Sorry," she said, though it was clear from her expression that she wasn't remorseful at all.

"It's accepted," Maddy said with just as much

guile. "We're curious about your plans. It's a fair question, Nathan."

"I'm not sure that's entirely true, and though my niece shouldn't have snapped at you, she was right about one thing; it's family business," he said.

After Nathan spoke, he turned to Nancy and smiled.

She looked at him so adoringly that I felt myself growing uncomfortable from the warmth. If I had to guess, I'd have to say that Nancy was going to figure prominently into the new plan. From the expression on Gina's face, it was pretty clear that she was beginning to realize it as well.

"You might as well go on and tell them what you have in mind, Uncle Nathan," Gina said. "Everyone is going to know soon enough, and you've kept all of us in the dark long enough."

He frowned at her, and then asked the other woman beside him, "Nancy, do you mind? This concerns you as well."

"Whatever you want to do is fine with me, *Uncle* Nathan," she said.

Gina cringed visibly as Nancy called him uncle.

He nodded. "Very well. As I said before, I decided that it was time to set things right, so I'm going to tear up my old will and write a new one."

"Who was the beneficiary before?" I asked, more out of curiosity than anything else. There was a fortune at stake, and I couldn't help wondering who was going to miss out on it.

He shrugged. "I don't suppose it hurts to tell you now, since it was written before Gina and Judson came into my life, not to mention Nancy. I left everything to my relative in Timber Ridge."

"I didn't think you knew who that was?" I asked.

"I didn't, and I still don't, but I left a provision in my will for Bob Lemon to track my heir down and give them everything I own."

"But that's all changed now," Maddy said.

"Indeed it has," Nathan said. "As soon as Bob and I have hammered out the details of an exact listing of my assets, I've decided to divide my estate into three equal shares." He turned to Gina and said, "You'll get a third," and then he looked at Nancy and added, "You'll get a third, and your baby will get the remaining third."

That struck like a slap in the face to Gina. "She gets more than me, and she's not even blood family?" Gina shouted, clearly blindsided by the new order of things.

"She's carrying Judson's child," Nathan said, clearly hurt by her reaction. "I thought you'd be pleased."

"Have you lost your mind? In what world would I be happy with that?" She looked harshly at Nancy. "We don't even know if that's Judson's kid she's carrying."

"I've never been with anyone but him, not that way," Nancy said, the level of her voice increasing to match her accuser's.

"Save it, lady, nobody here believes you."

Nathan said calmly, "I do."

I wouldn't have been surprised if Nancy had stuck her tongue out at Gina at that moment.

"Then you're nothing but an old fool," she shouted as she stood and stomped off the porch and into the house, "and I'm going to prove that she's lying."

"I'd better go talk to her," Nancy said as she started to get up.

"Do you think that's the wisest course of action at the moment?" I asked her.

Nancy stood and looked at the door as she spoke. "We may not agree about everything, but these two people are the only family I have in the world, and I can't stand the thought of something like money coming between us."

She smiled once more at Nathan, and then disappeared inside.

"Should you leave them alone like that?" Maddy asked.

"Perhaps you're right," he said as he stood as well. "I'm sorry you had to see that. I'm sure that once I explain it to Gina, she'll accept it as the right thing to do. I want to get this settled so I can destroy the current will and replace it with something that means more to me." He looked at the pizza sleeves at my feet. "I hate that we didn't touch those. I'd be happy to pay you for your trouble."

"Nonsense," I said. "They were a gift."

"Then I want to thank you for the thought," he said. "Can you two see yourselves out? I'd better go inside and make sure everything's okay."

After he was gone, I started for the back steps when Maddy grabbed my arm.

"We should go out through the house," my sister said.

I couldn't believe that my sister was suggesting that we intrude on their family's difficulties. "Are you insane? He wants us to leave them alone. That much was pretty clear."

Maddy's eyes were gleaming as she asked, "Aren't you the least bit curious what they're saying right now to each other?"

I shook my head. "We're not doing it, so forget it. Now come on. We have three pizzas we need to get rid of."

Maddy shrugged. "Is there anyone else we need to go see? We could offer these as a bribe for information."

"If there's anyone who can be swayed by pizza, I haven't met them yet," I said as we walked around the house to her car.

I saw the workmen diligently toiling to make an old house beautiful again, and I suddenly knew the perfect thing to do with the pizzas in my arms.

I approached them and asked, "Would you gentlemen be interested in some pizzas, free of charge, to a good home?"

"Are you kidding? We'd love it," one man said.

I handed them the pizza boxes out of the sleeves, and said, "I'm sorry I don't have anything to offer you to drink."

"We'll manage," the man said. "Guys, go get the crew inside. I'm declaring a break."

As they gathered around the food, Maddy smiled at me.

"What?" I asked. "I couldn't bear to see it go to waste."

"And that's one reason I love you, Sis," she said.

"I thought you had to because we're family," I replied with a grin.

"You think so? Ask them in there, and then come back and talk to me. Let's go back to the Slice and get ready for the evening crowd. You need to make more dough for deep dish pizzas, you know that, don't you?"

"I don't mind," I said. "It's what I do."

"It's what *we* do, Sis," she said as she drove us back to the Slice.

I wouldn't have minded being rich. There were a lot of things I might buy, including a new pizza oven, but if I had to choose between wealth and my friends and family, it would be an easy decision. Love trumped everything else, at least in my book, and I'd lived my life by that rule.

It was the only way I knew how to be, and I was thrilled by that realization.

When we got back to the Slice, I was surprised to find a large, muscular man in a dark coat and hat standing with his back to us waiting at the door.

I felt the muscles in my stomach begin to tighten, and then I realized that it was Art Young's driver.

"I've got a message for you," he said without preamble as he turned to face us.

"What can I do for you?" I asked.

"Mr. Young would appreciate it very much if you would join him in his automobile over there."

I looked in the direction where he was pointing and saw the long, black vehicle parked on the edge of the promenade.

Maddy asked, "Both of us?"

He shook his head. "No, ma'am. Sorry, but the invitation is for Mrs. Swift alone. My apologies."

Maddy looked as though she'd just gotten a get-out-of-jail-free card. "No offense taken. I've got work to do inside." As she started to unlock the door to the pizzeria with her own key, she said, "Don't be long. Remember, you've got dough to make."

Maddy was inside before we made it to Art's car, and I glanced back to see her face pressed up against the glass, watching my every step. There was no doubt in my mind that my sister's cell phone had the first two digits of 911 already punched in and waiting to be completed.

As the driver opened the door, I looked inside the car to find Art waiting for me.

"This is an odd summons," I said as I looked in.

"Would you join me for a moment?" he asked.

"What's the matter, are you afraid of being seen in public with me now?" I asked him. "You're not still upset with me, are you?"

He shook his head. "You know better than that, Eleanor. It is your reputation that I'm concerned about."

"It's nice of you to think of me, but don't do that again. I'm not afraid who knows we're friends, so it shouldn't matter to you."

Instead of answering, Art got out of the car and said to his driver, "Wait here. I'll be right back."

The driver looked at me with a hint of disbelief in his expression, though I was certain Art couldn't see it from where he was standing. Or so I thought.

"Save your opinions of my behavior for your own time," he said softly, and I saw the large driver stiffen.

"I'm sorry, sir. No disrespect intended."

"I'm sure he didn't mean anything by it," I said.

Art simply shrugged in my direction, and then

turned and stared at the man for a second and a half before dismissing him completely.

We moved to a bench on the promenade that faced a statue dedicated to the doctors who had died saving others from polio, an obelisk that I often admired. After a moment, Art said, "I respect those who behave selflessly, though I doubt I'll ever understand it."

"Given the right circumstances, I'm sure you'd be heroic yourself."

He laughed softly. "Eleanor, you give me too much credit."

"Could it be that you don't give yourself enough?"

He seemed to consider that, and then shook his head. "I'm not here to discuss my character. You're in some difficulty, aren't you?"

"No more than usual," I said, trying to keep my voice light as I said it. I didn't want Art to know just how deeply I'd managed to get myself involved in a murder investigation. Although he was on the opposite side of the law from our chief of police, neither man wanted to see me put myself in harm's way.

"Eleanor, I hope you respect me enough not to lie to me."

I let out a deep breath. If I was going to ask him to treat me as a friend, then I had to return the favor. "Okay, you're right. I apologize. Apparently Maddy and I have ruffled some feathers in our investigation."

"That shouldn't surprise you," Art said. I couldn't believe how dapper the man could look, how professional and businesslike he could act, and yet still be the same person who Bob Lemon—a man who had faced his own share of bad guys in the past—was afraid of.

"It shouldn't, but it always does," I said.

"You were threatened," Art said quietly.

I whirled around and looked at him. "How did you know that?"

"I didn't, but your actions made it a possibility, and you just confirmed it."

"Have you ever thought of being a detective?" I asked him.

His loud laughter caught me off guard. When he was able to compose himself again, he said, "You never cease to entertain me, Eleanor."

"What was so funny about what I said? You have the skills a good detective needs. You're persistent, observant, pay great attention to detail, and are able to make intuitive leaps based on limited information."

"Thank you for your praise, but I believe that particular job opportunity is forever lost to me. Do you have any idea who is threatening you?"

"No," I admitted. "Maddy and I each got telephone calls telling us to butt out, or we'd pay the consequences."

"Were those the caller's exact words?" he asked.

"No. Hang on, let me think about it." I put myself back in time and tried to recall the exact wording of the threat I'd received. It came back so vividly that I felt myself shaking upon hearing that voice in my mind again.

"I'm sorry. I didn't mean to subject you to that again." He must have seen my reaction, and was feeling remorseful about his question.

"It's fine. You can't help it if you don't know exactly what the person on the other end of the line said." I replayed it once more in my head, and then opened my eyes and repeated, "*Keep nosing around where you don't belong and you're going to pay for it.* That's it. I'm certain of it."

"Was it a man or a woman?"

"The voice was gravelly and pitched really low, so there's no way I can be sure of anything other than the threat."

He stared at me, and then nodded. "Do you have a guess?"

"Not a clue," I admitted. "If it matters, Maddy didn't know, either."

"Was her threat the same, or was it something similar?"

I didn't have to think about that for a second. "She got the exact same threat that I did. It was as though the caller had read it off a script."

Art frowned, and then looked around for a moment. I knew better than to interrupt him, but after a few seconds, he said, "I'll look into it."

"You don't have to," I said.

"It's what a friend would do," he answered.

Before I could say another word, he left the bench we'd shared to return to his car. I couldn't believe how quickly his driver moved to be sure that Art's door was open by the time he got there. My friend didn't look at his driver, he just slid inside, and the door quickly closed after him. The driver nodded in my direction, and I could swear he said *thank you* under his breath before getting in and driving off.

Chapter 15

"What was that all about?" Maddy asked me as I walked back into the Slice.

"Art wants to help us figure out who threatened us over the telephone," I admitted as I started back toward the kitchen. I wanted to make that biscuit-like dough again for the deep dish pizzas, and if I started now, I might have some decent crust by the time we hit our dinner rush.

"You're not serious, are you? Did you actually tell him that someone called us? I thought we were keeping it to ourselves."

I was getting tired of my sister's attitude toward Art Young, especially since he'd been nothing but helpful to us in the past. "I didn't tell him anything; he guessed it from my reaction. This is a good thing, Sis. He thought he might be able to help."

"That's too funny," Maddy said.

"What's that?"

"A man in his line of work acting like a detective," Maddy said. "Come on, Eleanor, you have to see the irony in it."

"I don't agree. He's just a friend doing us a favor," I said. "That's it. Don't read anything into it, Maddy."

"Okay, I'm sorry. I shouldn't have said anything. Goodness knows we can use all the friends we can get."

I smiled at her. "That's the spirit. After I make more dough, we might have a little time to chat about what we saw at Nathan's this afternoon."

"Forget that. I'm not willing to wait that long. We'll discuss it while you work. I can't believe how openly defiant Gina was with Nathan. He looked pretty shocked by her behavior, too."

"I'm not sure why he should have been," I said. "After all, Gina went from being his last living beneficiary to just getting a third."

Maddy nodded as she took a seat on the stool by the counter where I prepped my dough. "It had to be a shock for her to hear it out of the blue like that, and she didn't really have time to prepare herself for it."

"Especially if she really did kill her brother to get his share," I said as I measured out ingredients for the dough. I planned to make another batch tonight and let it sit out overnight to see if I could get the dough to rise any more than I had so far. What I was making at the moment was perfectly fine, but it wasn't good enough for my standards, at least not yet. I hoped with a little tweaking and a lot more practice, I'd be ready to serve three kinds of pizza at the Slice on a regular basis.

"Do you really think she could have killed her own brother for his share of an inheritance they weren't even sure they were ever going to get?" Maddy asked me.

"I'd believe anything from her. She's in debt up to her pretty little eyebrows," I said. "Being desperate makes people do some unimaginable things."

"How about our other suspects?" Maddy asked.

"I wanted to talk to you about that," I said. "I'm having a hard time believing that Nathan could have done it."

"Why do you say that?"

I shrugged. "Look at how far he's willing to support a woman who says she's carrying his nephew's baby. That sounds like an act of love to me."

"When you look at it from another angle, it could just as easily be guilt," Maddy said after a moment's thought.

I considered it, and as I mixed the dough with my hands to get the right consistency, I finally said, "You're right. We have to leave his name on the list."

"Don't forget, we've got Lacy White and Jack Hanks, too."

"I'm not about to forget them, or Nancy Thorpe, either."

"That just leaves Nathan's mystery heir," Maddy said.

"I have a hard time counting whoever that is," I said. "Nathan doesn't even know his cousin's identity, or if the family rumors are even true for that matter. And a lot of people would have to die before this cousin inherits anything, and quickly be-fore Nathan can write another will."

"It's a motive, no matter how slight it might look," she said.

"I'm not disagreeing with you. We'll have to keep it in mind." I had a sudden thought. "Hey, I know who might be able to help us find out who it is."

"Forget it. I can't ask Bob to help us dig this per-son up," she said. "We're still having a bit of a rough patch, and you shouldn't ask David Quin-ton, either."

"What on earth made you think I'd ask him?"

She smiled brightly at me. "Come on, we both know there's something there, no matter how much you deny it."

"Who's denying it?" I asked.

Maddy whooped with delight. "That's outstand-ing, Eleanor. You've got your spunk back."

"I don't know about that," I said, "but I'm plan-ning to enjoy his company as long as he's here."

"That sounds like a good idea," she said. "So, if we're not talking about Bob or David, and Art Young is already doing us a favor, who's left?"

"I'll tell you when we open for dinner. I'm ex-pecting her to come by the Slice this evening."

Maddy looked at me. "You're seriously not going to tell me until then?"

I laughed. "I'm evil, I know."

"I was just going to say that you're getting more like me every day."

"That's just cruel," I said, adding a smile to show her that I was just teasing. I could do worse than emulate my sister and the way she lived her life. Maddy put herself out there every time, and if it meant she was vulnerable, she didn't let that stop her the next time. Granted, she'd never lost someone she loved, but the principle was the same, and it would make me a happier woman if I could manage to apply some of the things I'd seen her do to my own life.

When Greg arrived just before we opened, I sent Maddy to the back to pick up some extra napkins.

"While she's gone, I need to ask you for a favor," I said.

"You don't want me to knock her off, do you?"

"Of course not," I said.

"Then I'm in. What can I do? Do you need someone tailed? Can I teach someone a lesson for you?" he asked as he slapped his fist in his palm. "I can do the rough stuff, too, you know, so don't be afraid to ask."

"You've been watching too many old movies," I said as I laughed out loud. "Just let me know when Karen Green comes in."

"That's it?" he asked, clearly disappointed with his assignment. "That's the only thing I can do?"

"For now, but I may need you to rough someone up later, so don't go far."

"I'm your man," he said.

I started laughing—I couldn't help myself—and then Greg began to laugh, too.

"What's so funny?" Maddy asked when she walked back out front with the requested napkins.

"I'd tell you, but you probably wouldn't get it. It's an inside joke," Greg said.

"I thought I was on the inside of everything," Maddy said, the dismay clear in her expression.

I couldn't let her think we were excluding her. "Greg just offered to pound someone for us if they need to be taught a lesson in manners. I think that's gallant of him, don't you?"

She shook her head. "Not unless he's going to use a baseball bat."

Greg said, "Hey, I'm a big guy."

"I know you are, but are you tough?"

He tensed his stomach and said, "Go on, take your best shot."

She just shook her head. "Save it, champ. You're right, and I was wrong. You're a real tough guy."

He nodded. "Believe me, I am, if either of you need me to be," Greg said.

"Need him to be what?" Josh asked as he came in.

"A tough guy," I said.

Josh looked at me and flexed an arm muscle. "You think he's something? You should see me in action. I may not be as big as he is, but I'm wiry."

"Somehow, I feel better just knowing you two are out here," I said with a smile as I retreated to my kitchen.

Greg came back a little while after we opened. "She's here."

"Thanks," I said. "I'll be right out."

I went into the dining room and asked Maddy, "Could you cover for me in the kitchen for ten minutes?"

She looked alarmed by my request. "Why? Where are you going? Are you sure you won't be any longer than that?"

"Relax, you aren't being punished," I said. "That special little helper I told you about is here, and the two of us need to talk."

Maddy looked around the pizzeria, and I watched as her gaze barely touched on Karen Green before going to another customer. "I don't get it. I don't see anyone here who might be able to help us."

"Karen took a class in genealogy at the college," I said.

"So you're going to ask her to help find Nathan Sizemore's long-lost relative," Maddy said, finishing the thought for me. "Do you think she can do it?"

"I don't know, but it's worth a shot, isn't it? Do you have any better ideas?"

"Not really." She handed me her order pad. "If you want to take her order while you're asking her for a favor, you'll need this."

"Thanks," I said. "I won't be long."

Maddy nodded and faded into the back while I drew a Mountain Dew from the soda station. It was Karen's favorite, so I wasn't exactly taking a risk by bringing her one.

"Here you go, compliments of the house," I said as I slid the drink in front of her. She'd been frowning about something, but at the sight of the free soda, a smile bloomed on her face.

"That's so sweet of you," Karen said.

"Actually, I've got ulterior motives. May I join you for a minute?"

Karen appeared to be surprised by my request, but she nodded vigorously and pointed to one of the chairs at her table. "Please, I'd be honored."

"Don't be, I'm not all that special," I said with a laugh as I sat close to her.

Karen took a sip of her soft drink, and then asked me, "What can I do for you, Eleanor?"

"You told me that you took a genealogy class in the adult education program at the college, right?"

"Sure, I take lots of things there. Are you interested in tracing your family roots? We've got Swifts and Spencers all through the county society where I do most of my searches."

"Neither," I said. "There's someone else's family history I'd like you to trace, though, and I'd like you to keep it our little secret."

Karen nodded as she dug into her purse for a small notebook and a pencil. "All I need is a name and a birth date, and you'd be amazed by what I can turn up. The Internet has been a real savior for amateur genealogists like me."

"It's Nathan Sizemore," I said. "I'm looking for anyone living in town who might be related to him."

Karen started to write his name down, stopped and stared at her pad, and then finally looked at me without writing a thing. "Are you talking about crazy old Nathan, the man who lives on the edge of Timber Ridge? Do you mind if I ask why you're so interested in him?"

I had no desire to get into the reasons for my request then and there. "It's tough to explain. Would you mind doing it for me? I'd be happy to pay you for your time."

"That's not really an issue. How soon would you need it?" she asked as I watched her finally write Nathan's name in her book.

"Tonight, if that's at all possible."

Karen frowned. "Could I do the research, and then come by sometime tomorrow afternoon?"

"We'll be prepping for the Halloween Blowout," I said, "but if you don't mind a little chaos, that would be great."

"I'll see what I can do," she said.

"Wonderful. I really appreciate that. Now, what can I get you? Anything you want tonight is on the house."

"Anything?"

"Just name it," I said.

"I'd love one of those deep dish pizzas, with the works. Is that too much to ask?"

"Not at all. I'll go start on it myself. And Karen?"

"Yes?"

"Thank you," I said.

As she nodded, I went back to Maddy, where I found her struggling with a ball of the deep dish dough. "Thanks, I'll take over for you now."

She smiled, the relief spreading across her face. "It's about time. I don't know how you work with this stuff."

"Practice makes perfect."

I took the dough from her, and after a quick re-shaping, I worked it into the pan, making sure that the sides of the crust peeked over the top of the rim.

"How did you do that?" Maddy asked.

"I'd love to tell you, but I can't. It's a trade secret."

"You know what? I don't really care." She started laughing as she said, "Now I don't have to ever make them when you're not here." Changing her line of questioning, Maddy asked, "Was Karen able to help you?"

"She's going to check something out online and get back to me tomorrow," I said.

"Good. That just leaves the rest of our suspect list to go through. Not one of them has given us an alibi for the night of the murder. Do you ever get the feeling that we're just spinning our wheels here?"

"All the time," I admitted as I began layering sauce, toppings, and parmesan cheese into the pan. "We just have to keep stirring until something boils."

"Just as long as it's not us," Maddy said.

She went back up front to reclaim her spot there, and I began working on the rest of the pending orders. We were making headway on the case, I knew that much, but I wished we could see more progress.

Things had a habit of working out that way. We'd go days and even weeks without a real break, and then all at once we'd reach the tipping point and everything would start to make sense. I just had to believe that moment was in sight. If I didn't, it would drive me totally nuts.

* * *

We were an hour from closing for the night when Bob Lemon came into the kitchen. "Before you say anything, Maddy sent me back here to talk to you. Either she's worried about you being lonely, or she's beginning to tire of me."

"Did she make plans with you for later tonight when we close?" I asked as I put a thin crust pizza onto the conveyor.

"Yes, we've got a date to watch a movie at her place."

"Then you're good. When she starts breaking dates for no good reason, it's time to move into action, because your walking papers won't be too far behind."

"That's good to know," he said. "I need to speak with you, so I'm glad we've got this opportunity to chat."

"Why? Are you thinking of proposing?" I'd been kidding him, but from the look on his face, I saw that I'd hit home with an errant shot. "You're not, are you?"

"Would that be such a bad thing to have me as a brother-in-law?" he asked, fighting to hide his disappointment at my reaction.

"Are you kidding? I'm fine with it. It's my sister that you might have a hard time convincing," I said as I added a pizza-melt sandwich onto the conveyor. I had a gap in my oven schedule, and I'd been trying to come up with new sandwiches to match the deep dish pizzas we were going to start offering. If I had to revamp my entire menu to stay in business, I'd do it.

"You don't think she loves me, do you?" Bob asked. It was as though I'd just told him he was going to die before sunrise tomorrow.

"Are you kidding me? She cares more about you than she did for at least two of her ex-husbands, and that's really saying something."

"Then what's the problem?"

I frowned at the oven, willing it to finish a pizza I could cut and bring out, anything to spare me from having the conversation I was currently embroiled in. "You don't want to know."

"Trust me when I tell you that I do." There was no denying the plea in his voice as he said it.

"Bob, I think you two are wonderful together, and if you asked my sister under a lie detector test, she would have to agree. But that doesn't mean that she's ready to get married again, no matter what she might say under oath."

"I just assumed that she is joking when she makes all those cracks about wedded unbliss," he answered.

"Maybe she is, and maybe she isn't. I can't speak for her, but if you are determined to ask her to marry you, be prepared for either answer, because I'm not even certain she knows what she'd say if you asked her."

Finally a pizza came out, and I pounced on it as though I was starving and it was all for me.

"So, what do you recommend?" Bob asked.

"Folks seem to really like the deep dish I just started serving," I said.

"That's not what I'm asking, and you know it."

"I do, but it's the only answer you're going to get from me."

He pulled a small felt box out of his pocket, weighed it in his hand, and then asked me, "What am I supposed to do with this?"

The door opened, and I saw Maddy coming.

"I'd put it away quickly, for now," I said as I handed the pizza to my sister, providing a distraction at the same time as it required a delivery.

Maddy looked at me, then at Bob, and finally back to me. "What are you two talking about back here?"

"My menu," I said.

Maddy raised an eyebrow as she looked at me. "Really?"

"Among other things," I amended. "Now, would you mind delivering that pizza to its rightful owners while it still has some semblance of being hot and fresh?"

"You got it, boss."

As she left, she winked at Bob, who didn't react one way or the other, an odd reaction coming from him. Maddy glanced at me and gave me her best quizzical look. I just shook my head, and she walked out looking bewildered.

"I'm sorry I couldn't be more help," I said.

"It's not your problem. It's mine," Bob replied.

As he headed for the door, I asked him, "Is that why you came back here, to ask for permission to marry my sister?"

Bob looked startled by the very idea of doing anything like that. "No, not at all. I learned something you might find interesting today. Funny, I nearly forgot all about it after our little conversation."

"Believe me, information is one thing I'm lacking these days. I'll take whatever you've got to give me."

"A friend discovered something today and passed the news on to me. It was given to me in trust, and I hope you'll respect that."

"I won't tell a soul," I said as I took another pizza out of the oven. This one was for Karen, and it had to go through one more time before it was ready to be served.

"I mean it. I could lose a great deal if this information was ever traced back to me, Eleanor."

I looked at him for a moment, and then said, "Bob, you've given me information before without making me swear some kind of oath of honesty to you. It all boils down to this: either you trust me or you don't. If you do, tell me whatever is on your mind, but please, if you think I'm going to blab it all around town, you're best off if you just walk away right now."

"Eleanor, why do you and your sister both have to make things so hard on people who are trying to help you?" he asked, the frustration coming out in his voice.

"Are we still talking about me, or did this conversation just take an abrupt shift back to my sister? I'm fine, either way. I'm just trying to keep up."

He laughed and shook his head, and then actually managed to find a smile for me. "You're right. I shouldn't be taking my aggravation with your sister out on you. I trust you, Eleanor."

"You're sure?"

"I'm positive, and I make a great portion of my living being a good judge of character."

"Then tell me what you've got," I said.

He was about to say something when the kitchen door opened again, an act that shut him right up again.

I was beginning to wonder if I'd ever hear what he had to say.

Chapter 16

"Eleanor, I've got a request for six more pizzas before we close," Greg said as he came through, "and I need to know if you can fill it."

"Let me check my dough first," I said as I poked my head into the refrigerator to take a count on available balls of dough.

"I can come back later," Bob said.

"You stay right there," I commanded, popping back out for one second.

As I looked for more dough, I heard Greg say, "She's scary, isn't she?"

"Nothing like her sister, though," he said.

"I can still hear you both," I said from inside the fridge. "Yes, we can handle it. What is it, some kind of party? I thought those didn't start in earnest until Halloween tomorrow."

"I guess they're getting a jump on things," he said.

"How do they want them?" I asked.

"Your choice," he said. With a grin, Greg added,

"I'd make them all garbage pizzas so you can charge them the max."

"It's always good to get your opinion," I said with a fake smile.

"So, you're going to do what you want, anyway," Greg answered.

"You've got it. Now go."

After he left, Bob asked, "Do we really need to do this now? I can come back later when things aren't so crazy around here."

"I'd love to hear what you have to say, but then again, I'm not the sister you really need to worry about pleasing, am I?"

He grinned at me. "You're probably the only one I have a shot with."

"Trust me, you're going to have to try a lot harder with me than you ever have with my sister," I said.

"I didn't mean it that way," Bob said, and then he finally saw my smile. "But then you knew that, didn't you?"

"Sorry, I guess I've got a cruel streak."

"I won't comment on that one way or the other, but I will tell you what I found out. Gina Sizemore's credit debt was paid off in full as of one P.M. today."

That was right before we'd had our meeting with Nathan, Gina, and Nancy, and I wondered if Gina felt she could speak a little more freely now that her debt was gone. It could explain why she'd been so vocal with her uncle, but it didn't explain her willingness to alienate his affections. I was certain she was counting on a great deal more money once he was gone. What I wasn't at all sure about was if she was willing to help that time come early.

"Does that help you and Maddy in your investigation at all?" Bob asked, and I suddenly realized that he was still standing there watching me.

"It might. Thanks for sharing," I said as I began to work on pizza crusts.

He nodded. "It was the least I could do."

"Don't kid yourself. You could have kept it to yourself. Thank you."

Bob nodded and then started for the door.

I couldn't let him leave like that. "Bob?"

He stopped and turned back to me. "Yes?"

"Don't give up, on either one of us. You're special to Maddy and me both. You know that, don't you?"

"But not in the same way," he answered with a smile.

I threw a towel at him. "Dream on, sport."

After he was gone, Karen's pizza came out of the oven for the second time. It was a bubbling pan of goodness, and if I hadn't made it special for her, I would have been tempted to sample it myself.

I grabbed a few hot pads and took it out to her personally. "Here you go, compliments of the Slice."

She nodded with a little less enthusiasm than I expected.

"Is something wrong, Karen?"

"No, not at all. I just realized that I have so much to do if I'm going to help you, I'm not sure I have time to eat it."

"Please, stay and enjoy it."

"Only if you'll join me," she said.

I knew I surprised her when I said, "Let me clear it with Maddy, and then I'll grab another plate."

Maddy wasn't thrilled about being banished to the kitchen again, but at the moment, I didn't care. She had a date tonight, and I didn't have a single plan other than to go home, take a shower, and read a good book. It wouldn't kill her to do a little more kitchen duty, and I had to eat something before I went home, or the cookies in my pantry there wouldn't stand a chance.

When I came back, I served us both slices of the delightful pizza, and then we began to eat. The tastes and textures were getting better and better, and I was beginning to be proud of my new addition.

After I'd finished a bite, I said, "You have a lot of interests, don't you?"

"I don't know. I come across something when I'm reading, and that triggers something else, and then I'm off to the races."

I took a sip of my soda. "What made you interested in genealogy?"

"I've never had much of a family," she said solemnly. "I thought it might be nice to know that there are other people out there I'm related to that I haven't met yet. I envy you and your sister," she said.

"Really?"

"You're both such important parts of each other's lives," she said. "Not everyone has that."

"I guess you're right," I said. Our tone had gotten rather intense, so I decided to change the subject. "That explains that, but what about auto mechanics and law? You were taking a class on money management as well, right?"

"That's next semester," she said. "I'm not sure about that one. The class is overbooked, so I'm going to have to get a waiver from the professor." Karen looked around the restaurant at our meager attempts to decorate for the Halloween festivities. "I like what you've done with the place," she said with a smile.

I looked around, too. "It's got that certain something, doesn't it? We decided to go minimalist this year."

"It works for you," she said. "You're dressing up for the Blowout tomorrow night, aren't you? It should be fun."

"I haven't even thought about a costume yet, but I'll come up with something. How about you?"

She looked at her pizza, and then said softly, "I was thinking about being Cinderella. Is it tacky for a grown woman to dress that way?"

"It depends. Is your princess going to be the least bit sleazy?"

"No, never. I could never imagine doing that."

"Then you'll be a delightful Cinderella," I said as I touched her arm lightly.

My approval seemed to mean something to her, because she smiled.

"I think you should go all out," Karen said.

"That's my sister's area of expertise," I said.

I saw Maddy waving at me from the back. "As a matter of fact, it appears that she needs me in the kitchen right now. Will you excuse me?"

"I've got to run, too," she said as she stood and

collected her books. "I had a delightful time, Eleanor."

"As did I. I'll see you tomorrow."

As Karen left, I made my way back to the kitchen. "What is it?" I asked Maddy.

"Oh, nothing, as long as you don't mind me ruining those pizzas you're making. You send the deep dish ones through three times, right?"

I raced past her. "Twice," I said as I pulled one out on its third trip, smoking and topped with a black substance that was unrecognizable.

Oh, well. My break had been fun while it had lasted. As I made a replacement pizza for the one Maddy had just ruined, I wondered if I'd ever get out of my kitchen for more than an hour or two a day.

Maddy came back into the kitchen after we locked up. "Anything I can do to help make this go faster?" she asked me.

"You can go ahead and send the guys home," I said. "I've got this covered."

"Got it." She leaned out through the doorway and said, "Okay, the coast is clear. You can go home."

When there was no response, I said, "You already let them go, didn't you?"

Maddy looked a little embarrassed when she admitted, "I knew we were nearly finished, and they both had things to do tonight. I'm sorry, Eleanor. I don't mean to keep overstepping my bounds."

"Why don't you go, too?"

She looked surprised. "You're not firing me, are you? I said I was sorry."

I had to laugh. "Maddy, there's nothing much left to do here, and Bob told me you have a date tonight yourself. Go home. I'll see you tomorrow."

"Are you sure?"

"I'm pretty certain that's what he said, but you can call him and ask him yourself if you'd like."

"I mean about leaving," she said.

"Go. Now."

She kissed my cheek. "Thanks, Sis. I love you."

"I love you, too."

After Maddy was gone, the Slice seemed awfully quiet as I balanced out the cash register and put the deposit in our safe. I lingered in the back, trying to find things to do, but finally I had to admit that I was finished.

Why was I suddenly so reluctant to go home?

And that's when it hit me. I was getting tired of being alone. Having David Quinton join me after work had already become something that I looked forward to, and the first night he was going to be absent, I was shocked to realize that I was feeling lonely.

After giving myself a pep talk, I left the Slice and drove home. I was a grown woman.

I could spend the evening by myself if I had to.

I just didn't want to.

When I woke up, I said, "Happy Halloween" to myself, and got ready for a very big day. We'd have our regular opening time for lunch, but our dinner shift would be hit or miss, serving our little ghost pizzas for a dollar each and contributing the profits to the Helping Hand Fund, a program set up to relieve some of the burdens of the very poorest in our community. It was a charity I fully supported, and I was happy for the opportunity to contribute my little bit to it. I completely understood the desire of some folks to help others in foreign countries, but I had a hard time doing it when I knew that kids within ten miles of me were going to bed hungry at night, or being forced to I was making a difference, no matter how little I managed to contribute every year.

After my shower, I realized that in the rush of everything that had been going on over the last week, I'd forgotten to get a costume, and for the first time in years, I felt like dressing up. I went through my closets, trying to come up with something I could put together, but I wasn't having much luck when my telephone rang.

"Happy Halloween," Maddy said.

"The same to you. What are you dressing up as this year?"

"I'm going to be Tinkerbell."

"Excuse me? You're kidding, right?"

She laughed. "No, I picked up some gossamer wings, and I'm doing the coolest makeup. The outfit shows off my figure, too."

"Not too much, I hope. We've got kids coming to the Slice." My sister had been known to get carried away in the name of Halloween.

"It's in perfect taste," she said. "Well, it should at

least pass inspection. How about you? What did you come up with?"

"I haven't," I reluctantly admitted. "I forgot to do anything earlier, and now it's too late."

"Nonsense," she said. "Give me twenty minutes, and I'll be right there. We can come up with something together. It will be like old times. We made our costumes at the last minute more than once in the old days, remember?"

"See you then," I said. When Maddy and I were kids, we couldn't always afford the latest and greatest in costumes, so we'd started a tradition of making each other's outfits for Halloween. In our own little world, the sister who helped the other achieve the best look got a third of that sister's candy, so it had been serious business between us. Sadly, Maddy usually won. She had a knack for seeing the potential in a pile of junk, and I almost always had a costume cooler than anything we could have bought at the store.

I grabbed a yogurt and added some cold fruit to it, and then scanned the newspaper as I waited for her.

When Maddy showed up, she looked absolutely adorable. Her costume shimmered as she moved, and her eyes were highlighted by a skilled makeup job. Something was missing, though.

"Hey, where are your wings?"

"I had to take them off. They're murder to drive in. Do you like it?" she asked as she twirled around, her skirt flaring as she did.

"It's perfect. You're going to have all the boys in town chasing after you."

"It's not the boys I care about," she said with a wicked grin. "It's the men I'm after."

"Not just one in particular? What's Bob going as?"

She shrugged. "He won't tell me, but he bought his costume at a big shop in Charlotte, and I can't wait to see it."

"You're really good for him, aren't you?"

She shrugged. "Honestly, we're good for each other. He's probably a better man than I deserve."

The admission was unusual for her. "I find that hard to believe."

"It's true," she insisted.

"Then why don't you treat him better than you do?"

Maddy bit her lip, and then said, "I wonder that sometimes myself."

"Could it be that your heart can't take being broken again? It's almost as though you don't want to get your hopes up this time."

She thought about that, and then said, "I honestly don't know. You could be right, Eleanor."

"He loves you, Maddy," I said.

She looked as though she wanted to cry when she heard me say that, something I didn't want. Making my voice lighter, I asked, "But then, who doesn't? You're going to be the hit of Halloween."

"Not if I can help it. Now let's see that closet of yours. Not the good stuff, either. I want the things you're ready to take to Goodwill."

After going through every item of clothing I had in my possession, Maddy frowned at the lot of it. "There's not a great deal here to work with, is there?"

"Sorry. I suspected that it was too much to ask."

"Nonsense," she said. Maddy frowned at it all, and then looked intently at me. "I'm going to suggest something to you, but if it's a bad idea, tell me up front and I'll drop it. Will you promise to do that?"

"I'm listening," I said. It was hard to tell what my sister was about to suggest, but her warning gave me more than a little pause.

"Do you have anything of Joe's that you kept?"

"No," I said firmly. "I won't do that."

"Fine, it was just an idea."

I explained, "Maddy, the things I've kept aren't for mocking, and that's what would happen if I wore them for Halloween."

"I said I was fine with it." She kept looking at my clothes, and finally said, "This is hopeless."

"Well, we both know I can't wear anything you've got." I could, if I was going for a laugh. My sister was tall and slim, whereas I was a good deal shorter, and curvier than she'd ever been in her life.

"Let's see your basement," Maddy said firmly.

"There's nothing down there that I can wear," I insisted.

"Well, the same goes for up here. Come on, what have we got to lose?"

"I don't have to dress up this year," I said as I reached for a pair of blue jeans and a T-shirt. I was still wearing my pajamas in the hopes that my sister would find something better for me to wear.

"Go on, put those on first. I have an idea. I'll be right back."

"Where are you going?"

"Trust me," she said.

That's when I knew I was in trouble.

I dressed as usual for a day of making pizzas and had just about resigned myself to being plain and boring when she came back upstairs carrying something.

"These are yours, aren't they?" She was carrying a paint-splattered pair of white overalls and an equally cruddy hat in her arms.

"Yes. I wore them when Joe and I painted the house."

"Any sentimental value to them?"

I thought about it, and then shook my head. "It was miserable standing on a ladder trying not to fall and cutting in paint around the edges of all the woodwork. I would have donated them long ago if I thought anyone would be interested in them."

"Put them on. I need to get my makeup kit, and we'll finish it off."

"That's it? I'm going as a painter?"

"Hey," she said, "don't be so critical, I didn't have much to work with here, and at least people will know that you made some kind of effort."

"Okay," I said. "I'll try anything at this point."

"Trust me, you'll look adorable."

I pulled my overalls on over my jeans, and there was so much paint on the legs that they crinkled as I walked. Next, I put the hat on, tucking my hair back in a ponytail before I did, and then I looked in the mirror. It wasn't bad at all, once I had it on.

Maddy came back, not with her makeup, but with some small plastic containers of the craft paint sold at craft stores.

"I found these in my trunk," she said. "They'll be even better."

"Whatever you say."

"I love it when you say that," Maddy said. "Now sit down on the bed so I can get to work."

"Why don't we go downstairs?" I asked. "That way we won't have to worry about spilling any paint up here."

"It's all water based, so it will come right up."

"But there's no reason to take the chance." I started downstairs, with Maddy close behind.

After taking a seat at the kitchen counter, I turned my face to her and said, "Knock yourself out."

She took out an old pie tin and asked, "May I use this?"

"Be my guest."

Maddy squirted dollops of paint from several little bottles, and then took out a small paintbrush and started making sweeping dabs on my face.

After half a dozen strokes, I said, "That's enough."

"Just one more," she said as she dragged one across my nose.

"That's too much."

She shrugged. "See for yourself. I think you look adorable."

I couldn't imagine that was true, but I walked into the hallway and looked into the mirror framed by quarter sawn oak, anyway. I had to admit it. She'd done an excellent job.

"It looks great," I said. "Thank you."

"You're very welcome. Now, are you ready to make some pizza?"

"I'd better be," I replied.

"That's the spirit. Did you make a sign for your trick-or-treaters for tonight?"

"No, I figured I'd just keep the porch light off. I don't think any kid in town goes door to door trick-or-treating anymore. Why should they? They get more goodies at the Blowout than they'd ever get walking through our neighborhood."

"You know, sometimes I kind of miss the old Halloween," she said.

"If you come to my door later, I'll find something I can give you."

"I might just take you up on that. I'll see you at the Slice."

"Okay. Maddy? Thanks for doing this."

She smiled brightly at me. "Are you kidding? You know me. I live for things like this."

"I know. And when you think about it, why not? You're really good at it."

"It's not just about wearing costumes," she explained as I locked the house behind us. "It's a chance to live outside our regular lives, you know?"

"I know you've always felt that way."

She looked hard at me. "You have, too."

"But not for a while," I said.

"Maybe again, though."

"Perhaps," I said.

We were walking to our cars when I spotted a vehicle driving erratically toward us. I wasn't sure who the driver was, but when it stopped in front of my place with two tires on my lawn, I easily recognized her.

It looked like one of our suspects was coming to pay us a visit.

Chapter 17

"I wasn't going to stop, but I saw you standing there, so I thought you should know what's happened," Nancy Thorpe said as she got out of her car. "I'm leaving Timber Ridge, and I'm never coming back."

"What happened?"

"She tried to kill me," Nancy said, her voice shrill and full of fright.

"Who did?" I asked.

"Gina. Who else?"

"Take a deep breath and tell us what happened," I said.

She took a look at our outfits, and then said, "I forgot it was Halloween, can you believe that?"

"It's not important. What happened?"

"I was on the stairs going down when that crazy woman tried to shove me. I'm lucky to be alive."

"Are you sure it was intentional?" I asked.

Nancy looked at me with crazy eyes. "I'm telling you, that's what happened. Don't tell me that you're taking her side, too. Nathan believed her when she said it was an accident, but I felt her hand on my back, and trust me, it was no accident."

"Do you think she was doing it to try to get rid of the baby?" I asked. I couldn't believe anyone would be so callous, but if Gina had killed her brother, what was a little more blood on her hands?

"If that's why she did it, the joke's on her, then. There never was a baby."

"What are you talking about?"

"I lied," she said.

"About being pregnant?" Maddy asked.

"About everything. I went out with Judson twice, and we just didn't have enough of a spark to keep it going. He was estranged from his sister at the time, so she had no idea. When I found out that he was dead, I wondered if there was an angle I could play."

There must have been a look on my face that showed my disapproval for her, because she added, "Hey, I'm not exactly proud of myself for trying to take advantage of an opportunity like that, but it was worth a shot. Not anymore, though. I'm getting out of Timber Ridge, and I'm never coming back."

Nancy got into her car and drove off, leaving two grooves of chewed-up grass in her wake.

I looked at Maddy and said, "Can you believe that?"

"The fact that Nancy lied, or that Gina tried to kill her imaginary baby?"

Was that what the world was coming to? "Both, I guess. What is wrong with people?"

Maddy shook her head. "That's not the way to look at it. The question is, what's wrong with these people? Not everybody's like them."

"I sincerely hope not. Is there any chance that Nancy could have been mistaken about Gina?" I asked.

"Anything's possible, but from what I've seen so far, I'm willing to believe her. After all, she's leaving town. What docs she have to gain by spreading lies on her way out?"

I shook my head. "Think about it, Maddy. The woman lied about being in love with Judson, and she just admitted to us that she made up a false pregnancy. Does that really give her any credibility now? If she told me the sky was blue, I'd have to look up and see for myself."

Maddy shrugged. "You've got a point. Look on the bright side, though."

"What, that I've got to get someone to fix the tracks in my lawn?"

"Think about it, Eleanor. We have one less suspect now than we had before."

"That's true," I said. "It is nice to eliminate one instead of adding someone new to our list."

"Don't get too excited. Karen's supposed to report back today with news of her genealogy search, isn't she?"

In all the excitement, I'd forgotten all about the job I'd given our customer. "Then it's a wash. Come on, I need a little reality right now, and there's nothing like burying my hands in dough to get that."

* * *

Maddy and I parked side by side in the back and walked through the shortcut together to head for the Slice. Before we left our cars, though, my sister had taken a minute to reattach her fairy wings, and I had to admit that she looked adorable.

My costume was the best she could do on short notice, but hers was truly eye-catching.

"Let's go see Paul," she said as we hit the promenade.

I glanced at my watch and saw that we had a few minutes to spare. "Why not? I'm a little worried about him."

Maddy asked, "Do you think he'd really leave Timber Ridge?"

"You saw the look on his face after Gina visited the bakery. I wasn't sure he'd finish out the day."

We walked toward the bakery, and soon we saw Paul through the window, behind the counter. To our delight, he was dressed as a scarecrow, complete with straw flopping out of his sleeves and a floppy hat.

"You look adorable," I said as we walked in.

"Right back at you both. You two look great."

"So do you," Maddy said.

"Maybe, but to tell you the truth, this hay is driving me nuts," he replied with a huge grin as he scratched at his sleeves.

"Are you allergic to straw?" Maddy asked.

"No, thank goodness for that, but it keeps falling out on the floor. If the health inspector comes by today, I'm doomed."

"I think you're safe," I said. "If I'm not mistaken, he's still on his honeymoon."

"Then I hope he doesn't get a substitute, because if he does, I'm going to get shut down."

I looked at the array of his offerings and saw full trays of the samples he'd shared with us before. "They all look wonderful."

"Sorry I never brought samples by to taste like I'd promised. I've been off my game the last few days."

"We understand," I said. "How are you doing?"

Paul managed a slight grin. "I'm getting better. I think I'll live, and in all honesty, I believe that's all I can hope for. Would either one of you care for a taste? Take whatever you want; it's on the house."

"No thanks," I said as I held a hand up. "They look wonderful, but I've had my fill of treats for a while."

Maddy looked at me as though I'd lost my mind. "I don't know what she's talking about. I'd be delighted. Thanks for offering."

"You don't have to," Paul said agreeably. "It won't hurt my feelings."

"I'm not sure I could look myself in the mirror if I turned down one of your confections," Maddy said. "I'll pick from the adult menu."

He nodded and offered the tray to her. Maddy chose a zombie head, and I changed my mind and reached for one myself since they looked so good.

"You don't have to," Paul said. "Really."

"I don't see how I can pass it up," I said with a smile. I took a bite and tasted the delightful cherry and raspberry filling. He'd overstuffed them, and it literally oozed out onto my hand. "Everyone's going to love you."

"I hope so," he said.

After Maddy and I finished eating, I said, "We're saving two ghost pizzas for you tonight. You are coming, aren't you?"

"I'm not sure," he said. "You know my hours."

Paul was up and working at a time when most folks were fast asleep, and I knew he rarely stayed up past eight at night.

"Surely you can make an exception," Maddy said. "You were at the Blowout last year."

"How could you possibly remember that?" he asked.

"You were a skeleton," I said, suddenly remembering the dancing bones of his costume, perfect for his tall and lanky frame.

"Very good. And you didn't dress up at all."

"Guilty," I said.

"Why the change?"

I was about to respond when Maddy waved her wand in the air, sending out little bits of glitter everywhere. "Haven't you heard, Paul? There's magic in the air today."

I stared at the glitter now scattered all over the floor. "Don't worry, we'll clean that up."

Paul just laughed. "Leave it right where it is. It complements the hay, don't you think? Happy Halloween, ladies."

"To you, too," we replied, nearly in unison.

When we left him, Paul was retrieving hay and stuffing it back into his shirt, a perfect scarecrow if ever there was one.

* * *

The lunch session at the Slice went fine, and I was pleased enough with my costume to come out every now and then to show it off, and to see what my fellow residents of Timber Ridge had managed to come up with. There were a few ghosts, goblins, witches, and zombies mixed in with a politician's mask and a few from movies I'd never seen, but I was surprised by such a light turnout. The air was festive, and I knew most folks were getting excited about the Blowout later that night. I kept watching the door, hoping that David would come through, but he must have still been interviewing candidates for the branch manager's job.

Maddy caught me looking once and said, "You could always call him and say hi, you know."

"Call who?"

"Don't play dumb with me, Sis. David will be here tonight."

"I know that," I said, pretending to be offended by her statement, but I wasn't fooling either one of us.

As the day went on, I realized that the lunch crowd was never going to reach our normal sales level for the day, and I knew that we'd be giving food away later by donating the proceeds to charity instead of keeping any of it for ourselves. It wouldn't do much for my bottom line, but Halloween was one of the few days of the year that I didn't watch my income so closely. I was in the spirit of things, and I wasn't about to let a little slow business get to me.

At least, not until Maddy reminded me of the real reason we weren't selling nearly as much as we were used to.

"It's not hurting us as much as I thought it would," she said. "At least not so far, anyway."

"What's that?"

"Eleanor, have you honestly forgotten? Gina is opening Italia's today."

It had truly slipped my mind, though I had no idea how that could have happened. "We still had our share of customers today," I said.

"That's because she doesn't officially open until tonight," Maddy said. "At least we weren't completely deserted, which is what I've been afraid of since we found out she was going ahead with the grand opening."

I glanced at the clock and saw that we still had half an hour before we were due to close the pizzeria for our break. "Maddy, this place is dead. Let's go ahead and shut down so we can check her place out and see how things are going over there."

"I've been waiting for you to suggest that for the last hour," she said as she quickly flipped our sign to CLOSED.

"I'll do even better than that," I said. "Tell you what, let's go right now. The dishes can wait until later."

"Are the paint fumes from the swatches I brushed on your face getting to you?" Maddy asked as she stared into my eyes.

"No, I'm fine. Why do you ask?"

"It's not like you to leave a dirty dish unwashed before you leave, let alone a sink full of them."

"Hey, people can change." I felt as though I'd already proved that.

"So I see," she said.

"Do you want to go, or not?"

"I'm right behind you," she said.

I locked the door, hoping that we weren't alienating any of our customers. Then again, who would notice? The promenade had folks drifting around from shop to shop, and I knew that some of my fellow tenants were taking advantage of the day to offer excellent specials to their customers. I'd tried it myself years before, without a great deal of success. I supposed most folks didn't associate Halloween with pizza.

As I thought, Gina had a crowd out in front of Italia's, but it was smaller than I'd been expecting. I was about to resign myself to standing in line out front when she spotted Maddy and me waiting to get in.

"I'm surprised to see you here," she said. Gina was dressed in a peasant outfit with her cleavage exaggerated outward, and so much of her left thigh showing that she had to be chilled to the bone in the brisk October breeze. It was absolutely not a kid-friendly outfit, but most of the men around us didn't seem to mind.

"I didn't think you were opening up until this evening," I said.

"Midnight, as a matter of fact. Dramatic, isn't it?" She waved a hand in the air. "This is a dry run. We're offering some excellent deals to get the word out, and then we're going to close from four until we open again at midnight. I'm sending everyone home to rest. We're going to have a busy night."

"Good for you. We thought we'd come by and show our support," I said.

Maddy snorted beside me, but if Gina heard her, she chose to ignore it. "How sweet of you."

I pretended to look around. "Where's Nancy Thorpe? I haven't seen her all day."

Maddy took the bait. "Eleanor, we saw her leave town this morning, remember?"

Gina's face clouded up. "That woman is delusional. Did she tell you that I tried to kill her?"

"It came up," I said.

"Well, she tripped over those boat shoes of hers and I tried to grab her shoulder before she fell. The idiot pulled away from me, and she nearly took a tumble. It was just three steps."

"How did Nathan react?"

Gina looked angry enough to spit. "He took her side, of course, until she started babbling about making the pregnancy up to trick him. He changed his attitude after that, believe me."

"Then I guess she and her phantom baby are out of the will," I said.

Gina looked smug as she admitted, "Uncle Nathan's making the final revisions to his will even as we speak," she said. "He's planning on signing it either tonight or tomorrow."

"Leaving it all to you? You must be so pleased."

"I don't know what he's doing, but I'm happy that fraud was exposed for what she really was."

An elegantly dressed man in a tuxedo called out to Gina, who held up one hand. "I'll be there in a second." She turned to us and added, "Sorry, but duty calls. It's amazing how many people in Timber Ridge love pizza, isn't it?"

Maddy started to say something nasty in reply—
I could see it in her eyes—so I grabbed her arm
and squeezed it. She got the signal, so I said,
"Good luck."

Gina pointed at the customers still waiting to
get in as she said, "It's sweet of you to say that, but
clearly luck isn't a factor at all."

As she turned away, Maddy started after her, and
I was glad that I'd kept a grip on her arm.

"She's not worth it," I said.

"I don't know. You could be wrong about that."

"Maybe, but it's too late now. Gina's already
gone."

"Fine, you can let go of me now. Is there any
place in particular you'd like to go for lunch?"

"I've got an idea," I said. "I've suddenly lost my
taste for crowds. Why don't we go back to the Slice,
make something with way too many calories, and
shut the rest of the world out?"

"That's the best idea you've had in weeks,"
Maddy answered.

It was just too bad that's not how it ended up
working out.

When we got back to the pizzeria, someone was
waiting for us there. "Art, we were just about to
have a quiet lunch. Would you care to join us?" I
hadn't even glanced at Maddy for her permission
to make the invitation. She'd been holding Art in
contempt for too long, and I had a feeling if she
took the chance to know him, she might get to like
him as much as I did.

"I'm sorry to say that I don't have time for that

at the moment. Eleanor, I'm afraid there's something we need to discuss," he said.

"I'll go inside and get started on our pizza," Maddy said.

"This involves you as well," Art said. "You should hear it, too."

"Whatever it is, Eleanor can handle it." She disappeared inside before I had a chance to say anything else.

I turned to Art and said, "I'm sorry. I don't know what's gotten into her."

"That doesn't matter," he said. "You need to come with me."

"Why? Did something happen?"

"I had someone who owes me a favor watch your pizzeria," he said.

"Without telling me? Seriously? What happened to our trust?"

"I did it for you," he said patiently. "And you should be glad that I did. He caught someone trying to break in the minute you left." I felt a chill of ice run through me as he said it.

"Who was it?"

"It's the gentleman we discussed earlier, Jack Hanks. He's being detained in my car, and I thought you might like the opportunity to speak with him."

I could barely contain myself as I said, "Let me at him."

When we got to Art's car, his driver opened the door instantly. I slid inside, and Art joined us. Jack Hanks sat there sullenly against the opposite door, and he barely glanced my way as the door shut behind us.

"Explain yourself," Art said softly.

Jack looked as though he'd been slapped.

"I was looking for something to steal," he said.

"From me?" I asked. "I don't have anything of value to you."

"You have a cash register, don't you? I'm betting you don't lock your money up between your lunch and dinner shifts. Am I right?"

Art coughed lightly, and the man came instantly back in line. "Sorry," Jack said, obviously reined in.

"I never thought about it before," I admitted. I promised myself that I'd change that habit immediately. I couldn't afford to lose a day's lunch receipts, especially with Italia's off to such a good start.

"Why me, though? I'm not in your usual hunting ground, am I?"

When Jack didn't respond, Art tapped him lightly on the knee. It was as though the touch was charged with high voltage. "Okay, there was more to it than that. You were making life unhappy for my friend."

"Which friend is that, Gina or Lacy?"

"Trust me, Gina's no friend of mine," he said sullenly.

"I thought you two were dating," I said.

"Off and on, but she wanted more expensive things than I could give her, and her nagging was driving me nuts, so I broke it off with her."

Somehow I doubted his spin on their breakup, but that didn't concern me at the moment. "So, that's when you took up with Lacy."

"It wasn't like that," he said. "We've been friends

since grade school. We watched out for each other when nobody else would."

I nodded. He was there to defend a friend's honor, a worthy duty that had been performed badly. "So you decided to make me pay for my meddling. Did *you* call me in the middle of the night?"

He nodded. "For all the good it did me. You wouldn't give up, so I thought I'd teach you a lesson the hard way."

I couldn't believe how cooperative he was being, so I decided to ask him the most important question of all. If I could confirm Lacy's story in front of Art Young, I knew that he had to be telling the truth. The consequences of being caught lying were clearly too much for the man to take. "Where were you the night of Judson's murder?"

"I was in Charlotte clubbing with Lacy after her doctor's appointment, and that's the truth."

I turned to Art. "Can that be confirmed?"

"It already has. They were both where they said they were."

I nodded. "It's fine, then."

"Is there anything else you'd like to ask him?" Art asked.

I was suddenly sick of the man's presence. "No, I'm finished with him."

Art nodded. "Very good. Why don't you go back to the Slice and join your sister for lunch?"

I didn't like the tone of his voice. "What's going to happen to him?" I asked as I gestured to Jack Hanks.

Art laughed softly, but there wasn't an ounce of humor in it. "You don't have to worry about him.

He'll never bother either of you again after he's shown the error of his ways."

I couldn't allow that to happen, no matter how I felt about this creep. "Please, I don't want him hurt, not on my account."

Art shook his head. "Eleanor, you do realize that he tried to rob you less than an hour ago, don't you?"

"I'm asking as a favor to me."

Art nodded, though it was clear it was a reluctant agreement. He turned to Jack Hanks and said, "You may go, but remember this. You owe this woman a great favor, and the best way you can repay it is to forget you ever met her. Do you understand?"

"Yes, sir," he said quickly.

"Then go."

He left so quickly I thought the door's hinges were going to snap off as it bolted open.

After Jack was gone, Art said, "I'm not sure compassion was the right instinct to have just then."

"Sorry, but it's all I've got. Thanks for looking out for me."

"It was no trouble at all," he said.

"Now, I would like to repeat my invitation. Would you like to have lunch with Maddy and me? Your driver can come, too, and we can make it a party."

"Thank you, but we have obligations elsewhere. Enjoy Halloween. By the way, I like your costume."

In all honesty, I'd forgotten that I was wearing it. "Thanks. Bye. And Happy Halloween to you, too."

I got out of the car, and it quickly drove away. I wouldn't have trusted Jack Hanks to tell me the truth without Art's presence, but I felt pretty good about what I'd been told. I sincerely doubted that he'd dare lie to my friend, and that meant that I could strike two more names off my suspect list. I wondered if Chief Hurley was doing any better than that, but I had to doubt it. It wasn't entirely his fault, though. I wasn't bound by any rules or regulations regarding my conduct. He didn't have the resources I had at my disposal. True, he had computers, databases, and experts at his finger-tips, but I had something just as vital, sources I could tap that he could never touch.

In all honesty, I didn't care who caught the killer, as long as one of us did before they could ever strike again.

Chapter 18

"There's somebody here to see you," Maddy said as I worked at forming the last of the spooky little ghost pizzas for later that night. We were just about to officially close for the evening so I could finish making the treats we'd be selling at the dance. They'd stay warm in the sleeves we had for delivering pizza, and that way I wouldn't be tied up in the kitchen all night and miss out on all the fun.

I wiped my hands on my apron. "That sounds great. Why don't you send him back?"

"What makes you think it's a man?" she asked.

"I'm just guessing," I said. "At least there's a fifty–fifty chance that I'm right."

Maddy grinned at me, enjoying torturing me a little when the opportunity presented itself. "Sorry, you chose the wrong half. It's Karen Green."

"Tell her to come on back," I said.

Maddy looked surprised. "Really? Into your kitchen? Are you sure? I didn't think you liked anyone back here but friends and family."

"It's Halloween. Let's live a little."

"Okay, I'll ask her."

A minute later the door opened again, and Karen stuck her head in. She was dressed in some kind of long burgundy robe, with a flickering light coming out of her tall hat.

"Come on in," I said as I formed another ghost. "I won't bite."

"If you're sure it's okay," she said as she took a few tentative steps in.

"Yes, I'm pretty certain I won't bite you."

"That's not what I meant," she said as her cheeks reddened a little.

"I know that. Thanks for coming." I studied her costume, and then said, "You're not a princess or a wizard, I know that much."

"That's more than anyone else has been able to come up with," she said.

"Hang on, I'll get it." I took in the entire ensemble, wondering how the flickering candle matched the rest of her outfit. That's when I got it.

"You're a giant candle, aren't you?"

"Bravo," she said.

"I love the Christmas light on top," I said.

"I like your painter's costume, too," she replied.

"It's not so much a costume as something I wear when I'm painting," I admitted.

"The streaks of paint on your face really sell it, though."

I had to laugh at that. "I'd like to take credit for it, but it was Maddy's idea." I looked at the notebook in her hand and asked, "Did you have any luck?"

"Some," she said. "I'm going to need more time,

but I do have it narrowed to the Parsons branch of Nathan's family. There was a streak where the men had only daughters, so the Sizemore name was absorbed into the Parsons family and the Harpers along the way. I'm fairly certain I'll be able to find something more specific for you in a few days. I hope that's good enough for now."

I thought about the Parsons and Harpers who'd been around Timber Ridge, but for the life of me, I couldn't think of any descendents still in town. I hoped it wasn't a dead end, for Nathan's sake, at least.

"Thanks so much," I said. "I appreciate what you're doing."

"No need to thank me," she said. "I love this kind of thing." Karen looked around the kitchen, and then said, "Sorry I can't stay longer, but I have things to do before tonight's Blowout."

"I know exactly what you mean," I said.

After she was gone, I struck another suspect off my list. If a wizard at genealogy like Karen couldn't track Nathan's relative down, there was a very good chance that even if the person was still alive, they most likely had no idea that they were related to the land baron.

That left just two suspects on my list: Nathan himself, and his niece, Gina. The more I thought about it, I had to believe that Gina had killed her own brother for the sake of a bigger stake of potential inheritance. It was going to take patience on her part to wait until her uncle died, but she didn't have any competition left to take any of her ill-gotten gains.

Then another thought struck me. What if she

wasn't in the mood to wait? Nathan had reported that he'd had a near miss on his lawn mower, and if Nancy was to be believed, Gina had had a hand in her near tumble down the steps. Also, Gina had taken great pride in announcing that Nathan was in the process of finalizing the changes to his will,

My heart started beating like a hummingbird's wings. I felt that if I didn't act immediately, my new friend wouldn't have a chance. He could be dead before the clock struck midnight if he'd already signed the papers for his new will.

I came rushing out front to find that Greg and Josh had already left for the festivities.

"Come on, Maddy. We need to go," I said.

"What happened?" my sister asked me as she dropped the broom she'd been sweeping with.

"Gina killed Judson, and now she's going to go after Nathan." I explained my logic to her, and she didn't question my explanation. "Where do we go, though? They could be at Nathan's house, or there's a chance he's at Italia's."

"We could go check out Italia's together," she said, "and then go to Nathan's to make sure he's all right."

"There's no time," I said as I grabbed my jacket. "I don't like it, but we're going to have to split up."

Maddy nodded. She had no problem with making quick decisions, something else I'd always admired about her. "I'll take the house, you take the pizza place, and we'll meet back here if we both draw a blank."

As I locked the door behind us, I said, "Be careful."

"Right back at you," she said.

Italia's was closed, Gina had told me that it would be, but I knew the back way in.

As I moved to the rear entrance, I thought I caught a glimpse of someone inside. Their door, unlike ours, had its own window in back, and I saw a flicker of light come through the frosted window. I wanted to turn and run for help with every fiber of my being, but I knew if I didn't distract the murderer, it might be too late.

It took me a moment, but that's when I realized that the murderer wasn't Gina, or Nathan, either. I knew it without a doubt now.

And as the pieces fell into place, I was amazed that I hadn't seen it before.

I tried the doorknob, and was relieved to find it was unlocked. I hoped that would be the murderer's mistake that ended up unraveling the entire plot to gain Nathan's fortune. As I crept in, I could see that Gina was in the kitchen, her face pale, even under the makeup. There was a fire in the wood-fired oven, and a few logs waiting to be fed into the mouth of the fireplace.

"Eleanor Swift," she said, darting her eyes quickly to the right, "what are you doing here?"

"I came to see if you needed any help," I said as I looked around for the killer.

Gina was trying to signal me, and I realized that she was looking steadily into the dining room as she spoke. "Thanks, but I'm just finishing up. I'm about to go home myself."

"I'll walk you out," I said, motioning her toward the door with my hand.

She shook her head. "Thanks, but I've got it covered." She mouthed the words, *Go get help* to me, but I refused to leave.

"I don't mind pitching in," I said. "Then we can go to the dance together."

"I can't," she said, the tears thick in her eyes.

I knew there had to be something that the killer was using to hold her there, and if I left them alone, Gina would most likely be dead by the time I got back with reinforcements. It was a chance I couldn't take.

It was time to end this charade.

Taking a deep breath, I called out, "Karen, I know you're in there. You might as well come out."

Karen Green stepped out of the shadows, pulling her hat off and throwing it to the ground as she walked, shattering the flickering bulb on top. "You just couldn't leave well enough alone, could you, Eleanor? I knew I should have taken care of you when I had the chance."

"First things first. Let me have your cell phone," she commanded as one hand came out of her robe holding a handgun.

I had been trying to call Maddy on speed dial, but that wasn't going to happen now. I tossed her my phone, purposely underthrowing it in an effort to get her to lean too far toward me, but she surprised me by stepping forward and plucking it out of the air. With a quick glance at that exposed pizza oven's fire, she flipped it into the opening, and I saw it melt from the sudden and intense heat.

When Karen turned back to me, she asked, "How did you know I was behind it all, Eleanor?"

"A lot of things started falling into place," I said. "You were too eager to help me, and the courses you were taking finally clicked in my mind."

She smiled. "You picked up on that, did you? You're smarter than I gave you credit for."

"What are you talking about?" Gina asked, her voice filled with fear.

"Patience," Karen said, and then turned to me. "I never dreamed I'd given you too much information. Most people don't listen at all when I talk. It was your bad luck to be one of the few who do."

"What classes?" Gina asked.

Karen explained as though she were talking to a child. "I took an auto repair class, and I learned how to disable Nathan's brakes on his mower. The mechanism is easy once you know how a car works."

"It was premature, though, wasn't it?" I said. "You nearly killed Nathan while Gina was still alive."

Karen didn't like me pointing out the flaw in her plan. "How could I have known he'd use his riding mower to blow the leaves into piles? If he'd waited till spring, my plan would have worked beautifully."

Gina was starting to see how insane Karen really was. "When were you going to kill me?"

"After a suitable period, you were going to have an accident, but then that all changed when I saw Nathan coming out of Bob Lemon's office. I knew that I was almost out of time, but it's still going to work out just fine. Imagine how appropriate it will be for you to die where your brother passed away.

He turned his back on me, and it was so easy to hit him from behind with that chunk of wood, I could barely believe my good fortune."

"How was I going to die?" Gina was breathless as she waited for the answer.

"I wasn't sure, but most likely it would be some kind of suicide. I should have taken a nursing class; maybe you could have overdosed on something."

I couldn't believe this woman. "So, you used the community college system to plan your rampage. What were the other classes for?"

She smiled as she said, "The law class was to help me figure out how to beat Nathan's will, and the money management was so that I'd know what to do when I inherited it all."

"There's one thing I don't understand, though," Gina said incredulously. "Why should he leave anything to you?"

Karen grinned at me, but there wasn't a great deal of sanity in it. "Do you want to tell her, or should I?"

I didn't want to give her the satisfaction. "Gina, this is Karen Green, your long-lost cousin, and another of your uncle's heirs."

Karen laughed. "You are very clever, Eleanor. I thought I hid the truth rather well today, but clearly I was mistaken."

"You almost had me, and then I remembered the last Parsons I knew. She taught me in kindergarten, and I'd almost forgotten her. We always called her Miss Garnet, but she was your aunt, Garnet Parsons, wasn't she?"

"You actually remembered," Karen said. "Not

many folks even knew her last name around here when her teaching name became so accepted."

I had to keep her talking. I knew if I could stall her long enough, Maddy would realize that the house was a dead end and everything was happening at Italia's. "You must have been shocked when Gina and Judson showed up on the scene."

"I didn't know they existed any more than Nathan realized that we were related," she agreed. "He'd filed a copy of his will to preapprove his probate, and I stumbled on it after I discovered that we were related." She looked disgusted as she added, "I was going to be rich until those two showed up."

Gina turned on her. "That's why you killed my brother? For money?"

"Don't act like you're so holy, Gina," she said. "You got Nathan to pay off your debt, so it's not like you weren't getting anything out of it, either. We're not that different, when you get right down to it." She looked around the restaurant. "This place had to cost a fortune too, so I knew that I had to get rid of you before you spent what was rightfully mine."

"Yours? He doesn't even know who you are. Are you completely insane?"

"Don't call me that," she snapped. "I'm not crazy. I fooled all of you, didn't I?"

I nodded. "Nobody thinks you're crazy," I said calmly.

"Speak for yourself," Gina said. That woman didn't know when it was in her best interest to keep her mouth shut.

"What are you planning to do with us?" I asked her.

She shook her head sadly. "I'm sorry, but you know too much, Eleanor, and she's in the way of my inheritance. There's no other way around it. You're both going to have to die."

"Let's not be hasty here. You can have it all. I'll sign whatever you want me to, just don't kill me."

Karen seemed to consider it for a moment, and then said sadly, "Sorry, I can't trust you with the truth."

"How about me?" I asked, trying to distract her long enough for Maddy to go to Nathan's, then realize that she was in the wrong place and come to Italia's, hopefully with reinforcements. "Where are you going to get the pizza you like so much if you get rid of me?"

"I'll be sorry to miss you, but Maddy's getting better at it every day. She might not be as good as you are, but she'll get there."

While she'd been talking to me, I'd seen Gina slowly reach back toward the fire for one of the burning logs. I wasn't sure how she planned to grab it without scorching her own hand, but I had to keep Karen distracted long enough to give her time to do something. It was the only real chance we had.

"Don't kid yourself, Karen," I said. "Maddy will close the place down if something happens to me."

"I won't let her do that," Karen shouted. "Stop saying things I don't like."

It was time for me to act.

I yelled, "Karen, look out. Chief Hurley's going to shoot you!"

As Karen spun around to see a man who wasn't there, it was the opportunity Gina was waiting for. With no hesitation whatsoever, she reached into the fire, screamed as the flames hit her hand, and retrieved a burning log quickly enough to hurl it at Karen.

It was one of the bravest things I'd ever seen in my life, even if it was done out of a sense of pure self-preservation.

As the log flew through the air, Karen whirled around and fired a shot at Gina. She went down, but there was nothing I could do for her. The only thing I could think of was to make sure that her sacrifice wasn't in vain. The wood hit Karen's chest, and as she struggled to put out the flames licking at her robe, the gun flew out of her hands.

The log wasn't finished with its purpose, though. A nearby tablecloth caught fire as the log rolled past it and ended up wedged against the heavy fabric of the curtains.

I didn't have a second to waste. I jumped toward the gun, but Karen was too fast for me, and too close to it. Ignoring the flames leaping up her robe, she grabbed for the weapon, and I fought to get control of it.

"You're burning up," I said as the heat of the robe hit my face. I could feel the hairs on the back of my hand start to burn from the proximity of the flames, and yet she was still fighting me. How could she take the pain? "Let go, Karen, or you're going to die."

"Not today," she said as she kept wrestling me for the gun. Where was she getting this strength? No matter what the source, I knew she couldn't keep ignoring the pain forever.

My life boiled down to getting control of that gun, regardless of what was going on around me. I could see the flames and smoke begin to fill the restaurant, but I refused to let go.

I was starting to wonder if any of us would make it out alive when I finally got control of the gun.

As I pointed it at her, Karen finally realized what was happening to her. She began to scream, ripping at the robe in an effort to get it off her. I ran to the nearest fire extinguisher to try to help her, but as I grabbed it and turned it upside down, I looked up just in time to see Karen swing a chair at my head. If I hadn't stepped back at the last second, I knew in my heart that I would have been hit.

I ducked, and the strike was so close that I could feel it knock my painter's cap off. Without another thought, I shot her in the face, not with the gun, but with the fire extinguisher, and then I put her clothes out once she was down on the ground.

I stood there staring at her for a few seconds, wondering what I should do next. In a heartbeat, I knew that there was only one thing I could do. I wasn't about to save myself and abandon the woman who had tried to save me. If Gina had the slightest chance of surviving, I was going to see that she got the opportunity.

I rushed to Gina's side to see if there was anything I could do to help her, worried that I was too late.

As I knelt down beside her, I saw that her arm was burned, and one shoulder was leaking blood. I started to cry when I saw her eyelids flutter, and then she looked at me. "Where is she?"

"She can't hurt you anymore," I said.

"Thanks," Gina said.

I started to get up, when she grabbed my hand. "Don't leave me."

"I'll be right back. I need to get something to put on your shoulder." I ran to a table and grabbed a cloth napkin that was untouched by the fire. I planned to carry her out of there if I had to, but I didn't want her to bleed to death as I did.

I pressed it against her shoulder, and she winced in pain.

"Sorry," I said, "but I'm getting you out of here."

"Save yourself," she said softly as the flames began to lick around us.

"You helped me," I said. "Now it's my turn."

As I thought about carrying her out of there, I realized there was no way I could do that. The front of the restaurant was now engulfed in flames. If we were going to make it, we had to go out the back way.

"This is going to hurt," I said as I reached under her arms and started to drag her out the back.

I knew I had to be hurting her, but there was nothing I could do about it. As we made our way back into the kitchen where the flames hadn't expanded yet, I started to feel the heat slacken. It gave me strength to keep going, but I wasn't sure we were going to make it before the flames or smoke overtook us. I was exhausted from the ordeal, but I forced myself forward, until we reached the door.

I was about to open it when the door burst open and Timber Ridge's volunteer fire department came rushing in.

To my surprise, the first set of hands that reached me were David Quinton's. It appeared that he'd thrown himself after them in search of me without the least bit of regard for his own safety. I was just glad I'd been able to meet him at the back door.

As he helped me outside, paramedics began working on Gina immediately. I'd done all I could. Now it was in their hands.

David helped me to my feet as he said, "Eleanor, you're okay." As promised, he was dressed as a gangster pirate, with billowing clothes, a plastic sword at his side, and a fedora instead of a head-band.

"I survived it, anyway," I said, coughing from the sting of the smoke in my lungs.

After a nearby paramedic gave me some water, he asked, "Are you okay?"

"I'll be fine," I said as the water instantly soothed my ragged throat.

"I don't know about that, but you'll do for now."

I looked at David and asked, "How did you know I was here?"

"Maddy called me when she couldn't get you on your cell phone. What happened to it?"

I pointed toward billowing flames still burning inside. "Karen threw it in there."

"Don't worry, we'll get you a new one."

"That doesn't matter. Nothing does, right now."

I felt the cool night air envelope me. The smoke and fire had taken their toll on me, and I felt myself weaken at the knees.

David was there, and he grabbed me before I could fall.

And to be honest, I didn't mind, not one bit.

He looked a little shy all of a sudden. "Sorry about that."

"Why are you apologizing for keeping me from falling?"

I looked up at him, and wondered why it had taken me so long to see what had been right in front of me all along.

He must have seen something in my eyes. "I'm afraid it's a little too late for me," he said solemnly. "I fell a long time ago."

And then he kissed me.

I had to admit—even with my shortness of breath—it managed to steal the last bit of breath away from me.

It had been worth waiting for.

Chapter 19

I was still trying to catch my breath when Bob interrupted by grabbing us both wildly. "Maddy's not in there, is she?" He was dressed as a king, with royal robes and a crown. The man was nearly in tears, and I could see that his legs were fighting to keep him standing.

I turned to look at the firefighters still battling the flames inside.

I was about to tell him that my sister was safe when two EMS personnel put the gurney that Gina was on into a waiting ambulance.

"It's her," Bob said as he started toward Gina.

"It's not Maddy. She's safe," I said as another coughing fit overtook me.

Bob looked at me and then the gurney as they moved it into the ambulance. "Are you sure?"

"I'm positive," I managed to say.

That's when Maddy appeared, so delicately beautiful in her costume, looking as though she'd just stepped out of a fairy tale. "Eleanor, are you okay?"

I didn't get a chance to answer as Bob cried out, "You're all right!" sweeping her up into his arms as he said it.

"Of course I am," she said, fighting his embrace. "I wasn't anywhere near the fire. Put me down."

After he did as she asked, my sister looked at me and asked, "Eleanor, you look rough."

"I'm a little tired, but I'll be fine," I said, and then I coughed some more.

A second gurney came out of Italia's, and there was no mistaking the scorched robe that Karen had been wearing. I wondered if she would be able to survive the ordeal she'd caused, but her welfare wasn't my concern anymore. She'd abused our relationship and had tried to kill me. What happened to her next didn't matter.

"Was Nathan all right when you got there?" I asked her.

"He was a little startled when I burst through the door, but it didn't take me long to bring him up to speed."

"Yeah, about that. I was wrong. Gina was innocent." I wanted to tell them all how heroic she'd been, but I didn't have the breath to say any of it.

Maddy nodded. "We figured that out, too. Too many classes Karen took pointed the finger at her, didn't it?"

"Sis, you listened to me?"

"I hear more than you might think," she said with a smile.

Nathan finally joined us, his hair disheveled and a wild look in his eyes. "Where's Gina? Is she alive?"

"She got burned and shot in there," I said, my

voice quickly fading. I had to get the rest of it out before it was gone completely. "They took her away in an ambulance. Nathan, she put herself in harm's way trying to save us both."

"She's a Sizemore, isn't she?" he said proudly. "I'm going to go see her."

"We'll give you a ride," David said.

"Why are we going to the hospital?" I asked him.

David looked into my eyes and said firmly, "Because you need to be seen by a doctor, and I won't take no for an answer."

Everyone looked at me, waiting for some kind of reaction, but all I did was smile. "You know what? That sounds like a good idea."

Maddy said, "Don't worry about the food, Eleanor. Greg and Josh can sell the ghost pizzas."

"Okay," I said as one of the paramedics finally got around to me.

I squeezed David's hand and said, "Sorry about that dance I owe you."

He laughed a little too loudly as he answered, "There will be plenty of time for that later."

As they put me on a gurney, I thought about insisting that I could ride to the hospital with everyone else, but it was just starting to hit me.

I'd nearly died in there and, at least for the moment, I was done taking chances.

I was cleared by the hospital personnel after a thorough examination, and I changed into some fresh jeans and a T-shirt that Maddy had picked up from my place on the way over. They all insisted that I go home and go straight to bed, but I wasn't going anywhere until I found out how Gina was doing. I heard one of the doctors say that she'd been lucky. They'd brought in extra staff for Halloween mishaps, so she went to the head of the line.

Kevin Hurley came in a little later, and sat down beside me. "You okay?"

"I think so," I said.

"Karen Green, huh?"

"Yes." Neither one of us were spending many words with each other, me because every syllable seemed to hurt, and him because our chief of police was reticent by nature.

He nodded, then said, "I'll need a statement."

"Later," I said.

"Good enough." He turned to go, and then said, "Glad you're okay."

I grinned over at David, who had been watching us the entire time.

"Me, too," I said.

The doctors came in ten minutes later and talked to Nathan briefly.

I held my breath as I waited for him to fill us in. Nathan was crying when he turned to us, and I prepared myself for the worst.

"She's going to be all right," he said. "The bullet didn't hit anything vital, and as soon as she's discharged, she's coming back home with me. That's where family belongs: together."

I couldn't agree with him more.

There would be plenty of time tomorrow to deal with what had happened, but for now, I had just one goal in life, and that was to share a dance with David Quinton.

There was music playing over the loudspeakers, and I offered my hand to him.

He didn't get it at first. "Do you need some help standing up?"

I just smiled at him. "No. I want that dance."

He grinned at me as he pulled me into his arms. "I can do that."

As we moved slowly in time with the music, he said, "Sorry it's not the Halloween Blowout."

"I'm not," I said. "This is better."

As we danced on, he said, "You know what? You're right."

Tonight might have marked the end of the month, but in my life, it was the perfect time for a new beginning.

It didn't take a wall of flames to tell me it was time to tear down the last of the walls protecting my heart and let someone else in.

I'd come too close to dying not to take advantage of every second I had left.

It was a gift I meant to cherish every chance I got.

My Very Own Version of Deep Dish Pizza

I know that Chicagoans are justifiably proud of their deep dish pizza, but living in the South as I do, it's not always easy to come by. Over the years, I've created my own version of deep dish pizza, and I've found that it takes the edge off of any hunger! The crust tastes like a blend of pizza crust and biscuit to me, and the layering of desired toppings are varied enough to suit just about anyone's taste.

Since I don't claim to be an expert, I've substituted an eight-inch square baking pan for the standard deep dish pan, but a cake pan will do just as nicely. Also, I put just one layer of toppings, the way my family likes, but if you're in the mood to eat, by all means add another layer to the pie!

½ cup warm water
⅛ ounce active dry yeast (½ packet or 1 teaspoon;
   I like the pizza dough yeast)
2 tablespoons extra virgin olive oil
2 teaspoons table salt
3–4 cups bread flour, sifted with salt

In a large mixing bowl, combine the warm water and yeast, stirring it in until it dissolves. Next, add the olive oil and mix briefly. Now add 2 cups of the sifted flour and the table salt, and mix until it's all incorporated. Slowly add more flour until the dough loses some of its stickiness. You can do this in a mixer with a dough hook as well.

On a floured surface, turn out the dough and incorporate more flour until the dough loses its tackiness. Knead the dough just long enough to incorporate the flour.

In a bowl that's coated with cooking spray, drop the ball of dough in, spray it, and then cover it with plastic wrap. It needs time to rise to double its original shape, which can take from one to four hours. I like to put the bowl in the oven with just the light on. This keeps it out of the draft and also allows enough warmth.

As it rises, prep the other ingredients, which follow on the next page.

My Very Own Deep Dish Pizza
Filling and Topping

Note about my ingredient list

This is based on personal preference, and will depend on what you like on your pizza. It's also important to note that the amounts given are all approximate. Making your own pizza should be a fun experience, so I don't like to put too much emphasis on exact amounts when I'm adding my toppings. In fact, sometimes I make a "garbage" pizza for my family with whatever meats and cheeses are available in the fridge that night!

½ pound sausage, mild or hot, out of casing
1 tablespoon butter
3 tablespoons olive oil
4–8 slices mozzarella cheese
2–4 ounces Romano cheese, grated
2–4 ounces parmesan cheese, shaved or grated
4–6 mushrooms, sliced
12–18 pepperoni rounds
1 green bell pepper
1 small onion, white or yellow
1 jar pizza sauce, 8–14 ounces, depending on taste

While the dough is rising, I like to prep my filling. Mild sausage is a favorite at my house—but hot will do just as well—so I take 2 sausage links, about half a pound's worth, and squeeze them out of their casing into a skillet, heated to medium. I use turkey sausage, so a little olive oil helps the browning process. After the sausage is browned, I put it on a paper towel, clean out the skillet, and then add 2 tablespoons of olive oil and 1 tablespoon of butter. Once the butter's melted, I add 4 or 5 sliced mushrooms and let them sauté until golden. After that, I add 1 small coarsely chopped onion and green pepper, and sauté them a little longer in the pan.

When the dough has risen, turn it out onto a floured board and start shaping it for your pan's general size. Spray the pan with cooking spray, then coat it lightly with cornmeal so the pizza will release. Place the dough into the pan, and then shape it until it comes 1–1½ inches up the side of the pan.

Add a layer of sliced mozzarella to cover the crust, and then put the cooled sausage directly onto the cheese. Next, add pepperoni rounds and then a dusting of Romano cheese. After that, layer the vegetables sautéed earlier, then add pizza sauce from the jar. This is a matter of taste, so add as much—or as little—as you like. After that, add a covering of Romano cheese, and then finish it up with the parmesan cheese. I like the flakes because of their texture when they melt, but grated works just as well.

Cooking time varies for many reasons, but my general rule is to preheat the oven to 450ºF and let the pizza bake for 40–55 minutes, depending on the amount of toppings, the thickness of the dough, etc. I always set the timer for 25 minutes the first time, turn the pizza in the oven, and then check it every 5 minutes after that. When the crust is golden brown and the cheese is melted and has started to brown, I take the pizza out and put it on a cooling rack for 5 minutes before we eat. This helps the juices of the pizza reincorporate into the pie.

After that, serve the pizza in thick slices, and enjoy!

Yield: The dough above makes one eight-inch square pan pizza, with a little left over.

Cozy towns like Timber Ridge, North Carolina—the home of Eleanor Swift's delectable pizzeria, A Slice of Delight—don't take well to prima donna celebrities. So no one is particularly pleased when TV host and famous chef Antonio Benet roars into town for a book signing and manages to insult Eleanor, her deliciously saucy sister Maddie, and everyone else within earshot. Insults are one thing, however . . . but a cold dish of murder is quite another . . .

Eleanor knows she's on the menu of suspects who would bury a kitchen knife between the rolling-in-dough chef's shoulders. But so is Beth, the owner of the bookstore, who may have some deep secrets to dish. Or Benet's personal assistant, who very well may have had it with pampering his blowhard boss . . . and may even have some pie-in-the-sky ambitions of his own. And then there's the TV producer—is it true the crusty chef was bellowing about going to another network before he reached his premature expiration date?

With her freedom—and even her looking-good-for-a-minute-there love life—on the chopping block, Eleanor's got a seriously full plate. The only way out of this mess is a pretty tall order: deliver the real killer before she finds a knife in *her* back.

Please turn the page for an exciting sneak peek of Chris Cavender's REST IN PIZZA coming next month!

Chapter 1

At first glance through the large front window of A Slice of Delight, it looked as though the person inside the pizzeria was simply sitting at a table in the dining area, waiting patiently for food to be delivered.

But the pizzeria wasn't open yet and wouldn't be for hours.

A closer look revealed the chef's knife stuck all the way to its handle through the victim's chest, pinning the patron upright in place to the back of the chair, like a butterfly in a collector's case.

The murder weapon, taken straight from the kitchen but never before used in such a grim and dreadful fashion, was one all too familiar to the owner of A Slice of Delight.

There was no movement, no sound, no life surrounding the victim.

Murder had come back to the sleepy little town of Timber Ridge, North Carolina, and despite the warmth of the day, its cold breath was having its way with the citizens there.

One Week Earlier

"How's the lunch crowd doing out there now? Are we going to be able to take our break anytime soon?" I impatiently asked my sister, Maddy Spencer, who also happened to be one of my employees. I'm Eleanor Swift, and I normally work the kitchen while she handles the dining room of my pizzeria, A Slice of Delight, located on the Square in the heart of Timber Ridge, North Carolina. My younger sister is tall, thin, and blonde, three things that with all certainty could never be used to describe me. Maddy had come to help out when my late husband, Joe, had been killed, and she had kept everything going until I'd been ready to face the world again, and much to my delight, she'd decided to stay.

"We're all good. Greg is the only one out there besides me, Eleanor," Maddy answered. Greg Hatcher, along with Josh Hurley, were our only other two employees at the time, and though we were pressed on occasion with such a small staff, it allowed me to run the pizzeria on a tight budget, keeping my expenses pared to the bone. We didn't deliver pizzas or sandwiches anymore as a general rule, but if the occasion merited it, and the income it generated was large enough, I'd been known to make an exception from time to time. We'd had some bad experiences in the past with our deliveries, and it was something I wasn't willing to take a chance on these days without a proportionally sized payoff on the other end.

I glanced at the clock and saw that we still had seven minutes until we were officially due to close for our one-hour break, but that was just too bad. For some reason I needed a break, and after all, if I couldn't change our hours whenever I wanted to as the boss, what good did all the headaches I got do that also came with the territory? "Go ahead and tell Greg to flip the sign and lock up," I said.

Maddy didn't wait around for me to second-guess myself as she bolted for the front with a grin on her face. She knew enough to take a golden opportunity like that when she saw it. Greg was a student at the local college, and Josh would be going even farther away himself soon. It meant that I'd be losing my connection to the nearby high school, and I always tried to keep at least one high schooler on the payroll all of the time, but for the two of them, I'd make an exception. I knew this "family" of employees wouldn't last forever, but I wasn't about to hurry the end of this particular era. That was the sad truth of it. Whether they were good, bad, or indifferent, no staff ever stayed the same. At least I had Maddy, a constant in my life since she'd first come to work for me.

Greg came into the back whistling and put his apron on the hook by the door. He was a big guy and could look fierce when he wanted to, but I knew that under that tough exterior was a gentle soul. "Thanks for the break, boss. You don't even have to pay me for the time I'm missing," he said with a smile.

The funny thing was, Greg had more money than I did. He'd come into an inheritance from his grandparents a while back, and I had worried that he'd leave me once he didn't need his job at the Slice anymore, but to my great delight, he'd decided to stay. The only thing that was really different about him was that he didn't have to scrounge food in my kitchen anymore, though that never stopped him from trying. Old habits died hard, I knew.

"Is there anything in this joint to eat?" Greg asked, reinforcing my last thought about him.

I looked around and said, "This is your lucky day. We've got a large cheese pizza nobody picked up, but I doubt it's any good now. It's been sitting there on the warming rack for awhile."

"How long has it been?" Greg asked, standing close to me. Sometimes I forgot just how tall and broad-shouldered he was, but it was pretty obvious when I had to look up to see into his eyes.

"I'd have to say at least forty minutes. Let me make you a new one before Maddy and I take off."

"No, it's fine," he said, grabbing up the box. "I like a pizza that's room temperature now and then. Good thing Josh is in class, or I'd be fighting him for it. I might grab a soda on the way out though, if you don't mind."

"Be my guest," I said.

Maddy came back just as I finished washing the last of the lunch dishes. Most days we made something at the Slice and ate right there, but today we were treating ourselves to a lunch out on the town. Well, Brian's Diner wasn't exactly high-class dining; it was actually more like a greasy spoon café, but at least it wasn't a pizza or a sub. As much as I loved what we offered at the Slice, sometimes I just had to get away, and Maddy was all for it, especially since I'd offered to treat.

"Let's roll, Eleanor. Aren't you ready yet?" she asked. "We don't want to miss our reservation."

I looked at her and smiled. "Since when did Mark Deacon require lunchtime reservations at Brian's?"

Maddy grinned at me. "He doesn't, but I'm hungry, and I didn't want to sound like a pig. Are you coming, or what?"

I had to laugh. "I'm right behind you. Do you want to drive, or should I?"

"I will," she said as she shucked off her apron and grabbed her purse. "No offense, but sometimes you drive like an old woman."

"How could I possibly take offense to that? It doesn't even apply to me, since I'm not all that old," I said.

"You're older than me," she said with a laugh. "That's really all that counts when it comes down to it, isn't it?"

I fought to hide my own grin as I double-checked everything. The conveyor oven was turned off, and the toppings were wrapped and stored in the refrigerator. "Did you grab the till from the cash register?"

She snapped her fingers in the air. "I knew I forgot something. I'll be right back."

We'd been robbed once before, which have given me enough incentive to install a safe from Slick's Hardware Store in our storeroom. Even with the generous discount my friend, Slick, had given me, it had still cost more money than I'd been comfortable spending, but in the end, I suppose that it was better than losing everything. "The money has to actually be in the safe for it to be protected, you know that, right?" I called out to her, not able to hide my laughter.

Maddy came back thirty seconds later, long enough for me to open the safe's door and make room for the cash till. As she slid it into place, I waited, then shut the door, spinning the dial twice for good luck.

"Now, who's ready to eat?" I asked. "I thought you were as ready as I was to get away for an hour." I glanced at my watch, and then amended, "Well, fifty-seven minutes, anyway."

Maddy arched an eyebrow. "Just for that, I'm going to order two specials. Especially since you're paying."

"Order whatever you'd like," I said with a grin, and then quickly added, "as long as our total bill isn't over twelve bucks."

"Is that with tip, or without?" she asked.

I grinned at her. "No, I'll cover the tip, too."

"Gee, Sis, you are all heart," she said.

"Come on, let's go before something comes up."

"Are you expecting anything to?" Maddy asked as we walked through the Slice, turning off lights as we went.

"I never expect it. That's why I'm always so surprised when something does," I admitted.

As I let us out the front door and locked it behind us, I nearly ran Cary Wilkes over. Cary owned a multi-state cleaning agency, but my ties to her were more personal than that. Her son, Rick, was away at college now, but he'd worked at the Slice before leaving home, and we'd become friends during his time at the pizzeria. Cary had been working on loosening her apron strings since he'd gone away, with admittedly marginal success so far, but clearly still not enough for Rick's taste.

"I'm sorry, Cary. I'd love to stay and chat, but we're closed for lunch, and Maddy and I have someplace we need to be," I said. There was no way I was going to work through our lunchtime, not even for a friend. My sister and I hadn't had a real break for the past several days, but I'd grown too used to the time off in the middle of the day since we'd implemented it to ever go back to our old hours. Most days it gave us all a nice hour away from the pizzeria, but sometimes we had to use it for sleuthing. Maddy and I were crackerjack amateur investigators, but only when the crimes involved us. The rest of the time, we did our best not to poke our noses into other people's problems. We managed to have enough on our own.

"Don't worry, I already ate," she said as she pulled a large envelope from her purse. "Rick wanted me to give this to you. I didn't even realize that it was your birthday, Eleanor."

"It's not for another two weeks," I said, taking the card from her. I slid it into my back pocket, something that clearly disappointed Cary. From the intent look on her face, it was clear that she was curious about what it said inside.

"Aren't you going to open it?" she asked eagerly.

"I will, but not until my birthday," I said with a smile.

"That's the way the Spencers do it," Maddy said. "No cards opened early, and no presents enjoyed until the thank-you notes have been written."

"The Swifts feel that way, too," I said, since I'd

implemented the rule right after marrying Joe. He'd thought I'd been joking at first, but it didn't take him long to realize that I hadn't been kidding, and he quickly indulged me.

Cary grinned despite her disappointment. "You two are a real pair, aren't you?"

"Jokers, maybe," Maddy said as she glanced over at me. "I'd say that's a good fit, wouldn't you?"

I decided her question really didn't need an answer, so I turned to Cary and asked, "How's Rick doing these days?"

"I'm not sure he's eating enough, or getting enough sleep," she admitted, the worry showing in her face instantly.

"I'm sure that he's fine, Cary," I said, patting her hand. "I'm just curious, but why didn't Rick send my card directly here to the Slice instead of sending through you? He knows my address."

Cary looked uncomfortable by the question, and I had a suspicion I knew why. I asked a little strongly, "You're still giving him space, aren't you?"

"Hey, I'm working on it," she said as her cell phone rang. As if arranged by providence, she started to answer it as she said to me, "Sorry, I've got to take this."

Cary was deep in conversation as she left us, and I had to wonder if some of it was so that she wouldn't have to address my question.

After she was out of sight, Maddy said, "I'm amazed Rick stayed close enough to Timber Ridge for his mom to drop in on him whenever she wants to. I figured he'd go to the school in Hawaii or Alaska."

"We should cut her some slack, Maddy. She

doesn't have anyone else, and Rick knows it. He wouldn't go very far away to be cruel. He loves her, even if she does have a tendency to smother him."

"Well, she should give Rick his space and get someone of her own," Maddy said. "After all, even we've both managed to do it."

I wasn't sure I liked the assumption in Maddy's statement. "Slow down there, Sister. I never said I had anyone in my life."

Maddy arched one eyebrow toward me as we walked down the promenade toward the shortcut to our parking area in back. "Really? What would David Quinton say if he heard you say that?"

David had courted me for years, to no avail, and then he'd left Timber Ridge to try to make a fresh start. When he'd come back later, he was a changed man, and if I were being honest about it, maybe I'd changed some, too, in the time that he was gone. I'd been so in love with my late husband, Joe, that I couldn't imagine anyone else in my life, but David had somehow managed to find his way in. We were taking it slow though—glacially, in Maddy's opinion—but I was letting him into my heart a little bit at a time, and it was honestly the best that I could do. "He'd understand. He knows how I feel about him." I turned to look at her and asked, "Speaking of men in our lives, how are you and Bob getting along these days?" Bob Lemon was an excellent local attorney, and the current object of my sister's affections. The question was fair game, since Maddy had been the one to bring our love lives into the conversation. After all, I figured that the more I could distract Maddy from asking questions about my private life, the better.

My sister didn't answer as quickly as I expected her to. "I'm not sure, to be honest with you."

That was an odd reply, even for her. "What do you mean?"

Maddy frowned, and then said, "I thought we were in a good place, but he's been acting kind of odd lately. Eleanor, we both know that I've been married more than a few times before, but I still can't figure that man out. You'd think I'd getter better with practice being around them."

"More than a few times? Did you just say that?" I asked with a grin.

"Okay, so it's four times, but who's counting?" Maddy asked.

"Not me," I said. "All I can think about right now is lunch."

"I'm right behind you."

As we walked down the promenade toward the shortcut together, I glanced back at A Slice of Delight. The previous occupant had painted the building mostly blue, and Joe and I had learned early on that it would have been prohibitively expensive to get rid of, so we'd kept it as is. I'd grown fond of it over the years, and doubted I would change it even if I could afford to now. We stood out among a cluster of shops and businesses, and really, what more could I ask for? The other buildings, normally sharing sidewalls and standing shoulder to shoulder, allowed a single break from the walls that touched on either side. Maddy and I used the bricked shortcut every time we came or left the pizzeria. In order to get there from the Slice, though, we had to pass several other shops along the way. One of the buildings, a now-defunct exclusive wine and cheese shop that had lasted just six months, had lost its previous sign of The Winey Husband and was now going to reopen as a bookstore, something the square sorely needed, in my opinion. Adding even more to our excitement, the new owner was a friend of ours named Cindy Rankin. Her husband had died unexpectedly, and she'd come into some money from an insurance policy that she hadn't even known he had. After a year spent mostly in mourning, Cindy had decided it was time to get on with her life. It had been her dream to own a bookstore someday, and despite a generally gloomy financial outlook, Cindy had gone for it.

I was about to comment on how brave she was to Maddy when the door of the bookshop opened, and Cindy herself came out.

"I'm so glad I ran into you two," she said. "I was just coming down to the Slice. I'm in trouble, and I desperately need your help."

"What's going on?" I asked Cindy as Maddy and I walked inside. Visions of our lunch out dissipated like morning mist. "It looks like you could open today."

The new bookstore was in great shape as far as I could tell, with row upon row of shelves made of polished cherry wood and filled with books. There were clever signs above each section, with categories written in script on large bookmarks hanging from the ceiling. One corner of the place was devoted exclusively to reading, with big comfy chairs and a fireplace giving the entire space a warm glow, and another nook housed a coffee counter and pastry display area. Soft music played in the background, and the only thing out of place was a stack of boxes near the register.

Cindy frowned as she looked around. "I wish. We're seven days away from opening, whether we're ready or not."

I couldn't imagine what else she might be hoping to do in that brief amount of time, but I remembered when Joe and I had first opened A Slice of Delight how I found myself constantly wishing that we had one more week. Joe had assured me that no matter how prepared we thought we were, that extra week would never come. The only way we'd managed to get everything right was actually opening our pizzeria for business. "What can we do to help?"

"I just got a call from a publicist from one of the big publishers. They want to feature one of their A-list writers for my grand opening."

"Is that actually a problem? It sounds like a wonderful opportunity," Maddy said as she picked up a mystery and started flipping through it. My sister was a nut for mysteries, and despite her brash and bold outward appearance, she favored cozies, especially craft-based and culinary mysteries above all else.

"You'd think so," Cindy said with a worried expression on her face, "but I don't know anything about cooking, especially Italian fare."

"Why should you have to?" I asked. "Leave that to the celebrity author. No one expects you to know how to cook or bake. After all, you're not making your own pastries, are you?"

"Of course not. Paul is supplying them."

"Good choice," I said. Paul was a good friend of

ours, and he happened to run the best bakery, Paul's Pastries, in our part of North Carolina. "He makes our sandwich rolls for us. Trust me, you won't be disappointed."

"I'm not worried about that," she said. "The problem is, they're sending Antonio Benet, and I understand he can be difficult at times."

"The guy from the Food for Thought Network?" Maddy asked.

Cindy nodded. "Have you seen his show?"

"I've watched it a few times," Maddy admitted. I knew she was addicted to all of the food-related channels on television.

"Then you'll be perfect," Cindy said with delight.

"For what?" Maddy asked, the suspicion clear in her voice.

"To help me," Cindy said after taking a lungful of air,. "Ladies, I hate to ask, but I need you both."

The poor girl looked as though she were about to collapse.

"What's your concern?" I asked.

"This," Cindy said as she thrust a sheaf of papers toward me. "The whole thing just came today."

I took the offered sheets of paper from her and scanned through them as Maddy read over my shoulder.

It appeared that Chef Benet was going to be promoting his new cookbook, *A Taste of Italian Heaven, Benet Style*, and he had a very specific list of expectations of any venue he'd be visiting.

"It looks pretty clear to me," I said as I scanned the list. He wanted cooking equipment, including a portable oven and other kitchen tools, to enable him to host a demonstration. I had a feeling Cindy could round up what she needed in town without much trouble at all.

"Flip the page," Cindy said ominously.

I did, and saw that the chef was more particular than any diva I'd ever imagined. The next page contained his list of personal demands, and they sounded as though they'd come from a madman holding hostages instead of a cook preparing a meal. I stopped after reading the first one. "He expects you to have a full kitchen mock-up for his demonstration? Where are you going to put it all?"

"I'm moving the middle of the store into storage for now, but that's not all. Keep reading."

I did, and soon saw the reason she'd probably wanted to talk to us. "You want us to be his assistants, don't you?" The contract stipulated that two trained cooks had to be at his disposal to do his prep and clean up, and to basically keep him happy the entire time he was in Timber Ridge. He also required a greenroom before his "performance," and another kitchen, one with an electric pizza oven, at his disposal off-site to test some new recipes.

"I know it's a lot to ask," Cindy said. "You can say no if you want to. I'll manage somehow."

"You can do it. We have faith in you," Maddy said, and I shushed my sister.

"Don't worry. We'll help," I said. I'd had Joe to fall back on when we'd opened our place, but Cindy had no one but her mother, Janet. If I could, I was going to be that rock for her. Cindy had lost her husband, but that didn't mean she had to lose her dream. If I couldn't help out another widow when she needed me, I wasn't sure I could justify occupying space in this world.

Maddy touched my arm and whispered, "Eleanor, can we talk about this first?"

"I'm sorry," I said to Cindy. "I should correct that. I'll help, but I really can't speak for Maddy."

"I'm in, too," my sister said, though in my mind she still sounded a little reluctant.

Cindy didn't hear it in her voice, though, or chose to ignore it. "You two are lifesavers," she said with a broad grin.

"When do you need us?" I asked.

"The day before the signing would be great. Not all day, but just to make sure I've got everything I need. Chef Benet is coming in later in the day, but his front person will be here early. I feel bad about having you shut down your restaurant for two days."

"We can't afford to do that," I said. "But we shouldn't have to. Maddy and Greg can run the Slice while I'm over here, and we can shut down during the few hours he needs for his demonstration the next day. At most we'll lose three or four hours, and we can afford that to help a friend."

Cindy hugged me and then Maddy in turn. "I can't thank you both enough."

"We're happy to help," I said.

Maddy and I left, and once we were out of sight of the bookstore, I turned to her and said, "You really don't want to do this, do you?"

"What are you talking about? I'm happy to lend a hand."

"Madeline Spencer, I know you better than that. What's wrong?"

My sister shook her head. "I just hate to see you

lose sales you can't afford to give up. I don't have to remind you how close we balance between red and black ink every month, do I?"

"There are more important things in this world than money," I said.

Maddy grinned. "In that case, how about a raise?"

I wasn't entirely sure she was serious, so I chose to treat it as a joke. "You know what I mean. Is that really it?"

Maddy frowned, and then stared at the brick pavers under her feet as she finally admitted, "Sis, I know how you feel about widows. Why shouldn't you help her? I admit that I'm a little worried about Benet, though."

"Why is that?" I asked. I'd have to catch one of his television shows before he came to town, but weren't all of those TV chefs perky and happy all of the time?

"From what I've read on the Internet, he's a bigger prima donna than seven divas in the same room."

"He can't be that bad, can he?" I asked.

"Trust me, if what I've read online is even close to the truth, he's worse. Much worse. That's what I was trying to warn you about. I'm thrilled to give Cindy a hand. I just wish she'd asked us to help stock shelves or something."

"It'll be fine," I said, wishing that I could believe it. After all, how bad could it really be?